THE MURDER PROPHET

SHERRY D. RAMSEY

First Published in 2014 by Sherry D. Ramsey
Copyright ©2014 by Sherry D. Ramsey
Cover Artwork copyright ©2014 by Sherry D. Ramsey
Print ISBN: 978-0-9938973-0-6
Ebook ISBN: 978-0-9938973-1-3

Email: sherrydramsey@gmail.com
Web: www.sherrydramsey.com
Cape Breton, Nova Scotia, Canada
Ramsey, Sherry D., 1963-, author
The Murder Prophet / Sherry D. Ramsey

For my siblings,
Denise, Gary, Darren, and Krista,
who taught me that a diverse group of characters
really can work well together

TABLE OF CONTENTS

Just take a trifling handful, O philosopher!
Of magic matter: give it a slight toss over
The ambient ether—and I don't see why
You shouldn't make a sky.
　　— Mortimer Collins (1827–1876)

But really, most of the time, magic sucks.
　　— Kit Stablefield (2027-)

ONE

Day Tripping At The Office

I was beginning to think I'd go mad if I had to hear the goose scream *"Hiii-yahhhhhh!"* one more time. The Darcko & Sadatake office sat mostly deserted, with everyone else out on various jobs, leaving me holding down the fort and the reception desk. There'd been no assaults on the fort yet, probably because of the pounding spring rain streaking the front windows. Even the phone sat as quiet as a dead thing on the desk. I didn't mind, since I hate phone duty. I'd clipped my nails, checked the charge on my .368 LaserWaster, and browsed my email. I worked a page of Anagrammatics—with paper and pencil, yes, because that's the only civilized way to do puzzles—and listened to the soothing cadence of the rain outside and the not-so-soothing sound of the goose playing video games in the back room.

Not that I have a problem with the animals who were affected by the meteorite spores, or their descendants. They didn't ask for what they got, any more than the rest of us did. It's just that they're relatively scarce, and I hadn't been around a lot of them until lately. We'd had a family dog around the time the spores happened, and overnight, he

1

developed human-level intelligence. At first it was great—we taught him to talk, he learned to use the TV remote, and he seemed even more like one of the family. We changed his name from 'Hotdog' to 'Frank,' at his request. There was always a tension, though, like he wasn't sure how he fit in with us any more. Eventually he...moved out. I'd say "ran away," but that sounds more like a regular dog, who wouldn't leave with luggage.

Anyway, I stayed away from magic-sapient animals after that. You can't avoid them entirely, but you can generally ignore them. When I joined the offices of Darcko and Sadatake, "Security Consultants," a year ago, that changed. It takes some serious focus to ignore a talking goose with an addiction to video games, especially when he's essentially the office mascot and considers you a friend. The talking, the games, the friendship; those I can accept most days. I never get used to the hands, though. They just look *wrong*.

The goose in question waddled in from the back room, which also serves as the lunch room. I heard him coming. I hadn't known, before I came to D & S, that a goose has claws on its feet, and they sound a lot like the tick-tick of a dog's paws on a tile floor. He paused in my doorway, pretended I'd taken him by surprise, and dropped into some kind of martial arts "guard" position. Those disconcerting hands were right up in front, looking totally out of place on the ends of his white-feathered wings as he bobbed gently in place for a few seconds, as if considering me. Then he erupted into a swirl of feathers, hands, and spindly orange webbed feet.

"Hiii-yahhhhhh!"

He fetched up on the desk, the tip of his carrot-colored

bill about six inches from the end of my nose, beady but intelligent blue eyes watching for my reaction.

I yawned, being careful not to suck in any feathers. "Hi, Trip."

"Come on, Kit, you've got to admit those are some killer moves!" he complained, pulling back from my personal space. His voice sounds pretty much like what you'd expect from a goose, a little squawky and crackly when he's upset. Well, all the time, really.

"Oh, killer," I agreed. "If the office is ever invaded by— what is it in the game? Flying ninja monkeys?—you can take point and we'll have nothing to worry about."

"Funny girl," he retorted, leaping down from the desk with his wings outstretched. When he wasn't actually using them, he could tuck his hands inside the soft sweep of his feathers. "You're nasty when you're bored, you know that?"

"I know." I sighed. "Sorry, you're right. I am bored."

He did that thing with his bill that signifies grinning. "They're still great moves. I can't wait to try them out on some little wanker who's got more to say than he should about a goose with hands."

I hid a smile. Trip had acquired the hands by magic, sure, but it was legal magic and I'm sure he'd paid well for them. Or I suppose my boss, Saga Sadatake, had paid. Not that Trip is his pet—I think the term "pet" goes out the window when the creature in question can carry on an intelligent conversation. But I wasn't one to ask Saga questions about his business or his goose's business, however you wanted to define their relationship. When you've got secrets of your own you tend to be reticent about sticking your nose elsewhere.

"Oh, that reminds me," Trip added, and waddled out of

the room again. He was back in a moment with a dust-laden magazine in hand. "I found this behind the cupboard in the kitchen."

I took it gingerly and blew some of the cobwebs and detritus away. It was the unfinished book of Anagrammatics puzzles I'd lost a month or more ago. "Thanks, Trip," I said, suddenly sorry I'd teased him. He has a good heart, for a goose.

The phone rang. Voice only, no vid. I went the same route. If they can't show me their face, they can't complain if I don't show them mine.

"Darcko and Sadatake," I answered, doodling a little stick figure on Kiku's notepad. I don't tend to go in for the whole chirpy *My name is Kit, and how can I help you today* schtick. When Kikufaax is at her preferred post at the reception desk, she tends to lay it on, like the happiest thing she's done all day is take your call, but from me, you get straight-up answering.

"I need to make an appointment," a thready male voice said. "And I need it soon."

"No, you don't," I said.

There was silence at the other end for a moment. "Excuse me?"

Childish, I know, but like I said, I was bored. "What I mean, sir, is that you don't need an appointment. We have walk-in service here; there's always someone in the office during normal business hours, which are nine-to-five, Monday through Friday."

"But will it be someone...I mean...this is very important. I'd like to speak to Mr. Darcko or Mr. Sadatake in person if possible."

"That would be *Mizz* Darcko," I corrected, "and you

don't want to get it wrong if she can hear you. All the investigators here are trained professionals, Mr...?" I let it hang.

He didn't jump at the chance, but he gave in when I stayed silent. "Coro," he said finally. "Aleshu Coro."

Good thing we weren't on the vid or he would have seen my eyes go wide. Coro was the millionaire CEO of MageData, Inc., one of a handful of database companies responsible for handling the NorthAm continent's RIMA—Registry of Individuals with Magic Abilities. Why he'd be looking to hire us, a relatively small-time, low-profile bunch of private investigators, I couldn't begin to guess.

I expended a little bit of magic energy to see if he was lying, not enough to make me sick, since I hadn't taken any Maginox® today. Just a quick scan—and read no hint of a lie. If it wasn't Aleshu Coro on the other end of the line, it was someone who could block my magic. I added a halo of dollar signs to my stick man doodle.

"Ms. Darcko and Mr. Sadatake should be in the office all day tomorrow," I suggested. For Mr. Aleshu Coro, they would be. "Would you prefer a time in the morning or the afternoon?"

"There's nothing today?" he pressed. "It's very urgent." Fear crackled in his voice like static, evident now that I was paying attention. He was well and truly scared of something, but I honestly couldn't get him in any faster. Anna Darcko was undercover and it could cost me my job if I tried to make contact. And Saga Sadatake was in Ireland looking for a runaway Transmute. He'd be home tonight, with or without her, but he couldn't get back sooner even if he wanted to.

"They're both out of the office today, and I have no way

to contact them," I said, sincerely sorry now that I'd recognized that static buzz of real fear. I added two wide eyes and a squiggly, down-turned mouth to my doodle. Trip snickered and I made a face at him. "They'll both be here first thing in the morning. That's really the best I can do."

He sighed, but as a man at the top of a company ladder he probably understood the futility of trying to get past the office border guards once the lines had been drawn. "First thing in the morning, I'll be there, then." He paused, then added, "If I'm still alive. Thank you for your time."

Coro broke the connection, and I stared at the dead receiver for a minute. Then I X'd out the stick man's fear-wide eyes.

———•———

Once I hung up the phone I logged directly onto the Netz and messaged LemurCandy. He's the office information hound, data retriever, and general Netz expert. It would look good to Saga and Anna if I had all the background work done before Aleshu Coro even set foot in the office tomorrow. Or at least, it would look bad if I didn't.

Lemur didn't have his Chatterz® open just then, so although I dislike wearing a faceskin where anyone might see me, I slipped the clear, thin film of bioplas over my face and pulled on my synth gloves. The familiar tingle rippled along my face and hands as the tiny, hairlike sensors connected. I called my favorite avatar up onscreen (she looks almost exactly like me, with just a few minor... adjustments) and spent a few minutes changing her clothes and hairstyle so she wouldn't look exactly the way she had the last time I'd met up with Lemur. Even in the virtual world, appearances count, and when you're using the Netz, if you're anywhere that offers a graphical interface, your avatar is, for all intents and purposes, you. I once read that people who create good-looking, well-dressed avatars become more confident and attractive in real life. While I didn't consider myself exceptionally attractive, virtual reality let me spruce myself up pretty good.

I went searching for Lemur in a few of his usual online haunts, hoping I wouldn't find him in any of the meat virtuals. He claims he only visits them in the course of his research, but I don't like the desperate atmosphere in most of them, the avatars "enhanced" out of all believable proportion, and the pick-up lines I've heard a thousand times already. Who cares if they're only looking for a virtual rendezvous and I'd never have to actually meet them? Most of them come off just like any slimy guy in a cheesy bar.

Not that it was any of my business what LemurCandy did, on the Netz or off. Just that—here's one of those secrets I mentioned earlier—I was pretty much in love with LemurCandy. Or at least as much in love as you can be with someone you've never seen, never met, never spoken to in realtime, and of whose gender you're not even completely certain. I thought he was male. I hoped he was male. He certainly *seemed* male and always wore male avatars. But these were the Netz, after all. You could appear to be anything you wanted, at least until someone managed to cajole or magick the truth out of you. And on the Netz these days, in the post-Spores, magic-filled world, anyone really *might* be a dog.

I figured if I ever did meet Lemur, it would be just my luck to have him turn out to be either female, gay, twelve years old, or a magic-sentient animal. At thirty-five, I'm still not attached, although I have it on reasonable authority that I'm not bad-looking myself. It just seems unlikely that my luck's going to change at this point.

Trip and Glaive would tell you that my personality is the defining factor there, and that luck doesn't really come into it, but how much weight can you put on the opinions of a goose and a former hit man? And I *do* have an attractive avatar, so that should count for something.

Anyway, back to LemurCandy. That's his default username, the one he uses with me and in all his dealings with Darcko and Sadatake, and the only name I have for him. Someday I'm going to ask him how he came up with it.

I finally found him in one of his favorite virtuals, but it was a mind virtual, not one of the meats, so I was secretly glad. This one called itself *Cogitario Now*—a little over-the-top for my liking—and sported a sumptuous decor in the style of an 18th century French salon, the virtual walls hung with richly detailed portraits of great thinkers and other period artworks, the muted brilliance of Persian carpets on the floors, and chairs scattered about in deliberately conversational groupings. There was also, of course, a marble-topped bar, which was where I saw Lemur.

<Hey, Kitano Kick-ass> he typed when he saw my avatar. The words appeared in a separate text chat window and his avatar threw me a friendly salute. "Kitano Kick-ass" is not my actual username, just what Lemur calls me. He has the advantage of me, since he knows who I am off the Netz.

Today he wore one of his favorite avatars; a lean but muscled bod in a pale green transform shirt and jeans, jet black short hair with an allover wave, and a smooth, chiseled face. The shirt enhanced the darker green of his eyes, and he winked at my avatar. I have myself convinced he favors wearing this avatar because it's what he really looks like.

<*What's the word from the office today?*>

<*It's not a word, it's a name,*> I answered. I moved my synth-gloved hands to make my avatar lean backwards against the bar and rest her/my elbows on the marble-texturized surface. I smiled, and the faceskin picked up the expression and translated it to my avatar's features. <*Can we get a room?*>

He raised his eyebrows, even though he had to know I just meant we needed a secure link, and nodded. A heartbeat later a security code flashed on my screen. I touched it, and the virtual's 18th century background morphed into a much more modern plush red velvet bedroom, complete with mirrors on the ceiling and ambient floor-lighting tiles. Lemur's avatar sat on the heart-shaped bed, and patted it invitingly.

<*Haha, nice try*> I typed, making my avatar roll her eyes. <*This is business.*>

LemurCandy shrugged. <*Can't blame a guy for trying,*> he said with a grin.

If I thought you really meant it, I thought, but brushed those fantasies aside. I made my avatar cross her arms and look businesslike. <*Aleshu Coro. What can you tell me?*>

LemurCandy's avatar jumped at the name and then went still for a moment.

<*What's wrong?*> I asked. <*He called the office today.*>

<*Oh, okay.*> His avatar sat smiling blankly for a moment or two, only his hands moving as if entering keyboard and touchscreen commands. I knew that somewhere, real-life-Lemur was accessing his secret databases and wherever else

he digs up information on people. Then the av's face came back to life.

<CEO of MageData, Inc.,> he said, <but you already knew that. Pretty private guy, keeps to himself, not out in the celebrity circles although he's certainly got the money to run with them if he wanted. He's on his third wife, she's French, no kids. Supposedly a lifetime contract this time, but they're easy enough to squirm out of if you really want to. Seems basically clean. He's registered as a level one Mancer, just a Talent.> LemurCandy chuckled. <Has the ability to bring on light rainshowers once a day.>

The chuckle bothered me. Sure, light rainshowers is a pretty meagre ability, laughable and fairly useless unless you're a farmer maybe, but it wasn't that. I have no idea if Lemur has any Mancer rating himself, or what he thinks of those of us who do, or what his magic abilities are if he does have any. Sometimes I get the impression that he looks down on Mancers in general, but I could be paranoid— reading a whole lot into it that just isn't there—one of the drawbacks of wholly cyber-interaction. After so many years post-Spores, Mancers are just part of society—hell, they figure ninety percent of the population has some magic ability now. But I still get the feeling that, instead of us pitying the mundanes, it's the other way around. The arrival of magic changed the world, in lots of ways that are good, and it also caused a lot of problems. If you ask me, most of the time, magic just sucks.

<What's up with Coro?> Lemur wanted to know, and I snapped out of my musings. Normally I would have told him what Coro had said, but the chuckle had left me piqued.

<Don't know yet, but I'll keep you posted,> I said shortly.

<Thanks. Could you send whatever background you have over to the office? Saga and Anna will want to take a look. Talk to you later.>

I didn't wait for his reply and broke the connection, then immediately felt stupid and childish. I peeled off the faceskin and gloves, rubbing my face to remove the sticky feeling—completely imaginary, or so I've been told. The quiet office felt eerie, as if ghosts whispered in the corners. And now I was mad at myself. I sighed, looking out through the rain-streaked front window at the colorless street outside. The rain seemed to have washed away every pigment but grey. Grey traffic, grey buildings on the other side of the street, and a few grey pedestrians.

The soundtrack of Trip's "Flying Monkey Ninjas from Wormhole 7" game trickled in from the other room, but I wasn't sure if the accompanying thumps and bumps were from Trip playing the game or practising the moves in real life. It annoyed me either way. I waited impatiently, clicking random Netz links until the data packet arrived from LemurCandy, copied it to both Anna and Saga with the message about Aleshu Coro and his appointment, and did one more Anagrammatic puzzle. Then I decided it was close enough to closing time, said goodnight to the goose, and went home in the rain.

It was the last "normal" day I'd see for quite a while.

TWO

Magic Sucks

The next morning I woke early, and lay in bed with my eyes closed for a little while, listening to the pleasing sound of it not raining. Thin light filtered through the blinds and fell in alternating pale and dark stripes across the bed. The quiet here was peaceful and lovely, not the lonesome quiet of an empty office.

I was ten years old when the wormhole opened just this side of Mars and the world went crazy. Scientists and politicians and clergy tried to keep everyone calm by telling us not to panic, because nobody knew what it meant yet. That worked—kind of—until the same wormhole disgorged an asteroid on a collision course with Earth. Then we learned what panic really was, until it gave way to pale faces and hushed voices as my parents tried to keep me from worrying.

For all the talk about satellite defences and such, there wasn't much they could do when an actual threat presented itself. They fired a couple of nukes but only one hit, and didn't take the thing out completely, just fragmented it. When they simulated and extrapolated, they figured out that it would likely impact in the Indian Ocean, which was better than somewhere on land. There were no options left but to sit back and wait, anyway. Nothing more they could do. We'd just have to sit tight and hope the damage was mild.

We got lucky, I suppose, that the pieces hit the ocean, but no one had counted on the Spores. Hell, no one imagined that such a thing was possible, with maybe the exception of a few science fiction writers, and governments aren't exactly known for listening to them. There was a lot of debate over whether the nuke had anything to do with the spores and their effects, but that question never did get answered and in the end it was moot anyway.

So we all know the rest of the story. The microscopic Spores end up in the atmosphere, spread around the world, and we all breathe them in without realizing what's happening. They activate some tiny, mysterious, dormant part of our DNA or brains or something and practically overnight, the human race has magic. So do a few animals who presumably had the necessary brain capacity or chemistry. And now that the genes are active, we pass them on in their active form. The scientists are still trying to work out all the permutations for recessive and dominant combinations, but they don't have any answers yet. Not that I really care.

All I know is that for me, magic sucks.

I rolled over in bed, facing away from the light. If I was lucky, I might get back to sleep for twenty minutes or so. Remnants of last night's rain-induced lethargy still lingered, and I thought I'd skip my run this morning. My mind refused to settle, though, still fixated on magic.

Consider my particular "gift"—detecting lies. It's a pretty strong Aptitude, enough to get me registered as a Level 4 Mancer in the Psych line. It's not infallible, and some people can use their own magic to fake me out. I also

13

can't tell when someone's just holding something back. That would probably take a full-blown, Level 5 Telepath, and thank goodness I'm not one of those.

Still, it isn't much fun going through high school being able to tell exactly when a guy is stringing you a line or when they like you so desperately that it's creepy. Knowing when compliments are phony, when friends are disloyal...I could go on and on, but you get the picture.

Sure, you could choose not to use it, but wouldn't that be sort of delusional? And of course when you're young you haven't yet mastered turning it on and off, so you have to take the Maginox® every day to keep from puking your guts up when the magic kicks in. And daily Maginox® use comes with its own special set of side effects—headaches, dizziness, a taste like burnt onions in the mouth, and overall sluggishness—which is why a huge percentage of the population have magic abilities that they never use and actually work hard to suppress. It's not so bad if you're just a Talent, because the Maginox® dose is low and the side effects mild, but for an Apt—a lot of the time it's just not worth the inconvenience.

"Good morning, Kit, the time is now six-thirty a.m.," the apartment AI told me in a revoltingly cheery voice, interrupting my trip down the rutted path of memory lane.

"Stuff it, Phoebe, I'm already awake," I muttered back. I rolled over again, but that put me facing the window that had brightened steadily as I ruminated. "Phoebe" is the name the apartment AI came with, and she doesn't respond to anything else. Believe me, I've tried. Not that there's anything wrong with the name itself. But shouldn't an apartment AI be sort of like a butler, with a name like Jeeves or Smith or Reginald?

"The rain has stopped and it's a lovely morning for your run," Phoebe replied, as chipper as before. "Rising now will allow you ample time to exercise and arrive at work on time. Or," a chiding note crept into her voice at this point, "I can prompt you again in fifteen minutes." The tone made it very clear that this would be a disappointing and unworthy choice.

"You're like the roommate from hell, you know," I told her. I have this perverse desire to just once hear her tell me off, but I guess that will never happen. The thing seems programmed to be impervious to insults, although sometimes our relationship gets a little strained. I'm not sure I made the right decision, setting up Netz access and automatic software upgrades for her a few months ago. With every upgrade she seems to develop more of a personality. One that unfortunately clashes with mine.

However, I keep her turned on because I really need her prodding some mornings, and this morning I wanted to be in the office and alert when Aleshu Coro arrived for his appointment. Reluctantly I rolled out of bed and into my runners just like she told me to do, and hit the streets. The rain must have stopped early in the morning, because although the pavement was dark and wet, most of the puddles were small. The air held an almost stinging freshness, though, and the thin layer of rainwater covering everything glistened in the morning sunlight.

I generally switch the brain into "off" mode when I run. I mean, I watch for traffic and obstacles and little old ladies, but apart from the general task of staying alive and healthy to run again tomorrow, I try to let my mind stay relatively blank, rebooting into a new day. This morning, though, my brain kept returning to my earlier musings and the overall suckiness of magic, poking at the past like a determined archeologist.

When they instituted the registration system for Mancers, it was all on the honor system, naturally. Still is, since there's no foolproof way to discern someone's magic ability short of having them demonstrate it or catching them using it. I was about fifteen when my ability manifested, and I had no trouble telling them about the lie-detection. One of the interviewers had the very same power, and they told me that someday, if I needed a job, I could get one just like hers with the government. *Wow, what fun,* my fifteen-year-old self thought.

By this time I had figured out that I couldn't tell when someone was holding something back, as long as it wasn't a real lie, and there was something else—a scary something else—that I wasn't so keen on sharing with the government. I gambled that the interviewer's ability worked the same way as mine, and kept my mouth shut about that. And it worked. As far as anyone knows, lie-detection constitutes the full range of my magical ability.

Stop thinking, I ordered my brain at this point. *What's done is done.* I forced myself to focus my concentration on the physical world of my run, and pushed into a sprint to reinforce that focus.

Last night's rain had washed all the litter off the streets and into the gutters, then overflowed the gutters, so I had to leap a few larger puddles here and there. The water must have ebbed and flowed a few times like a tide. This left an interesting row of garbage neatly ranged like beached seaweed along the sides of the road in a remarkably straight line. By tonight a crew would have been by to clean it up, and it would be converted, via the magic of a team of

Transmutes, into energy to run the city. If anything, people seemed more likely to litter now, knowing that it would be gone the next day. I rolled my eyes. Able to do magic, but still too lazy to find a trash can.

By the time I finished the five k and was turning the key in the door to my apartment, I felt better. I always do, although that knowledge, even combined with Phoebe's nagging, doesn't push me out the door every morning. The hot shower completed my return to normality. Under the pulsing water I decided that LemurCandy hadn't meant anything by his chuckle, that he wouldn't have been offended by my abrupt logoff, that I was through thinking about things I couldn't change, and that I wasn't going to let anything, not even Trip's ridiculous video game and martial arts obsessions, spoil my day.

———•———

Kikufaax was already behind the reception desk when I got there, which was a relief. Phone-answering and making nice with the clients is really not my thing. She, on the other hand, looked absolutely born for the job. Kiku is tall, almost six feet, so she tops me by a few inches and I'm no runt. She hangs model's clothes on a model's body, and the only time I've seen her break a sweat is when she's breaking someone else's bones. Her hair is jet black, glossy, and as straight as she is. I've never caught her in a lie, not to me, and not to anyone else. That's something in this business.

I guess we're good friends, although I don't tell her any of my secrets. That's one thing you want to avoid with someone who never lies. They can't—or won't—cover for you.

Kiku flashed me her brightest smile when I came in. She wore a black shirt of woven leather strips that didn't quite meet each other, joined with randomly scattered small silver links. Her long hair swept into a messy updo, the kind of thing I can never manage without the "messy" aspect completely taking over, and she'd clasped it in place with an ornate silver clip. Her eye makeup was smoky, her lips a glossy burgundy, and as usual she made me feel—entirely unintentionally—like I needed a radical makeover. She leaned toward me over her immaculately ordered desk, silver links tinkling slightly. "You bagged a big one yesterday," she whispered conspiratorially.

I chuckled as I hung my leather bomber-style jacket on the old-fashioned coat rack next to the door. "All I did was answer the phone. Although I suppose I saved Trip from answering it. Might not have gone so well if he'd picked up and yelled '*Hiii-yahhhhhh!*' at Aleshu Coro."

Video game music, faint and tinny, floated out from the back room and we both giggled. We got serious quickly when Saga Sadatake came out of his office, smoothing non-existent wrinkles out of his long black mandarin jacket. His greying hair has receded quite far back from his hairline, but his forehead remains smooth and his dark eyes bright. I think Saga deliberately wears the stereotype of the imperturbable, diminutive Asian man to lull people into a false sense of security.

"Good morning, Kitano," he said gravely. "Miss Kineall agreed to the terms and returned with me on the flight last night. She's extremely tired and staying at the Smith Street safe house right now. I wonder if you'd collect here there after lunch and escort her to the Registry? And stay with her until she's signed the contracts?"

"And ask the Reg Officer a few innocent questions about the contract to make sure they're playing fair?"

Saga winked at me. "An excellent idea."

"Sure thing," I said, before heading for my office. My desk looked spectacularly messy in comparison to Kiku's, littered with papers, files, data chips, case notes, and the wrapper from yesterday's lunch. I ignored all that and logged in to check my email and Chatterz® first. I told myself I simply needed to check for messages about a few of my current cases, but since I don't need magic to detect my own lies, I knew I was hoping for something from LemurCandy.

Nothing. I spent about thirty seconds brooding, then heard the front door open and decided to look busy tidying my desk. Through my open office door I saw Anna Darcko stop at the reception desk for a word with Kiku, and slip out of her long dark coat while they chatted. She'd pulled out all the stops for the appointment with Coro. Her shoulder-length, snow-white hair looked impeccably smooth and her suit was of real transform fabric, a swirling pattern of greens and greys with the characteristic sheen of transform. Transform fabric is made by magically transmuting relatively small amounts of raw material, as compared to traditional manufacturing. But while the transform shirt for LemurCandy's avatar was just a batch of electrons discombobulated in an interesting way, Anna's magic-sourced suit must have set her back what would amount to a week's pay for me. She caught my eye and smiled, and crossed to the door of my office.

"Would you sit in on our appointment this morning, Kit?" Anna has the most intensely blue eyes I'd ever seen. I have no idea if they're natural, or enhanced by tech or magic, but no one who meets her would ever forget them. Gold hoop earrings peeped out from under her fall of hair.

I hesitated. "I don't mind, but Saga didn't mention anything when I spoke to him just now."

She laughed, her caramel-coloured skin crinkling at the corners of her eyes. "That's because it's my idea, and I just had it. I wouldn't say I distrust big business on principle, but I'd like to have a little backup when I'm forming impressions of our Mr. Coro."

I smiled. "I'd be happy to join you."

As she walked away toward her own office, I wondered where she had her own .368 concealed—or if not the LaserWaster, what she was packing today. The tailored suit clung close to her curves, leaving little room for personal ordnance. I knew, because she'd told me once when we were in a very tight spot, that she always had at least one weapon on her person somewhere. In that case, she'd produced a razor-sharp throwing dagger at exactly the right time to save both our lives, so I was ready to take her at her word. For a mundane, with absolutely no magical ability, Anna Darcko can be one dangerous lady. As well as I get along with her, she's a person I never want to cross.

Since Anna obviously wanted my lie-detecting magic active in the meeting, I slipped into the bathroom and washed down a couple of Maginox®. I can sneak a basic check on someone and not feel much of an effect even if I do it without the medication, but nausea is never comfortable and I don't put myself through it if I have advance warning that I'm going to be magicking. And depending on what transpired in the Coro interview, I might be using my talent a lot. I'm one of the lucky ones who suffers very little in the way of Maginox® side effects right away, although I'd probably have to crash early tonight. No wonder most folks choose not to take it on a regular basis.

It wasn't long before the door opened again and Kikufaax's face lit up in greeting. Must be the great man himself. Aleshu Coro stepped over to the desk and leaned forward slightly to talk to Kiku. I almost fell off my chair.

He was LemurCandy's avatar. I mean, LemurCandy's avatar was him. A somewhat older version, to be sure, but the same body, same black hair, same...everything.

I'm sure I sat there with my mouth hanging open. Staring at the all-too-familiar body, this time covered not with a shirt and jeans, but an expensive shot silver transform three-piece suit, with a crisp white shirt and demurely patterned red and black tie. Staring at the short dark hair with that allover wave, peppered with grey in this incarnation, and the profile of the face I had talked to—or rather my avatar had talked to—a hundred times. If his eyes turned out to be green...well, of course they would. Lemur wouldn't have messed up on a simple detail like that, not when he went to such trouble to get all the rest of it right. But why would he want to look like Coro? For an instant I wondered if they were the same person, but I didn't see how that could be possible.

And then I realized that I'd seen pictures of Aleshu Coro once or twice in the news, but the likeness had never occurred to me. Now I just felt dumb.

Before Kiku could press the button to call them, Anna and Saga emerged from their offices and converged on Coro at the front desk. Anna didn't fawn, that would have been beneath her, but she greeted him warmly. Then she beckoned to me and I managed to arrange my face into something other than a shocked gawp and joined them. When Coro turned to shake my hand I was surprised to see that his eyes weren't green at all, but a dark, smoky grey. Fear shadowed them, making them even darker. His handshake was firm but brief, as if the social niceties had sunk far down his priorities list.

Anna led us all into what we fondly call the "boardroom," even though we couldn't fit the entire staff inside for a meeting. Those we held in the reception area or the lunch room. The boardroom was really just a spare office, with four comfortable chairs, a rolling bar cart, some artificial flowers and nice lighting. I took a seat in a brocade-covered wing chair near the door and tried to blend in with the dark, floral-embossed wallcoverings.

Saga offered Mr. Coro a drink, and when the client refused, settled himself in a chair and folded his hands placidly on his lap. "So, in what way may Darcko and Sadatake assist you?"

Aleshu Coro swallowed hard, his Adam's apple bobbing like something huge was trying to get past it. He looked from Anna to Saga pleadingly, and said in a low voice, "I'm hoping you might be able to save my life."

It felt like the room itself tensed, holding its breath. I know I did. Saga merely raised his eyebrows, and Anna allowed a slight crease of concern to wrinkle her forehead.

Coro continued, barely above a whisper, "I've had a message from the Murder Prophet."

And I knew without a shadow of doubt that he wasn't lying.

THREE

The Murder Prophet

Anna sat back in her chair and pursed her plum-glazed lips. She kept her voice a practised neutral when she answered. "When was this?"

Coro breathed deeply and blew it out in a long sigh before he answered, as if the initial revelation had been the hardest part. "Two days ago. It took me that long to discover that the police can or will do almost nothing to help me, and to find someone who might. You."

"The police can't offer you anything?" Anna asked. "I would think they'd be taking these messages seriously by now."

Coro set his face, the lines around his mouth pulled taut and determined. "They take them seriously, but they can't offer me anything except protection, and they don't have the manpower to offer much of that. Frankly, I could hire better bodyguards personally, if that's all I wanted. I want this person stopped."

"Why come to us?" Anna asked him. "We're not particularly well-known, I wouldn't think."

Coro shrugged. "You did some work for Hastings Wells. He was very satisfied, and recommended you."

Well, that answered that question. Wells was a corporate exec who'd been suffering at the hands of a hostile and corrupt Board of Directors. He'd come to us specifically because we weren't on anyone's radar, and we'd done some nice undercover work that solved the problem.

Saga turned his imperturbable gaze to me. "How many people have received messages from the Murder Prophet thus far?" I don't know why he always expects me to know stuff like that. This time, though, I knew the answer.

"Eight known here in the city. Of course there could be others."

Saga nodded. "And of those eight..."

"All have eventually been murdered, yes. Within a time frame mentioned in the message, however cryptically."

Aleshu Coro swallowed audibly.

A brief moment of silence followed, pressing down heavily on the room like a giant hand, and then Anna said briskly, "Well, this time it will be different. Mr. Coro, you want us to save your life. To do that we must discover who wants to end it. We'll need unlimited access to your business and personal files and information, as well as to your family, employees and acquaintances. We must be permitted to proceed unhampered, and you must not keep anything back from us. Do you understand?"

"Yes," he said, again in that voice that sounded like it hurt him to speak. He slumped inside his expensive suit like it was armor a size too big for him.

"And you'll agree to those terms?" Anna pressed.

"Yes," he said, a little more firmly this time.

She sat back and considered him for a moment, steepling her fingers and tapping them against her lips. "You haven't asked about our fee."

He shrugged. "The money won't matter if I'm dead. Whatever the fee is, I'll pay it. You know I have the means."

Saga leaned forward in his chair. His eyes twinkled with the excitement of a new challenge. "Did you bring the message with you?"

Coro nodded, and produced a slender, expensive-looking leather chip wallet. He carefully extracted one of the chips from its sleeve and handed it over to Saga. "The file is on that. You can keep it. I don't want to look at it again."

"Does the message mention a time-frame?" Anna wanted to know.

Coro ran a shaky hand over his face, pale beneath his black hair. "It contains the word 'fortnight,' but it doesn't say in so many words that that's how long..." His voice trailed away.

Anna shook her head. "As far as I know, all the messages have been quotations, difficult to apply to any given recipient. But as Kit says, if there's a measure of time mentioned, then invariably that provides a clue to when—"

"The recipient should conduct himself with caution," Saga finished smoothly. He likes clients to remain calm when they visit us, although he's always anxious to start a new case. Anna likes to lay the facts on the table. They're a strange pair, but their partnership seems to work.

"You were wise to come to us so quickly," Saga continued. "If you received the message two days ago, that gives us over a week before we should even begin to be alarmed. We shall meet with our staff to determine how best to conduct your case, and then we'll be in touch with you directly." He didn't stand or make any move at all, but it was clear the appointment was ending.

Aleshu Coro took the hint and stood, tugging his jacket down as if it helped him to compose himself. "Thank you so much," he said fervently, shaking all our hands again. His grip was firm, although his palm felt clammy. He took another deep breath, seemingly to ready himself to venture back out into the world, and I escorted him back to Kiku.

Once he was out the door I went straight to the kitchen and filled the coffeepot. After a moment's consideration, I picked up the phone and ordered pizzas to be delivered at lunchtime. I had a feeling we were about to have one of those staff meetings, and that it was going to be a long one.

———•———

Glaive Timesi started slowly shaking his head when Anna got to the part about the Murder Prophet, and kept shaking it until she noticed and frowned at him. "What?"

"I just don't see the point," he said. "Look, this Murder Prophet guy—"

"Or woman," I interjected.

"—or woman," he went on as if he'd been about to say that, "Has warned the intended victims of eight murders that we know about. They've still been murdered. The police have arrested the killers in two cases—"

"Three," I said. I'd had a brief exchange of messages with LemurCandy while we waited for Glaive to arrive at the office.

This time he shot me a look of annoyance and ran a hand over his grey-peppered short brown hair. "Three. Whatever. The rest are unsolved, no one has the faintest clue who's sending the messages, and at least in those two cases I mentioned, no one involved admits to knowing anything about them. The messages seem to have no connection to the killers, who have nothing to do with each other."

Anna cocked her head at him. "And your point is?"

He frowned and turned his palms up. "My point is, it's a waste of our time. Coro's going to get offed, and he might as well spend the next two weeks getting his affairs in order and having as much fun as he can. While he can."

Well, Glaive spent an indeterminate number of years in a government position that bureaucrats might call "targeted response agent" and the rest of us might call "hit man." I guess he has a unique take on matters of life and death. The fact that he always wears unrelieved black is, I'm sure, a holdover from those days, and might provide a little peek inside his psyche. If he has any magic ability, he keeps it as secret as he does the rest of his life. Which is to say, extremely secret.

You would think that having a former assassin as a co-worker would be awkward, or even troubling. It would, if Anna and Saga didn't vouch for him absolutely. I don't know what they know, but if they're okay with Glaive, then so am I. Even if sometimes I wonder whether he misses the option of solving problems via more direct and permanent methods.

We'd gathered, as usual, in the reception area, pulled the blinds and put the "back soon" sign in the window. This was interesting enough that even Trip had abandoned his video game in favor of sitting in. Every once in a while his eyes strayed in the direction of the back room, though, and I wondered how long he'd last.

Anna frowned and took a sip from her tumbler of water. "You're not usually such a defeatist, Glaive. Why this time?"

He shrugged his broad shoulders and sighed. "I'm not trying to be defeatist; just practical. I think it's an impossible situation, unless Coro goes into hiding or something. I know what you told him, but there's not even any real guarantee that he's got two weeks. It could be a complete coincidence that the other deaths occurred in the time frame the messages mentioned."

I shook my head. "Eight coincidences? Come on."

"Okay, but what if there's magic involved?"

Saga leaned forward in his chair. "What do you mean? We already know magic is involved if the Murder Prophet is a Seer. He or she is using that ability to predict the murders."

"Sure." Glaive nodded, brushing an imaginary speck of dust from his black pants. "But what if someone's using magic in some other way? Like a Psych influencing the killer to make the kill? Or a Chanter manipulating a weapon from a distance? Or even just a Shielder maybe knocking out someone else's protection? I don't know how to counter any of those things, do you?"

"Is any of that even possible?" Trip asked.

"Not legally, for certain," Anna said, tapping her fingertips together.

"Well, murder's not legal, either," Glaive said with a sardonic grin.

"Any of those things would take a very high level Mancer," Kikufaax said. "Using a weapon that way would be fifth-level enchantment." Kiku was a Chanter herself, although only a low level, so I figured she was probably right. Her own magic seemed to take the form of getting mechanical and electronic things to function for her really reliably, which I thought was pretty handy.

Trip turned to me. "Could a Psych do that, Kit? Mentally make someone kill someone else?"

I shifted uncomfortably in my chair. "I don't know. Mine is a different kind of Psych ability...I can't influence people, only read them. I don't know much about the other side. But I don't *think* so."

"There are so many nuances in the ways abilities manifest, so many shades of power and influence, it's hard to say if they'll ever be completely understood or catalogued," Saga added.

The goose nodded and looked thoughtful.

I glanced over at Kiku's computer screen, where the message from The Murder Prophet glowed, black letters stark against a pale background:

> *Phlebas the Phoenician, a fortnight dead,*
> *Forgot the cry of gulls, and the deep sea swell*
> *And the profit and loss.*
> *A current under sea*
> *Picked his bones in whispers. As he rose and fell*
> *He passed the stages of his age and youth*
> *Entering the whirlpool.*[1]

We'd checked the reference, of course. It was from the early 20th century poet T.S. Eliot, part of his poem "The Waste Land." One of the previous messages had also been taken from this particular poem, but none of the others. I suppose it's a bit of a challenge to find poetic references to death that also contain a particular time frame that matches the one you're looking for. When it came to that, why was the Murder Prophet, whoever he or she was, sending these obscure messages anyway?

I realized I had zoned out of the conversation—probably the effects of the Maginox® manifesting—and forced my attention back to it. Saga put an obvious end to further dissent or discussion by saying, "In any case, we have agreed to try and assist Mr. Coro—for a healthy, open-ended fee and a generous retainer, I might add—and so I am putting everyone on this case for the next few days. Finish up anything you must this afternoon, and tomorrow we will make a concentrated effort."

He turned to me. "Kit, once you are finished with Ms. Kineall this afternoon, will you contact LemurCandy? I want everything, and I do mean everything, about the other murders and about Mr. Coro, as soon as possible."

"Sure, no problem," I said. I wondered why he always tagged me to contact Lemur. It wasn't like Kiku or Glaive couldn't do it just as well. And the thought of seeing Lemur just now made me squirm a little. Our contact this morning had just been text, but for an in-depth research session we'd probably have to go virtual. I wondered if he'd be embarrassed that now I knew he'd chosen Aleshu Coro as his avatar.

The pizza arrived, and we shared out steaming slices as we discussed a few ways of tackling the investigation. We debated the relative merits of spiriting Coro away for safety if the fortnight deadline approached before we made progress—but he'd have to agree to that, too. Once Glaive accepted the fact that Saga and Anna were committed to the case, he put aside his objections with good grace. We may all be mercenaries at heart here at Darcko and Sadatake, but we act like professionals.

Well, most of the time.

When the pizza and discussion had run out, I left for my appointment with the runaway Transmute, Idala Kineall.

———•———

Idala was only eighteen, and I knew from her file that her Transmute powers had manifested after puberty, which happened in some people. It was actually better that way, I thought, because babies who could do things with their minds without understanding what they were doing could cause all kinds of disasters. The parents had to make tough decisions about using magic-dampening drugs as well as the Maginox® with its many and varied side effects. No, late-onset was better for everyone.

Except, of course, for the person enduring it. Trust me on that one.

What I knew about her, from the report Saga had shared with me, was that she'd come into her powers, become rebellious (big surprise there, what sixteen-year-old isn't rebellious?), said she'd never work for the government, and run away.

Naturally, a certain percentage of the population— probably about half—has figured out ways to monetize their magic abilities. Alimentals run restaurants, host cooking shows, own catering businesses. Ecos grow crops or magically harvest resources. Shielders offer physical protection services or go into police work, Chanters build and fix things. Some, like Psychs, have a harder time getting anyone to pay for their abilities, and have to be careful to stay on the right side of the law. All the rest have low-level abilities or ones that are too specific to be broadly useful, or are Mundane, with no magic at all.

Transmutes are expected to work in government jobs; comprising just six percent of the entire population, they're simply too valuable to waste. So far, transmutation is the magical ability with the most practical applications. It isn't like they aren't well-paid—show me a down-and-out Transmute who's even barely within the realm of sanity and I'll find him or her a good-paying job within twenty-four hours. Once someone realized that a Transmute could transform raw matter into energy with no waste products, the global energy crisis simply went away. A team of five Transmutes on a shift could churn out enough power to run a good-sized city easily, and that was also the end of the garbage problem.

It was just that the idea of spending every day turning garbage into something you can't even see doesn't appeal to everyone. I know it wouldn't to me.

It's obvious why the government hates to let one go, even though they make a big song and dance about everyone being entitled to use or not use their powers in whatever way makes sense to them. So every time a Transmute decides to run, the suits hire someone like us to hunt him down and offer him a very lucrative contract. *Very* lucrative. There's no force or coercion, oh no, because if word of that got out, there'd be an uproar. But they tempt them, and for most folks it's just too hard to resist.

Especially if being on the run hasn't been going so well. Saga says the best time to "catch up" to them is when they're just about ready to give up and go home anyway. They'll take a less lucrative contract then, and be happy about it.

Don't get me wrong, Saga's not a bad guy. But D&S is a business. As long as it doesn't cross a certain line, and sometimes if it just barely puts a toe across that line, we'll take the job and do our best for the client.

Anyway, back to Idala Kineall. She'd been on the run for

two years, a pretty good stretch for her age. Even though Saga said she had come back with him willingly, I half-expected that she'd be gone from the safe house when I went to collect her.

I was wrong. She sat in the kitchen, still in a faded pink silk kimono, nursing a coffee with her feet up on the table. Her toenails were painted a brilliant glittery purple, but her feet were clean. Her shoulder-length hair hung lank and wet from the shower. It would probably dry to a medium blond.

"Hello, Ms. Kineall," I said, plastering my best professional smile on my face. "I'm Kit Stablefield, and Mr. Sadatake asked me to make sure you get safely to the office this afternoon and get your contract in place."

She quirked a cynical half-smile. "So they'll pay up on his bill?"

I kept my own smile in place. "Something like that. And to be sure that you get a fair deal, what Mr. Sadatake offered you on the government's behalf."

She lifted the coffee cup and sipped, but her eyes flicked to the latched back door.

"It's locked on the *inside*, Ms. Kineall," I told her. "This house keeps you safe, it's not for keeping you prisoner. You could have left anytime through the night, and you can still leave now if you want. No-one's forcing you to do this."

The kid lowered her coffee cup. A drop fell on the well-worn pink silk, but she didn't seem to notice. I didn't think she had makeup on. If she did, she hadn't done a very good job with it.

"Might as well sit down while I finish this. There's at least another cup left in the pot," she offered with a negligent gesture in the general direction of the countertop.

33

I pulled out a chair across from her and sat down. We had no particular appointment at the government office, and she wasn't dressed yet. Despite her glance at the door, I figured her mind was made up.

"You a Mancer?" she asked, tilting her head to one side as she appraised me with clear hazel eyes.

I nodded. "Psych line, level three. I can tell when someone's lying."

She chuckled. "That might be handy."

"Sometimes." I shrugged. "Sometimes it sucks."

"Yeah, I can imagine."

My arrival obviously hadn't nudged her into any more of a hurry, so I got up and fixed myself a coffee, too. The caffeine would help banish the Maginox® drowsiness for a while. When I sat back down, she had the good grace to take her feet off the table, and leaned forward with her elbows in their place.

"When I was in Ireland," she said slowly, wrapping her hands around her mug as if they were cold, "I worked for a little while in a pub called The Chant and Cup. The tips were pretty good, and the owner wasn't much of a jerk. In fact, at first I didn't think he was a jerk at all. Of course I didn't tell him I was a Transmute; after all, that's what I was running away from, right?"

I nodded. If she wanted to talk, I felt I owed her the courtesy of listening.

"I didn't think he had any magic, this guy, or if he did he never talked about it. One day he was talking about how he'd love to have an apple. A crisp, fall apple like the ones he used to pick straight from his grandfather's backyard apple tree in Hazlemere. He went on about those apples all day, described them perfectly. When he went home for supper I took some of the leftovers from the grill and made him an apple. I made it exactly like the one he'd described. Exactly, you know?"

I thought I could see where this was going, and I felt sorry for her. Really. I mean, it was a stupid thing to do, but she was eighteen, right? Who doesn't make a fool of themselves for love when they're eighteen, even if it's by way of something as simple as an apple?

"When he came back I gave it to him." She sipped her coffee again. "He thought I'd run to the grocer's and bought him an apple, but when he bit into it—he just looked at me. He knew. He absolutely knew I must have transmuted it."

I felt I had to say something. "And he fired you?"

"No," she said, shaking her head. "He asked me to marry him."

I thought about it for a minute. "But he wasn't all that interested in you before that, right?"

"Exactly."

"So you figured if you were going to be with someone who only wanted you for your magic, you might as well be getting paid for it?"

She smiled, a real smile this time. "I thought you might understand."

"Are you ready to go now?"

"Just give me fifteen minutes to get dressed and get my things together. This is a pretty nice place, you know."

"You'll be able to afford a place a lot nicer than this with your new job," I said.

She looked around, considering. "I guess so. I just wonder what it will cost me."

And we both knew she wasn't talking about the money.

FOUR

Nana Nina

It all went swimmingly when I took Idala to see the suits and get her contract signed all nice and tidy and legal. We didn't talk any more about serious stuff after she went to get dressed. When she came back downstairs I'd finished the coffee and cleaned out the pot, given the place a once-over and checked all the door locks. She'd changed into black jeans and a mock transform turtleneck in green paisley, had her hair slicked back in a ponytail and looked like a perfectly normal teenager. Talked like one, too, all the way downtown, music and movies and what Ireland had been like, and I let her. This was going to be the new normal, so we might as well start letting it happen.

The meeting went smoothly, the contract was fine, and I signed the invoice before I left. She gave me a little wave in farewell. I wished I didn't feel like I was selling her out. I wished I had talked to her more about how hard it is to decide what to do with your life, and how it's okay sometimes to make mistakes in those decisions. But she didn't ask, and it wasn't part of my job.

It was late afternoon when I left her, and I felt unsettled. The prospect of going back to the office for half an hour didn't appeal. I stood indecisively on the corner of the street and pondered my options. All around, people were already hurrying home to their after-work lives, picking up kids, cooking dinner, making plans for the evening. The sun flared in my eyes for a last moment as it started the slide behind the building across the street from me, and as soon as it was gone, the air chilled and shadows sprang to life.

I really didn't feel like going back to the office—by the time I got there, it was likely everyone else would be gone. And I was in no real hurry to get home. The meetup with LemurCandy could happen anytime during the evening, as long as he was online, and I have to say I'd hardly ever gone looking for him that he wasn't online somewhere. That was one of the reasons I really hadn't believed he could look anything like that avatar, but I kept telling myself it was entirely possible that he had a whole home gym right there in his computer hideaway, and worked out regularly from a vantage point where he could still see the screen. In real life, he'd be as fit as his various avs.

Yeah, right.

Anyway, I didn't have to get home and get in touch with him right now. All things considered, I decided that it would be a good time to go and visit my grandmother.

———◆———

Seemed like every time I ended up at Nana Nina's apartment, she knew exactly what brought me there. I'd asked her before if she had Seer magic, but she always laughed it off.

"I just know my girl," she'd say. And, I mean, we're talking about my grandmother. I wasn't going to use my lie-detecting magic on her. I knew that she was a registered Mancer, but not in the Seer lines, so it could have been true

—or she could have just been holding back, on the government as well as on me. And since the state had to just let it slide, I did the same.

Anyway, I pulled out my cell and called Nana Nina to let her know I was coming, and fifteen minutes later I knocked on the door of her apartment. I've got a key to get into the building, and it works on her door, too, but that's only in case of an emergency. I'd never think of just barging in.

When she opened the door the fragrance of freshly-brewed coffee greeted me as warmly as she did. She looked as spry as ever, blue eyes twinkling as she gave me a hug, and stepped back to let me in to her open, airy space. Late afternoon sunlight laid bright tiles on the floor, broken only by the silhouette of her easel set near the bank of windows. She'd divided the loft-style space into furniture-defined 'rooms,' and the only walls surrounded a tiny bathroom. Now that I was inside, the aroma of tacos hit me, too, and I saw that all the fixings waited for us on the dining room table. She'd managed all that in the few minutes since I'd called her? I don't know how she does it at her age, but then, if anyone was going to surprise me, it would likely be Nana Nina.

She'd been born Nina Morow eighty-six years earlier, and although she'd married, she hadn't changed her name. She'd had about a dozen careers, from nursing to construction to art, and as I understand it, she dove headfirst into the fray when computers came to the forefront, blogging from day one and writing open source code. Now she did what she wanted, but what she most liked to do was keep busy. She worked out regularly, wore her hair in a chic layered cut, and painted colorful abstracts for a local gallery.

She motioned me over toward the table, which she'd also managed to set with a hand-embroidered tablecloth and colorful stoneware plates and mugs. As she fetched a fragrant covered pan from the stove, she said "Kit, you know I'm always so glad to see you. But when I do, it usually means you're down in the dumps, so that kind of takes the fun out of it, you know?"

She gave me a grin to let me know she didn't really mean it and set the pan on the table. The seasoned meat still sizzled inside. "We'll eat up, first," she instructed, "and then we'll chat about what's bothering you over the coffee."

"Nothing's bothering me," I lied quickly.

"Sure," she said, "Just an old lady's imagination. Eat a taco, dear."

I grinned, already feeling better as I spooned salsa, shredded cheddar, lettuce and sour cream onto my first taco and wrapped it in a soft, warm tortilla. She was a hard lady to feel glum around. Which I suppose really was the reason I was here.

"How's work?" she asked, as she poured tall glasses of iced green tea for us and started building a taco for herself.

I raised my eyebrows and shrugged. "Interesting lately. We're looking into this whole Murder Prophet business. Or we're about to start."

She frowned and shook her head. "Something weird about that whole thing, Kit. I don't get the motive."

"Neither do I. Neither does anyone, as far as I know. That's what's going to make it difficult."

"How's that young man...the one with the strange name? FerretSnacks?"

I almost snorted green tea through my nose.

"LemurCandy!"

Nana Nina beamed. "That's him! Is he helping you with this case?"

"I'm going to contact him when I go home."

She nodded knowingly. I shook my head. Nana Nina had run into us one night when we were meeting in one of the meat virtuals for cover. I didn't recognize her. Her avatar looked about twenty-four, slim, with long, dramatic red hair and a drink in one hand. She recognized me, though, (like I said, I'm usually not at pains to conceal my identity online) and came over to say hello.

Shocked as I was to meet my grandmother in a place like that, looking like she did, (and not daring to ask—or really wanting to know—what she was doing there) I had the presence of mind to introduce her to Lemur and we made small talk for a few minutes. She took a shine to him, and ever since then she always asks about him. I thought back. He hadn't been using the Coro avatar that night, but a different one.

"He seemed like a nice young man, Kit. You still haven't met him in real life?"

I gave her a look. "I'm perfectly happy the way things are, Nana."

She gave me a look right back. "Oh, not perfectly, dear. Don't try to fool an old woman, because you're the one who ends up looking like a fool."

I laughed. "All right, then. Not perfectly happy. I still have to listen to that goose playing video games all the time."

She laughed, too. "And put up with all your other co-workers' annoying little ways."

"And have trouble finding the perfect pair of jeans."

"And have to clean the toilet from time to time."

"And listen to ads on the vids."

We were both giggling by this time, but Nana sobered first. "Is that really all, honey? I know something deeper's bothering you. I could see it in your eyes when you first got here."

"Are you sure you haven't developed some kind of Seer magic?" I kidded her, but my heart wasn't in it.

"Quite sure," she declared. "I'm much too old to be developing any new magic. But grandmothers have a special kind of insight when it comes to their children and grandchildren. Better than magic." She reached across the table and patted my hand briefly.

I sighed and finished off the green tea, leaning back in my chair and savoring the dregs of honey that had pooled at the bottom. "I guess that's it...the magic. I know most people think it was the best thing that ever happened, but a lot of the time I'm still not so sure."

She nodded. "Let's get that coffee and take it into the living room," she suggested. "These chairs aren't the most comfortable thing under my old bones."

Nana Nina was exaggerating; she was practically in better shape than I was—would be in better shape quickly if I quit running, I thought—but I agreed and she pulled two steaming mugs of coffee from the perc and brought them into the area of the loft she called the living room. Somehow a plate of carob-chip cookies materialized on the coffee table. I settled myself in the big saffron-colored armchair and she sat on the bright red couch across from me. Nana Nina likes color, and being in her apartment is like walking into an Impressionist painting.

She put her slipper-shod feet daintily up on the coffee

table. "Now, what's got you thinking about magic today?" she asked.

I thought of Idala Kineall, so cynical already at only eighteen. "I had to take a runaway Transmute in to sign contracts," I said.

"She went willingly, of course."

"Yes, she did. But...did she have any other real choice? That's what bothers me."

Nana nodded. "You don't remember much about the days before magic, do you?"

"No, I don't."

"You were only ten when the meteorite hit." She closed her eyes and thought for a moment. "It changed everything. And then again, it changed nothing."

I frowned. "What do you mean?"

"It changed everything because the human race was altered in a fundamental way, and a lot of things about the way we perceive ourselves changed. Magic cut across every racial and tribal and societal line we'd ever used to define and separate ourselves. It affected almost everyone in the world, and the handful it didn't affect had nothing in common that anyone could point to and say, 'that's why they're different.' So the ideas of race and of racism changed.

"But what they turned into was just another way to separate and define and catalogue us. Even plug us into a new kind of hierarchy. Psychs and Seers, Shielders and Transmutes and Talents and Mundanes, and levels of ability in each. Now we're more defined by magic than by color, but we're still labelled. And magic has its own costs, which limit our ability to use it, so it couldn't fix everything. There used to be poverty. There's still poverty. There used to be homelessness. There's still homelessness. There used to be crime. There's still crime."

She took a long pull of her coffee. "The thing is, I think it's in our nature to be dissatisfied. We either don't like what we have, or we want what someone else has. No one ever gets exactly what they want, so no matter what the human race has or does, the underlying problems are still there. So that's why I say that everything changed, and nothing changed."

"But at least now we have some control over how we get defined," I protested. "If I don't want to be labelled as—I don't know, as a Seer, then I can just deny that I have that power. It's pretty hard to prove me wrong."

Nana shook her head. "But what kind of choice is that? The choice to live a lie? I don't see how that makes you any more free. And you have to live with denying something intrinsic to who you are."

I sighed. "No, I suppose you're right." I looked up to find her staring at me intently. "What?"

"Oh, nothing, dear. Do you think the girl made the right choice?"

"The girl?" For a second I couldn't think who she was talking about. "Oh, the Transmute. I guess so. I don't really know. I guess I wished she could have made it for different reasons."

"Well, we all have our own reasons for the choices we make, Kit," Nana said. "I think in the end it doesn't matter if anyone else understands why we make them, as long as we understand ourselves."

I looked at her hard for a moment. Was she trying to tell me something that she didn't want to come right out and say? But she looked totally innocent, sitting there with her coffee and her trendily-cut white hair and an EZ-med implant in her left arm, half-smiling indulgently at me.

Grandmothers are masters of deception, and don't let anyone tell you different.

FIVE

A Little Taste of LemurCandy

It was after dark by the time I left Nana Nina's apartment, and I caught a magicab back home. They're expensive, and I don't like the way they make me feel—kind of fuzzy-headed, afterward—so I don't use them often. I also don't know why they're called magi*cabs* when they aren't any kind of a vehicle, just a little booth with a teleportation spell inside it. Nana Nina had managed to cheer me up some, but I still felt like I had to keep busy to keep the dark thoughts at bay.

My apartment seemed dull and empty after spending time in Nana Nina's colorful space. Don't get me wrong, I like my place. I always feel, however, that it's more like the "before" picture than the "after" in an apartment makeover. The furniture is comfortable rather than stylish—I think Nana Nina actually used the word "utilitarian" once, and she was trying to be kind. Maybe I should invite her to turn it into an "after" picture for me some time. But that time wasn't now, so I turned on all the lights, then turned my back on it and sat down at my computer.

"How was your day, Kit?" Phoebe asked me.

"Great."

"You have no personal messages," she told me cheerfully.

"Gee, thanks," I muttered.

"Current energy use is unwarranted," Phoebe continued. "Shall I reduce ambient lighting to optimal levels?"

I sighed. "Sure."

The lights dimmed, but now it seemed darker than ever after I'd had them so bright. I decided it wasn't worth fighting with Phoebe over and logged in to my accounts.

The apartment AI wasn't through, however. "Foodstuffs on hand are low. Shall I compile a grocery list?"

I looked up, although since Phoebe was only a disembodied voice, there wasn't anything specific to glare at. "Yes, and please shut up now! I have work to do and unless there's something urgent, I'd like some quiet."

I don't know how an apartment AI voice can give the impression of offended silence, but Phoebe can. I massaged my temples in tiny circles while I counted to twenty, and went in virtual search of LemurCandy.

It didn't take long; he'd left signposting so I could track him down. That made my heart flutter a little although I reminded myself sternly that we were working a case together, so it only made sense to make it easy to find him. He was in another of the mind virtuals, *Consider the Implications*, one of his favorite haunts. This one styled itself to look like a university faculty lounge, with burgundy tufted-leather armchairs, floor-to-ceiling bookshelves, high windows and chandeliers. Here the discussion usually turned to politics, which was fine for a time but I couldn't take a whole lot of exposure to the chatter. They had a bar, and that's where I found LemurCandy, talking to a grey-haired avatar who looked a lot like those posters of Albert Einstein. You know, the ones with the really wild hair and eyes balanced on the tightrope between genius and crazy.

The guy nodded a hybrid greeting/farewell and walked off as I came up.

This time Lemur didn't look anything like Aleshu Coro, for which I was thankful. Coro and LemurCandy seemed to have completely different personalities, and I would have found it difficult to merge the two in my mind now. Honestly, I hadn't taken much of a shine to the real Coro, and somehow his looks had lost some of their attractiveness, too.

This was an avatar I'd seen Lemur wear before, but not as often as the Coro. Now he had short brown hair with just a hint of curl where it fell over his forehead, and an average build, not as muscled as the other one. When he turned to greet me, though, I realized with a shock that the eyes were the same. Green and somehow knowing. I shook that thought aside. This was a world made of pixels and projections, no matter how sensitive the faceskin you used to run your avatar. There was nothing about this or any avatar that could reflect what LemurCandy was really like, and I'd be better off if I got that fact through my thick head.

<Hey, it's Kitano Kick-ass,> he typed, grinning as usual.

<You don't look like yourself tonight, Lemur,> I replied with a smirk. *<Or, wait, maybe you do? You don't look like Aleshu Coro, at any rate.>*

He had the grace to look sheepish. *<Hey, I just picked that one at random. He wasn't bad-looking, after all.>*

<But you knew who it was.> I'd seen his reaction when I'd asked for information on the name.

His avatar looked away. *<It was something I read online.>* The words appeared more slowly than usual, as if he was confessing something reluctantly. *<That choosing a powerful or attractive avatar can affect your personality in real life.>*

I almost choked, since I'd read—and taken to heart—the same advice. But I just said *<Interesting. I actually like this one better.>* This new avatar might not have the style of Coro's, but since I'd cooled on Coro, it was true.

<Really? Thanks!> His avatar looked pleased.

Dance music started up in the background, and I muted it. My annoyance tolerance seemed to be at its limit for the day.

<Has Saga been in touch with you?> I asked, *<Or Anna?>*

He shook his head. *<Not since this morning. What's up?>*

Since we were standing at the bar, I had my avatar order a drink, a Mystic Summer, for verisimilitude. Sangria and lemon juice with a shot of *aratalel*. I honestly don't know how people got along without *aratalel* before the advent of magic. I knew as soon as I ordered it that I shouldn't have, since it made me want the real thing. Oh, well, maybe I could convince Kiku to go out for drinks after work tomorrow.

<Saga and Anna took Coro on as a client,> I told LemurCandy. *<He's had a message from the Murder Prophet that pegs him as the next victim in about two weeks' time. We're apparently going to save him. And solve the mystery of the Murder Prophet messages into the bargain.>*

LemurCandy's eyebrows went up, which was the least I would have expected. Secretly, I had some sympathy with Glaive's initial opinion, that it was a completely lost cause, but I hadn't wanted to give him the satisfaction of saying so at the meeting. And with Anna and Saga set on it, there wasn't much point in arguing. I wondered what LemurCandy would think of the idea.

I waited while he considered. Then he grinned. *<This isn't going to be easy, you know.>*

<What would be the fun if it was?> I asked, sipping my drink. My brain really wanted to taste it, but I just couldn't fool my taste buds into thinking it was real.

<Want to come on a little preliminary look-see?>

I blinked. LemurCandy had never invited me along on any of his information-gathering forays before. I asked, he investigated, reported to me, and I relayed the data back to the office. That was the drill.

<I wouldn't know what I was doing,> I protested, although actually the idea sounded exciting. Maybe I needed to do something different to shake off this funk. Maybe I just wanted to hang out with Lemur as long as I could.

<You won't have to actually do anything, just tag along,> he assured me. *<I can hitch your profile to mine, and you'll just follow.>*

I shrugged, not wanting to appear too eager. *<Sure, if you want to. I don't have anything else to do tonight that can't wait. Can I finish my drink first?>*

He laughed. *<You should have time while I link up our protocols. Oh, might as well take some Maginox®, too, just in case.>* His avatar looked mine up and down. *<I guess you're dressed okay.>*

<Gee, thanks,> I retorted. *<I suppose I could always go and dress up like Aleshu Coro's wife instead.>*

He stuck out his tongue at me and then his avatar spent the next few minutes arranging peanuts on the bar in silence. I knew that was because Lemur was busy in real life at his computer doing whatever technological "magic" he had to perform to join up our protocols, but it was a little disconcerting anyway. I'd have been happier if he'd just pulled the avatar and left me alone at the bar. I could have talked politics with Einstein-guy for that long.

49

I did slip off the faceskin long enough to wash down a couple of Maginox® like he'd suggested. Two doses in one day meant I'd crash hard tonight, but I wasn't going to let this opportunity slip away, even if I had no idea what I might need magic for. *Just in case*, he'd said. But just in case of what?

When LemurCandy's avatar came back to life, he asked, *<Ever gone outside the grid before?>*

<I don't think so.> I didn't even really understand what he meant by that.

<Okay, well, it'll be a bit confusing. Just relax and don't try to do anything. Enjoy the ride,> he said, and reached out and took my avatar's hand. I was about to say okay when the Netz exploded inside my head.

The mind virtual, the bar, Einstein-guy, LemurCandy's avatar and my drink all disappeared in—well, I was going to say in the blink of an eye, but I didn't have time to blink. It was there, and then it was gone, and I felt like I'd fallen into a black hole. Images flashed through my vision at such speed that I felt blinded. The physical me at my desk reflexively put a hand up to the faceskin to pull it off, but I stopped myself in time. I desperately didn't want to mess up the first time LemurCandy had invited me along on something.

My avatar still clutched LemurCandy's hand, but that's one of the things you get used to pretty quick in virtuals—the odd melding of self and avatar, so that it's perfectly normal after a while to think of yourself as having four hands or two faces. I satisfied myself with putting my real hand on my real cheek. It felt like I had to hold the faceskin in place or it would be whipped away by the speed at which we were moving.

Virtually, of course. I reminded myself that I was actually sitting at my desk at home, in front of the computer. But it sure didn't feel like that.

After a moment the things flying past my vision clarified into pathways, variously colored blue, yellow, green, pink, orange—I wasn't sure that there was a finite number of variations. They weren't the wire-frame tunnels used in early attempts to visualize the Netz. It was more like being inside a glowing, 3-D subway route map.

LemurCandy veered left into a blue one and I almost screamed. My avatar's hand clenched his. At least he wouldn't have heard me, but my avatar's expression mirroring mine via the faceskin would no doubt give it away. He would never let me live it down. I kept my lips firmly clamped shut.

After that the turns came with blinding speed and frequency. I had the thought that I would never find my way back, which was stupid, because I wasn't actually *going anywhere* and all I had to do was take off the faceskin and I'd just be back in my apartment. But the sensation of movement was so real, that's how it felt.

We finally emerged from the maze of intersecting paths back into a static virtual, the digital pathways morphed back into streets, and we fetched up outside a huge building. It stood many storeys high, its colonnaded facade styled to look like it had endured decades of use. Wide stone steps led up to double glass doors. I realized that LemurCandy was smiling at me and I took a deep breath. *<So that's what it's like outside the grid, huh?>*

<Yup. It's the only way to travel. Come on. This is the Library.> He ran up the virtual stone steps of the building and I followed a little more slowly, trying to calm my

pounding heart.

Inside, instead of books, workstation terminals lined the walls, although they floated in space, not attached to anything. The walls themselves were a multiplicity of screens, and many avatars stood at terminals using them to look up information and read what displayed on the screen near their terminal. Lemur crossed to one and began pecking at the keys.

<What are you doing?> I asked.

<Asking for a chronological correlation of all Netz references to The Murder Prophet since the first appearance,> he said.

<But that will take years to sort through!>

He shook his head, still typing. *<If you just tried to do a Netz search from your computer it would,>* he said, *<but in here, there's a more complex filtering system available. Since we're actually inside the Netz, I can tap into the data and discard irrelevant references faster.>*

I frowned. It wasn't exactly an explanation. *<How does that work? Could I do it?>*

He glanced at me and grinned. This new avatar had a pretty nice smile. *<It takes some practice.>*

<Okay, whatever.> I looked around the room idly at the other users, hiding my disappointment. Had he brought me along just to show off? For personal reasons, or so that I'd report back to Anna and Saga how dedicated and talented he was?

<I mean, you could try it, you just wouldn't be as fast,> he amended.

Not wanting to look childish, I said, *<Sure.>*

He pulled one of the free-floating terminals over next to his and showed me how to tap into the data stream. Since he was searching the Murder Prophet refs, I typed in

Aleshu Coro's name.

It *was* faster. I guess the difference was that I wasn't reading things physically off the screen at my computer, I was actually getting the data directly through the faceskin and synth glove interface—somehow. I felt deeper inside the Netz than I'd ever been, like I'd tapped into some dense inner current of the data stream. Almost a trance, a dream-state, where time moves differently, or is irrelevant. It felt sneaky, too. I liked that. I sorted through a lot of Aleshu Coro's life in an amazingly short time.

I still didn't see any reason why someone would want to kill him. Whatever motive existed, no Netz data seemed to point to it.

<*Got 'em,*> LemurCandy said.

<*Now what?*> I asked.

<*On to the next stop. I want to check on a tracer I sent out.*>

<*Okay.*> I had no idea what a tracer was or where we had to go to check on it, but I'd said I was along for the ride and I wasn't ready to go home yet.

We left the virtual building and LemurCandy took my avatar's hand again when we reached the "street" outside. He did something, and then without warning we were back in the labyrinth of flashing pathways, and my main concerns were holding tight to LemurCandy's hand and trying not to get a headache. I felt certain if I did, it would be a real one, not the virtual kind.

This time we settled in front of an apartment building. It was nice, virtually constructed of light-colored bricks and landscaped in a minimal way with a few small trees and shrubs, and gravel to keep the virtual weeds down. I'd had no idea that places like this existed in the Netz, that people took the time to craft actual cities for their interactive "rooms" to exist in. I'd heard of games that did this, sure, but this didn't feel like a game. I thought I might have a better understanding now of why some people spent so much time on the Netz. It wasn't just part of the real world; it had become a whole world of its own.

I said as much to LemurCandy as we walked up a few flights of stairs inside the building. *<Some of it's the product of Psych magic,>* he explained. *<Virtuals have been around for a long time, but they always came from hours and hours of work using graphical imaging software and reams of program code. Some Psych Mancers have become so attuned to it there's a new term for them—Netzers. They can tap into the ambient Netz magic and create stuff like this using their own illusion magic. But it's persistent magic in the Netz then, part of the virtual infrastructure, and anyone can use it.>*

<I didn't know that.> Most of what he'd just said didn't even make sense to me. My ignorance was embarrassing. How could I have missed all this? I looked around the hallway we'd reached. It was long and narrow, carpeted in swirls of blue and green and yellow. Light spilled up and down the walls from conical sconces, and doors waited at even intervals. It looked like a nice place to live. I suspected most of the apartments looked nicer inside than mine did in the real world.

We stopped at the last door on the left. Bright, blue-tinged light leaked out underneath the door. LemurCandy's avatar still held my hand, but he put his other one up against the door and pressed it there for a moment. When it opened I realized why the light coming from underneath it was so bright. The entire inside of the room beyond was filled with computer screens.

Computer screens, and one avatar. I could just discern

the outline back-lit by the screens as Lemur dragged me over to be introduced. *<Kit, this is FallenElfGeek. FEG, meet Kitano Kick-Ass.>*

I wanted to protest, since that wasn't exactly my real username, but honestly I couldn't speak. FallenElfGeek really did look like an elf, all pointy ears and long intricately braided hair and soulful eyes. He also looked like a geek, wearing a black t-shirt that said **<1nT3nZ3 G33K>** in bright green letters, in case there were any doubt. His elf-like persona extended to the expression of thoughtful composure on his face.

But he sort of lit up when Lemur introduced me and he just said *<Kit!>* and rather surprisingly hugged my avatar.

I smiled and hugged him back, because I had no idea what else to do.

LemurCandy and FallenElfGeek quickly fell into a very technical conversation. I zoned out purely for the preservation of my mental health. I gathered that FEG had been helping Lemur try to trace the origin of the Murder Prophet messages, but it involved a convoluted system of backtracking, looping, and aliasing. Whatever that meant. It seemed to mean that it was hard to track. That much, I got.

Then FallenElfGeek proffered faceskins for us and put one on himself. I made my avatar take one and chose the "wear" command to put it on. At this point, what else could I do? I was in my apartment, attached via faceskin to my computer, and interacting over the Netz via an avatar, who was now putting on a virtual faceskin to interact with—I didn't know what. Some even deeper part of the Netz system? I hadn't even known about the kinds of places LemurCandy had already taken me tonight. But I wasn't about to back out now.

We put on the faceskins and LemurCandy told me, *<I think you'll be able to help with this, Kit.>*

I said, *<Really? I cannot imagine how.>*

He laughed. He must have thought I was making a joke.

Then we became completely incorporeal.

Of course, we were already completely incorporeal in the virtual, because our bodies were back at home. Now we became...I don't know. Data in its purest digital form, I guess. There was no longer any semblance of reality or nods to creating surroundings that mimicked, even in a superficial way, the real world. There was only data—I sensed rather than saw the presence of the data packets representing LemurCandy and FEG.

Even though I no longer had a virtual hand, it seemed like LemurCandy squeezed it encouragingly, then let go. The data packet that was LemurCandy moved away from us. I wondered briefly where he was going, but was too intrigued by what surrounded us to worry about it.

On all sides ran streams of numbers, digital code that somehow, through the faceskin, made sense to me. They were maps. They were instructions. They were pictures. They were statements of fact.

And some of them were lies.

My magic sensed it without conscious effort from me. I was glad I had taken the Maginox®. *<That one's false,>* I said, as a string of numbers streamed past me. It was as if the mental intention of the originator had imprinted itself on the command, tainting it with a visible aura of deception.

The stream I'd just indicated glowed red. *<I tagged it,>* FallenElfGeek said, somewhere inside my head. *<See any more like that?>*

I studied the numbers carefully now. Some emanated a stronger sense of deception than others. Those I picked out easily. In others, it seemed more removed, as if maybe they had simply iterated from a false one, not been directly created themselves by someone with misleading intentions. I became completely caught up in sorting and classifying them, entranced by what my magic could reveal.

Finally FallenElfGeek said that was probably enough, and when we took off our secondary faceskins, the streaming numbers winked out and we were back in FEG's monitor-lined virtual living room. FEG regarded one of the screens with a look of satisfaction. "That's taken care of a lot of garbage," he said.

"What kind of garbage?" I didn't even really understand what I'd been doing, and I didn't see LemurCandy anywhere. I wondered where he had gone.

"Well, all those things you tagged were backtracks, aliases—all kinds of deceptive message path manipulations."

Before I could ask what that meant, Lemur returned from another room in the apartment and asked, "How'd it go?"

"She was netzune!" FEG said, which I took to mean something good. LemurCandy clapped him on the shoulder, and we said our goodbyes. FEG promised to do some more detective work with this new information, and get back to LemurCandy in the morning.

Lemur and I walked down the stairs and out of the building slowly. He had taken hold of my avatar's hand again and I was trying to wrap my head around what had just happened.

<I had no idea that magic had permeated the Netz that much,>

I said, as we stood outside the building. It was full dark now, programmed to simulate the physical world, and streetlights glowed on standards high above our heads. Stars twinkled in the distance. Most of the buildings around us had lights in their windows. An avatar in medieval garb flew past, low over our heads, and settled on the sidewalk in front of a building a little further down the street. LemurCandy didn't even look up, so I assumed this was an ordinary occurrence.

Lemur nodded. *<I don't think people who aren't working in it realize what's been happening over the last ten years,>* he said. He spread his arms wide. *<Do you know, if all the power in the world shut down, the Netz would still continue to function? They'd run on the ambient magic that's been absorbed by the datastreams. And it's spreading. Your apartment could be completely dark, but your computer would still run if it was hooked into the Netz.>*

<What?> I stared at him. *<That's crazy!>*

He raised his eyebrows a little and grinned. *<Doesn't mean it isn't true. Who knows where it'll be in five years?>*

I was in no mental state to imagine.

<Anyway, I guess you'd rather just unskin from here than travel back?> he asked.

I nodded. Maginox® exhaustion grabbed me and shook me like a dog with a chew toy. It seemed ages since I'd had supper with Nana Nina, and aeons since I'd sat in on Aleshu Coro's appointment and taken Idala to the Registry office.

<I'll be in touch in the morning with a report,> Lemur said. *<Thanks for your help in there. You've made a new friend in FallenElfGeek.>*

<I can use all the friends I can get,> I said. *<Thanks for*

showing me some things I didn't know about.>

<No problem. Anything to stay on your good side.> He was still smiling, and I couldn't read those green avatar eyes.

I couldn't think of anything else to say, so I smiled back, reached up, and gently peeled off the faceskin. I suppose to LemurCandy my avatar simply winked out of existence.

I was back in my dark apartment, the only glow coming from the computer screen and a little from the streetlights leaking in around the window blind. I peeled off the synth gloves and left them on the desk. The Maginox® in my system had triggered a buzzing dizziness in my head now, and even that small amount of light made me want to clench my eyes against it. I managed to shut down my computer and unplugged it from the wall. What LemurCandy had told me about the magic on the Netz was just too creepy. Then I crawled into bed without getting undressed.

"Goodnight, Kit," Phoebe said stiffly.

I wished briefly that I could unplug her sometimes, too, and pretended to be already asleep.

SIX

I'll Shoot The Messenger If I Get The Chance

In the morning, I managed to get my run in again (two days in a row!) despite how tired I'd been the night before. Phoebe seemed to be over last night's snit and was as cheerful as usual when she woke me. I have to admit, even before I hit the pavement, I felt...buoyant. The trip "outside the grid" with LemurCandy last night had been, for all its strangeness and physical drain, fun. I ran longer than usual, caught up in a generally good feeling about the world, and then had to rush to shower, dress, and make it to the office on time.

Which was just as well, because I didn't have time to check my mail until I got to Darcko and Sadatake, and I was glad to have other people around me when I found what was waiting in my inbox.

My very own message from the Murder Prophet.

I don't know how long I stared at the stark black letters, not really comprehending what I was seeing. Or maybe not letting myself comprehend it. I swallowed hard a few times, my throat thick and constricted. It seemed to be full of my heart, pushing blood and adrenaline and denial through my veins. Even reading the message to Aleshu Coro had made my skin prickle, just because, although on its surface it was only a lovely bit of poetry sent as a warning, it didn't feel like that. It felt like a threat. Malevolent and menacing. And so did this one.

> *I have a rendezvous with Death*
> *At some disputed barricade,*
> *When Spring comes back with rustling shade*
> *And apple-blossoms fill the air—*
> *I have a rendezvous with Death*
> *When Spring brings back blue days and fair.*[2]

My eyes were still locked on the screen when Kikufaax came to my doorway, pulling a red leather jacket on over her cream-coloured cashmere turtleneck. "I'm making a run to Grounds Zero for real coffee—Kit? What's wrong?"

I swallowed hard once more so that my voice would have room to get through, and swivelled the screen so she could see it. "I got a message. Take a look."

Her eyes narrowed as she read it. She raised her voice loud enough to be heard all over the office and called, "Kit's office, everyone!"

It didn't take them long to congregate around the screen. My small office was packed, with five of us and the goose. Trip jumped up on my desk to see better. He shed some feathers, but I ignored them.

"Anyone else get one of these?" Anna asked.

Negatives all around.

"So why Kit?" Glaive looked at me almost accusingly. He moved away from my desk to lean against the wall and folded his black-clad arms. "What did you do?"

"What makes you think I did anything? I thought we were all working on this case as of yesterday afternoon."

"Of course we were," Anna said soothingly. She patted

my arm. "I think Glaive just meant, what did you in particular, do, that might have attracted attention?"

"It could be a fluke," Trip suggested. Everyone looked at him. "Yeah, I guess not."

"Hmmmm." Glaive stroked his stubbled chin with a forefinger. Glaive doesn't see any need to shave every day. I suppose there's a different standard for retired hit men than for other men. Or maybe it was trendy. "The police don't seem to have been treating these messages as threats, but it's hard to see this one as anything else."

Kikufaax sat on the edge of my desk and shook her head. She'd shed her jacket again. Her right foot, clad in a low-heeled soft leather boot, drummed a little staccato of agitation against the wood. "It doesn't have to be a threat. The timing certainly seems to be related to the Coro case, but that doesn't necessarily speak to the intent as well. It might or might not mean someone's telling us to stay out of this."

"Kiku's right," Anna said, frowning. She lowered herself gracefully into one of the "client" chairs in my office, smoothing the pleats of her mauve-patterned skirt with restless fingers that belied the calm in her voice. "There are two ways to think about these messages. They're either well-intentioned warnings to put the intended victim on guard, or they're threats designed to rattle the victim and make their last few days or weeks miserable."

"Elegantly put, Anna," Saga said, taking the other chair. "The question is, which?"

I waved a hand in the air. "Speaking as a recipient," I said, "it feels like a threat, and I'm feeling rattled *and* miserable. And in case anyone else hadn't noticed, look out the window—it's already spring."

"Not yet," Trip said.

Everyone looked at him again. He shrugged his wings. "The first day of spring isn't officially until March twentieth, and this is only the tenth."

"When is Coro's fortnight up, if that's accurate?" Glaive asked.

Kiku shot him a withering glance. "The twentieth. Didn't you figure that out already?"

Glaive shrugged. "No. I figured two weeks gave us more than enough time, once we put our minds to it. So I didn't bother with dates."

Anna fixed me with a serious look. "Don't worry, Kit. We're not going to let anything happen to you."

"Yeah," I said, "I wonder if anyone said that very same thing to any of the other victims?"

Trip waddled across the desk and patted me awkwardly on the shoulder with one of those weird hands. At least he'd had the good sense to get the Mancer to make them white, so they just looked like an extension of his white-feathered wings. Sort of. I couldn't imagine how creepy they would be if he'd had them flesh-colored. "I'm going to start practicing my moves even harder," he assured me. "And I'll be around, whenever you need me. I mean it. We're all in this together."

Well, I didn't burst out laughing, but it was close. No matter what I say about him, there's no way I'd intentionally hurt Trip's feelings, so I managed to clamp my lips together in some semblance of a smile and bite my tongue at the same time. The pain kept the laughter at bay long enough for me to get control, and then I just said, "Thanks, Trip. I appreciate it."

Glaive said, "Okay, so let's call it a threat. That means

that the Murder Prophet, whoever he or she is, has some interest in the murders, other than just being able to predict them."

"Or if not in the murders, then in the murderer," Kiku said.

Saga shook his head and narrowed his eyes. Although his demeanor stayed as outwardly calm as ever, the hard note of anger in his voice came through loud and clear. "There are multiple murderers involved, remember. It would be too much to believe that they are connected in any way other than through the person sending these messages. If that person is not the murderer in all cases, that theory fails. I cannot accept that these murderers are related by anything other than chance."

"Then we're back to the Murder Prophet," I said. "Personally, I don't care what his motivations are right now. I just want him stopped." I shivered. I didn't want anyone else receiving one of these messages.

"Glaive was correct to ask his earlier question, however," Saga said, turning to me. "What did you do yesterday, Kit? You seem to have attracted unwanted attention. That in itself could be a clue."

"Lucky me," I said. I leaned back in my chair and counted items off on my fingers. "I picked up Miss Kineall. We chatted a bit, not about the Coro case or the Murder Prophet. I delivered her to the Registry office as you requested. I had supper with my grandmother. I went directly home from there and went Netz-surfing with LemurCandy, looking for information relevant to the Coro case. I had a tiff with my apartment AI. I went to bed." I shrugged. "That's it."

Glaive snickered. "I've always said, Kit can piss off

anyone. Obviously, even a computer."

"Where did you go with Lemur?" Kikufaax asked, ignoring him.

"I met up with him in a mind virtual, then we went outside the grid—"

"Really?" Trip interjected. "I've read about that! It's supposed to be really cool! Do you think he'd take me sometime?" The goose was practically jumping up and down on my desk. Fluffy bits of white down fluttered over some of my papers.

"I'm sure he would, if you asked him," I said reassuringly. "It was definitely interesting. We went to place Lemur called the Library and sorted through data; Lemur was looking for references to the Murder Prophet and I did a search on Coro. Then he took me to a...a friend's house, I guess. Still virtual. The guy was trying to do a traceback on one of the messages from the Murder Prophet."

"Any luck?" Glaive asked.

I shrugged. "They didn't seem to have any real answers before we left. Then we went really deep inside the Netz and they got me to tag some of the data streams as true or false—I didn't even know my magic could do that—"

I stopped because I caught sight of Saga's face. Now he also *looked* angry. You have to understand, Saga is the epitome of imperturbable. Here's how I knew he was angry: a straight little vertical line bisected the space between his brows, and the corners of his mouth turned down about two degrees.

"What's wrong?" I asked.

"LemurCandy may have exposed you to a malicious Harmonized Divination Nexus," Saga said. "Do you know if he source-response vetted the data streams before he exposed you to them?"

I raised an eyebrow. "Once more, this time in some language I might understand?"

"Never mind. I will contact LemurCandy myself," he said, and stood. "Did anyone check with him to see if he received any messages from the Murder Prophet himself?"

"Not yet," Anna said calmly. "You go ahead and ask him." Those two had been partners for so long, they had learned some cosmic secret about balancing each others' moods. If one was angry, the other got preternaturally calm. And vice versa. More marriages would last if couples could learn that secret.

"I'm going to go get Kit a coffee," Kikufaax said.

"And a lemon doughnut?" I asked hopefully.

She laughed. "And a lemon doughnut. Anyone else?"

The others chimed in with their orders, following Kiku out of my office, and I had a few moments alone to collect my thoughts. I wanted to contact LemurCandy, but Saga was already doing that. I supposed I could try and get in touch with FallenElfGeek, but I wasn't confident I could find my way back to his apartment by myself and I didn't like to try without talking to Lemur first anyway. For all I knew, that was FEG's secret virtual hideaway, and they wouldn't appreciate my mucking it up for him.

But I didn't want to just sit there thinking about the message. I closed it with a vehement click, determined to put it out of my mind. I still had the data I'd filtered about Aleshu Coro to go through, sent to my own inbox in a secure packet from the Library last night. I set about opening it up and trying to arrange the data into something that made sense.

Coro's biography read like something out of a boring

movie about a guy with an almost-perfect life. He'd developed his meagre magic talent early, but not at such a young age that his parents had to deal with the medication issue. Top student, sociable, enhanced no doubt by the fact that his father was a well-to-do businessman and his mother a prominent environmentalist, although not the fanatical kind.

He started MageData, Inc. straight out of college, utilizing an innovative type of database he'd developed in a university computer course. Married his college sweetheart, an artist named Evangeline Harrington. The sweetness apparently didn't last, and they'd divorced about six years later. The ex-wife had dropped off the radar, gone off to Europe to pursue her art.

Second wife, Clarice Valencia, was a technician at MageData, and they married shortly after Coro's divorce, just when the company started to really become a leader in the field. A MageData subsidiary came up with a reliable genetic test to determine if a person had an active magical ability or not, and it was hailed by some as the first step toward a real magic-ability identification test. Not everyone thinks having such a thing is a good idea, but the governments want it so badly they pour a lot of money every year into funding the research. Me, I think if it ever comes it'll be such a massive invasion of privacy that they won't be able to implement it, since they still can't even force anyone to take the initial genetic test.

Anyway. Second marriage lasted ten years. MageData got to be the biggest in the field, and I guess Coro thought he deserved a new trophy wife. At least that had been the rumor at the time. Wife #2 got a lot of property, including a magically-created island near Fiji, so I don't imagine she spent a lot of time licking her wounds. Wife #3, Sandrine (née Allaire), had been in the picture for five years now.

At this point Kiku came back with my coffee and doughnut. I barely looked up to thank her, I was so deep in reading the data, but she didn't leave right away.

"You all right, Kit?" she asked, hovering in front of my desk. She twisted the plain silver ring she always wore on her right hand, a sure sign of her agitation.

I looked up then. "What? Oh, yeah, sure." I drew a deep breath and blew it out. "I was spooked at first, but the best thing for me to do is just keep working, keep my mind off it."

She nodded. "I'd be the same way. Anyway, don't worry. We've got your back."

"I know it."

She smiled then and left, but I'd heard the undercurrent of concern in her voice. Kiku was almost as unflappable as Saga, so it didn't exactly make me feel as much better as she'd probably hoped. I took a sip of coffee and then a big bite of doughnut. Powdered sugar and tart lemon filling...now *that* was comforting. I turned my attention back to the screen.

Numerous tidbits of information had made it through my filters but I didn't see how most of them could be useful to the case. Coro's favorite drink (something called a Bodyguard's Scabbard, which I'd never tried but sounded interesting), preferred avatars (one that looked just like him, and a blond male bimbo who seemed to get a lot of use), known usernames (apart from his corporate "Acoro" the only other he ever seemed to use was "PsychoticMuslinCrayon," apparently a holdover from his college days and linked to the blond avatar), and favorite color (blue).

There was also data on Coro's charitable donations (on which, I admit, he didn't stint) and "good works," which included youth facilities, university endowments, magic research grants, and the like. I only skimmed over those, because philanthropy is not generally the kind of thing that gets a person killed.

In fact, there was very little in the file to peg Coro as the kind of person who gets murdered with malice aforethought. Sure, he might have trampled on a few little people on his march to the top of the database ladder, but on the whole my impression was that he was a pretty nice guy. He had ethics. He had a conscience. He gave back.

I sighed and cleared the data off my screen. That had gotten me exactly nowhere, except for the two ex-wives, whom I didn't think were going to figure in this. One had likely been gone too long to be still holding a grudge, and the other had made out well enough on the deal to let bygones be bygones. We'd check them out, but it seemed like a dead end.

I shivered. What's with these expressions that we use all the time and then suddenly they take on a whole new meaning?

I shook it off and buzzed Kiku. "Anyone else tasked with talking to Coro yet?"

"I don't think so."

"I'm going to call him up, ask him about the company and stuff."

"Sure thing," she said. "Logical for you to do it, since you'll know if he's telling the truth."

I slipped into the kitchen and washed down a couple of Maginox®, then went back to my office, closed the door, and phoned Coro. He'd obviously left instructions for his staff because with an absolute minimum of runaround, for a company the size of MageData, I was talking to the man himself. He still sounded tired, but glad to hear from me.

The conversation followed pretty standard lines. I asked him again if he had any enemies, he said no, and then I asked him again in various ways, this time pinpointing specific possibilities like employees, members of MageData's Board of Directors, other business contacts, ex-wives and their families, personal acquaintances, etc.

He said no to all of them, and he was telling the truth. The guy really couldn't imagine anyone wanting to kill him, for any reason.

I got him to verify some of the information I'd found online, just to double-check and so that he'd know we were doing our job. I didn't bring up his favorite drink or the blond male avatar. He didn't have to know everything we knew.

And then we were done, and I didn't feel any further ahead.

Saga came into my office just as I hung up the phone. The angry line on his forehead had smoothed itself out again and he looked as serene as ever. "LemurCandy would like you to contact him as soon as possible," he said. He peered at me closely for a moment. "Are you all right, Kitano?"

I nodded. "Same thing Kiku asked me twenty minutes ago. I'm fine. What do you want me to do today?"

He tented his fingers, tapping them meditatively. "Actually, Anna and I are wondering if we should remove you from this case. Now that you've caught the attention of this person—"

"Oh, no, Saga, please!" I interrupted. "That's the last thing I want. I'll go crazy if I can't keep working—"

He interrupted me right back. "Crazy is preferable to dead, Kit."

"That's a matter of opinion." I stood up, not that I thought I could intimidate him in any way, but it felt like a stronger position. "Look, I'll be careful, I really will. But you've got to keep me on the case. I've got a personal stake in it now."

Anna poked her head in at the doorway, smiling that smile that on anyone else would be a grin, but she was just too classy for that. "I told you so, Saga."

He sighed. "Yes, you did. I still think I'm right, but—all right, Kit. For now. The first day of spring is not here yet, so we will assume that your danger is no more imminent than Mr. Coro's." He rapped his knuckles on my desk. "But I reserve the right to change my mind about this at any time."

"Understood," I said meekly. "So, do you have an assignment for me?"

He did not pause to consider. I expect he had everyone's tasks planned out for them already, and knew what he was going to get me to do if I balked at being sidelined. "I would like you and Glaive to visit the current wife. I have already cleared it with Mr. Coro, who does not think she will have anything useful to tell you." He made a face that told me exactly what he thought of men who underestimated what their wives might know.

"Okay. Is Glaive waiting for me?"

"He is finishing up a telephone call. You have time to contact Lemur before you go if you wish."

Now, how did he know I wanted to do that? If I asked him he'd only smile enigmatically, so I didn't waste my breath. I slipped on the faceskin, logged in, and LemurCandy messaged me immediately with a link to his location. I clicked it, and my avatar materialized in another one of the mind virtuals; this one mimicked a university campus and LemurCandy stood in a virtual classroom. The blackboard behind his avatar was covered with scientific-looking scribbles that meant nothing to me. LemurCandy wore the same avatar he'd had on last night. He looked worried as he tossed a stick of virtual chalk from hand to hand.

<Kit! Are you all right?>

<Of course I'm all right.> I felt a strange mix of annoyance and pleasure that he'd asked. *<You're the third person who's asked me that in the last half hour. It was only a message. Not like someone came to the office gunning for me.>*

<I know. But it mustn't have been very nice.>

I thought of the words again and shivered. *<No,>* I admitted, *<it wasn't. You didn't get one?>*

<Nothing. I feel like it's my fault, though.>

I frowned. *<Why?>*

<I took you to FallenElfGeek. Let you muck around with your magic in those datastreams connected to this freakazoid prophet. That could be how they zoned in on you. Saga reamed me out pretty good for that, and he's completely right.> The chalk disappeared and he stuck his hands in his pockets.

I shrugged, and so did my avatar. *<I also sifted through all that data on Coro at the library,>* I typed. *<It's not like I was exactly tiptoeing around, avoiding connections with him.>*

The avatar shook its head. *<Couldn't have been that,>* he said. *<Library accesses are identity-protected.>*

Glaive stuck his head in at my door. He'd added a black jacket to his already-ebony ensemble. "I'm ready to head out anytime."

"Give me one second."

He went out to talk to Kikufaax and I typed hastily. *<Gotta go. Will you be online later?>*

<Sure thing. Kit?>

<Yes?>

There was a long pause before anything else appeared on the screen, and the avatar just stood there with a blank expression.

The words *<Be careful out there>* finally appeared.

I half-smiled. Like I wasn't always, or tried to be. But all I said was, *<I will. Talk to you later.>* Then I signed off, grabbed my gun out of the bottom drawer, and followed Glaive out to his Cloudwalker.

SEVEN

Of Hit Men and Lovely Ladies

It annoys me sometimes, how a lot of things involving magic ended up with these cutesy names. I mean, you wouldn't see a non-magical vehicle ending up with a name like "Cloudwalker." Not unless it was something that could actually fly. The Cloudwalker series was just a ground-level glider that used two spells: one to recharge the matter-to-energy conversion inside the battery, and a second to give it lift, so it hovered about two feet off the ground.

I couldn't see the point—another spell to be recharged every time it got low—but they were surprisingly popular with manly men like Glaive. Might have been something about not leaving tire tracks behind, I don't know. They still left a traceable magic signature, so it didn't make you invisible or anything.

Men.

I shared everything I'd found out about Coro with Glaive on our drive out to the Coros' mansion on the outskirts of the city, in an area called Alchemist's Ridge. In truth, there weren't a whole lot of alchemists living out there. The alchemy involved, as far as I could see, was the magic of turning ideas into money. Everyone who lived in the area must have been very, very good at it.

Glaive listened impassively as he drove, interjecting a

comment or question now and then. I'd been a little nervous around him when I'd first learned about his background, but apart from being the strong, silent type (a temperament which I'm sure was as much deliberately cultivated as natural), he really seemed like a normal guy. Sometimes I even wondered if he'd made up the stuff about the clandestine government-sanctioned escapades of his past, but Anna and Saga seemed to think it was true, so who was I to doubt? Kiku and I often complained to each other that he was too taciturn and overprotective of us, but we managed to work well together in spite of that.

An ancient-looking stone wall broken by a ten-foot-tall iron gate surrounded the Coro place. The gate sported all the requisite swirls and curlicues unfurling around a massive letter "C," and the iron behemoth opened as we drove slowly up to it. No doubt we were being observed by unseen eyes. Inside the wall, tall, drooping willow trees showed branches furred with an aura of spring green as they budded out. We drove up a winding road through exquisitely manicured grounds dotted with surprising topiaries sculpted in the shapes of fantastic creatures. A dragon with widespread boxwood wings and menacing teeth. A mermaid combing viridian hair. A goat-legged satyr engaged in a static dance. I wondered if they were Coro's idea, or his wife's.

We rounded a bend and the house came into view, a woman standing on the front steps waiting for us. The house was my first surprise. It wasn't new, as these places go; the body of the house and the western wing sported the turreted style that had enjoyed a resurgence around the time of the advent of magic. As if everyone thought we were going to start living in castles and wearing medieval gowns and armor. The east wing was more modern, obviously added once the "Nouveau Magic" period had ended. The gardens fronting the house, however, were different again, with an English country feel. A boxwood-hedged knot garden wound around a fountain in the shape of a unicorn. Even after the topiaries, that one made me blink. Water spouted energetically from the creature's horn and looked extremely unusual erupting from that part of its anatomy.

I recognized the woman on the steps from Coro's file—his wife, Sandrine. She didn't descend as we drove up, just stood hugging herself in a moss green sweater that I would have bet a week's pay was cashmere, and a straight grey wool skirt. Worry had pulled the skin on her face and neck taut, so maybe it wasn't just the cool spring breeze that was making Sandrine Coro hug herself. Long blond hair hung in loose curls down her back and wisped around her face in the wind. Glaive got out first and walked over to her, hands in his pockets.

"Mrs. Coro?" he asked pleasantly.

I came up behind him as she was nodding. Her gaze flicked to me but didn't linger. A woman who'd rather deal with men.

"Your husband told you to expect us, I assume. I'm Glaive Timesi, and this is Kitano Stablefield. We're with Darcko and Sadatake."

She nodded. "Please come inside," she said. "We'll have tea while we speak." She wasn't asking if we'd like some. She was telling us the agenda. Politely, though.

We entered a foyer with a bright, mosaic-tiled ceiling that vaulted halfway up into the turret above it, and a floor so highly polished I was half glad my boots had non-slip soles and half mortified to walk on it with them. An elegantly curving stairway led to the upper reaches of the house, and a tree—an actual *tree*—starred with tiny white lights grew inside its curve, stretching green-trimmed branches to a skylight high above. Mrs. Coro led us past the stairs and into another room filled with soft-looking beige striped furniture and enormous and fragrant flower arrangements. Tastefully abstract paintings dotted the walls and a low mahogany table held a silver tea service and an assortment of mugs, cups, and glasses. She motioned us to sit near it, and lowered herself nervously onto a cream-and-ginger patterned divan.

"Would you prefer tea or coffee, Miss Stablefield?" she asked me, "Or perhaps some iced *sprakele*?"

I could see only the one pot on the table, a huge silver Victorian affair, but she'd asked, so I said, "The *sprakele* would be lovely, thank you." It was a while since I'd had the magically-produced drink, but as soon as she mentioned it I wanted some. "But only a small glass, please." I had to be careful since I'd taken Maginox® before my conversation with her husband, and that combination could produce a powerful intoxication.

She nodded and took up the teapot and a crystal glass, and poured out a full measure of the sparkling turquoise drink. Handing it to me, she looked at Glaive. "And you, Mr. Timesi?"

He looked discomfited. I knew from one of our past office parties that he hated *sprakele*. "Did you mention coffee, Mrs. Coro? But not if it's too much trouble..."

"No trouble at all. And please, call me Sandrine." She took up one of the manlier-looking coffee mugs and the same pot, and this time rich, dark coffee poured from the spout. She passed him the steaming cup and indicated cream and sugar on the table. "Not much of a talent," she said ruefully, nodding at the silver pot, "But it comes in handy once in a while."

Mrs. Coro poured herself what looked like green tea and left it unadulterated with sugar or honey. She sat with her back very straight and her hands clasped in her lap and asked, "Are you going to be able to save my husband?"

"We're going to do our very best," Glaive said smoothly, stirring his coffee. "But we do need your help."

He proceeded to ask her questions for the next half hour, about her husband, his ex-wives, the staff at the house, the people he worked with, their friends. It was very pleasant to sit in those lovely surroundings drinking *sprakele*, but it seemed more and more futile. Glaive was starting to think so, too; I could tell by the way the line of his jaw grew more and more pronounced. He was pretty much grasping at straws when he asked Mrs. Coro about her husband's activity on the Netz. "Does he spend much time in virtuals, games, alias lives, anything like that?"

She smiled and shook her head. "Oh, no, apart from mail and things pertaining to work I don't think he spends much time on the Netz at all. We might look something up from time to time, but that's it." She leaned forward to top up my glass of *sprakele* and Glaive shot me a covert look. I knew we were both thinking about that blond male avatar who seemed to get a lot of Netz time. I checked, but got no impression that she was lying. So maybe she didn't know about him at all. That might be interesting. The full glass of *sprakele* was tempting, but I didn't finish it off. I'd had a *sprakele*-Maginox® headache once before, and believe me, once is enough.

We took our leave shortly after that, driving back into the city through a perfect spring day. "So does she know, or not?" I said to Glaive as soon as we'd pulled out of the driveway.

He flipped on the radio and a blues-jazz fusion filled the air. "Good question. We should ask LemurCandy to check Mrs. Coro's database, see if she's got an avatar who frequents the same kind of places as his. If so, it's likely some game they're just playing with each other. If not..."

"She didn't seem to be lying about the Netz use," I mused. "Or anything else. Still, It gives us something interesting to check into, at least." I started to open my window to let in some of the fresh spring air but Glaive stopped me.

"Do you know how easy it is to assassinate someone through the open window of a vehicle?" he barked.

I shuddered and closed the window again. "No, I didn't. And I wish I still didn't. Don't be ridiculous, Glaive. Do you really think some nutcase is lying in wait for me in Alchemist's Ridge?"

He grinned. "No, I don't. But you received a death threat, or what amounts to one, and you're going to have to learn how to take precautions for a little while."

"Let me guess. You're just the one to teach me."

"No doubt about it. Do you know anyone else who knows more about killing people?"

I swallowed. I really didn't like thinking about that side of Glaive's old job, even though he had been an ethical hit man. I know that sounds like an oxymoron, but Saga assures me that he was, and if Saga says so, that's good enough for me. I just still try not to think about it too much. "No," I retorted, "and I don't care to. You'll have to do."

"Good. So start listening to me without any backtalk when I tell you things like that." He was still smiling, but I could hear the undercurrent of concern in his voice.

"Okay," I said meekly, and he gave me a crash course on self-preservation that filled the rest of the drive back into the city. Frankly, it sounded like a lot of work.

———•———

When we got back to the office, a message from LemurCandy blinked on my screen, asking me to get in touch with him. I got online, and it seemed like he'd just been sitting there, waiting for me. We chatted text-only this time.

<You okay?> he asked right away.

<Of course I'm okay. I was with Glaive. I hope everybody isn't going to start asking me every ten seconds if I'm okay, because I'll lose my mind.>

There was a pause. Oops. Maybe that had been a little harsh.

Then, *<Sorry. Saga showed me a copy of your message.>*

I sighed. *<Yeah, I didn't mean to snap. It's a little unsettling.>*

<I still think it's my fault,> he said again. *<I didn't check for a Harmonized Divination Nexus. It didn't even occur to me.>*

<Well, I've never even heard of one,> I said. *<What is it?>*

The cursor blinked in place for a few moments. *<It's a spell that can be placed on a message to see who's accessing or possibly interfering with it. It could easily have tagged you when you used your magic on it. Pretty high-level enchanting, but folks who can afford it use them fairly often.>*

<Don't feel bad. I probably wouldn't have thought to check,

even if I had known about it,> I said.

<It's my job to think of these things. If it's on the Netz, I'm supposed to know about it.>

<Nobody's perfect. I suppose now you won't take me surfing for information any more.>

<Not right away!> he said, but added a smiley face.

<I need you to check out a few more things for me, then,> I told him, and fed him the data about Coro's blond avatar and username and what we needed to know about Sandrine's online activities.

<No problem,> he said. *<Get back to you by tonight.>*

Trip waddled into my office just then and flapped up onto a chair.

Before he could open his bill I said, "Don't ask me if I'm okay!"

He looked hurt, as much as a goose could manage that.

"Sorry," I said. "I just don't want everyone treating me like I'm about to break down in a crying fit every second. Yes, someone might be planning to try to kill me. It's not like it never happened before. It's a dangerous job sometimes."

He tilted his head to one side. "Okay. It's just that we like you, Kit."

"I know. But Glaive gave me a huge how-to-stay-alive lecture already today and I think I'm good."

He waved his hands theatrically. "And I've got my killer moves," he said. "I've been practicing even more. I think I could take someone down fast with these things."

"I'm sure you could. And if I get into trouble, I'd want you right there with me," I said as sincerely as I could manage.

"I'll be here if you need me," he assured me, then

suddenly turned and dug a hand down into the space between the edge of the chair arm and the cushion.

If I'd told Trip the truth, I *was* feeling rattled. I was just trying to push it down, bury it so that it couldn't sabotage me. It was also true that I'd been in sticky situations before in this job, and instinct and adrenaline had always won out. I had to believe I'd come through this, whatever this was, okay as well.

Kikufaax came into my office with a thick sheaf of papers and folders in one hand and laid them on my desk. Kiku would be the first to deny that she's the secretary around here, and she really isn't. She's as much an operative as any of us, and I've seen her display some killer moves of her own. But she also likes to act the part. I guess it works out for all of us, so long as we remember it's just an act.

"Anna wants you to look these over," she said, tapping the stack with a perfectly-manicured fingertip. "See if anything jumps out at you."

"What are they?"

"The reports on the other cases where the Murder Prophet sent a message. At least, the ones that we know about," she said. "I've been through them myself and personally, I don't see much to connect any of them. Every pair of eyes might see something different, though."

I stared at the stack. It would take me the rest of the day to go through them with any level of thoroughness. "Anna's not just trying to make sure I stay where you all can keep an eye on me, is she?"

Kiku put her hands on her hips. "I have no idea, but she made me look through them, and Glaive's next on the list, so if that's the real reason she's doing a good job of hiding it."

"Okay, okay," I said, raising my hands in surrender. "Just checking."

"Hey Kiku, is this yours?" Trip said suddenly, holding out one of those strange hands.

She turned to look and took the tiny thing he proffered, her other hand going to her ear. "My earring! I didn't even know I'd lost it!" she told him, tugging at a bare earlobe. "Thanks, Trip."

He shrugged as she slipped the silvery circlet back into place. "Saw it when I jumped up on the chair," he told her. "You probably lost it in all the excitement in here this morning."

She left and Trip followed her. He paused at the door and executed a series of kicks and lunges, shedding a feather or two in the process. "Killer," he whispered to me from the doorway, and winked. "I'll keep practicing."

I followed him out and fetched myself a mediocre coffee from the kitchen, then sat down with the stack of papers Kiku had delivered. I was right. It did take me the rest of the day to pore over those files, and I refilled the coffee cup twice. But it was worth it. I found something that everyone else seemed to have overlooked.

EIGHT

Geographical Coincidences and Things That Go Bump In the Night

Only three of the Murder Prophet cases had been solved so far, and when I say "solved," I mean that at least the police had a suspect who'd been arrested and charged. The general consensus seemed to be that the only thing the murder victims had in common was the fact that they'd all had a message from the Murder Prophet. However, what I noticed—well, I suppose it wasn't actually something they had in common, it was more like a pattern.

I can't say it's something that the police missed, because I was in possession of a fact that they probably hadn't had time to consider—Aleshu Coro himself. Or rather, his message. When they'd correlated data on the victims so far, he hadn't even been in the picture yet. What I did was put him in that picture, literally.

I wanted an overview of the Murder Prophet cases, so I called up a map of the city and surrounding areas, laid a redline grid over it, and started plotting the cases onto the map. I used the victims' homes, not necessarily where they'd been killed, for the first go-round.

But since I had just been there recently, and he was our client, my eyes kept straying back to Alchemist's Ridge as I was placing the other victims. And what I noticed was that none of them were anywhere near Aleshu Coro's house.

Okay, so that might not seem strange at first glance. New Kendrickson isn't a huge city, but it's big enough. It stood out to me, because the other murders had cut across all social lines—racial, magical, economic—but the one thing they had in common was geography. They all clustered in the southeast section of the city, while Aleshu Coro lived 'way up at the northern tip.

Just for fun, and suppressing a shudder, I put a little X on the map to represent myself. It was just as far away from Coro as any of the others, but on the west side of the city, also outside the other cluster.

I sat staring at the map for a few minutes, then called Kikufaax in to look at it, too.

"Do you see anything unusual here?" I asked her.

She considered for a minute.

"Everyone's been saying they're random," she said thoughtfully, "But this doesn't look random to me."

"That's what I thought." I linked to the police public database and got the coordinates for all the murders in the city since the first one with a Murder Prophet connection. It took me a few minutes to populate into my map, but after about half of them had appeared it was clear that there was a difference. The others were geographically random as well as in every other respect, and ranged over the entire breadth of the city.

Kikufaax pursed her lips and regarded me thoughtfully, her eyes narrowed. "Two possibilities," she said. "Either it's a coincidence, and the Murder Prophet could foresee only these particular attacks because of some geographical constraint on the magic—"

"—which apparently doesn't apply to either Aleshu

Coro or me—"

"Or it's not a coincidence—

"—and he or she deliberately chose which ones to send messages to," I finished for her. "That's what I thought."

"The question is, what does that tell us?" Kikufaax sat on the edge of my desk and swung one leg back and forth slowly.

I leaned back in my chair. "Well, I don't buy it as a coincidence. I don't like any coincidences in murder cases."

She shook her head slowly. "Me, neither."

"So that must mean these victims were picked for a reason."

"Something to do with Aleshu Coro? A reason that sets him apart?"

"Maybe." I ran a hand over my hair. "And yet I don't know what."

Kikufaax stood up again. "I know one thing."

I raised my eyebrows at her.

"We need coffee," she said, flashing a grin.

"That I can believe." I followed her out to the kitchen. A weird-looking contraption sat on the counter where the coffee maker had been half an hour before, when I fetched my last cup.

It stood about three feet high, bright red enamel covering most of the outside. An impressive array of buttons and a small touch-screen ranged over the front, along with a clock and temperature readout. Three chrome spigots poked out from the front panel.

"What the—" said Kikufaax, stopping halfway to the counter.

I felt a panicky chill down my spine. If Saga had decided we were drinking too much coffee and wanted to put us all on health drinks or something—I'd probably have to quit.

"Isn't it awesome?" Trip bounded over from the game console. An occasional beep signalled that the Flying Ninja Monkeys from Wormhole 7 were on 'pause.'

"What the hell is it?" Kikufaax asked, leaving unspoken the rest of the sentence: *and this had better be good*.

"It's a Coffee Robo-Alimental!" Trip explained. "I bought it on MegaNetzMall. Well, I convinced Saga to buy it. You wouldn't believe the things it can do!"

"Can. It. Make. Coffee?" Kikufaax growled.

"Hell-lo? It's a COFFEE Robo-Alimental," Trip said. "Of course it makes coffee. Coffee is its specialty. Black, breva, iced, Irish, espresso, mocha—you name it! It also makes tea, green tea, chai, fruit juice, hot chocolate, lemonade, eggnog, and *sprakele*."

"Just like Sandrine Coro," I muttered, but they didn't hear me.

"But that's not the best part," Trip added.

Kikufaax had stalked over to examine it more closely. I sat down at the table, relieved. If it could make coffee, she'd have it on the job in no time. Kiku liked machines, and they seemed to like her. I always put it down to her ability as an Enchanter, although I'd never actually observed her using magic. Anyway, she liked playing office manager, and the ability to make the machines play nice complemented that perfectly.

"What's the best part?" I asked Trip, because I was afraid he'd bust if he didn't tell me. Cleaning up the feathers would take the rest of the day.

"If you make something and then change your mind, it can *change it for you*," the goose explained delightedly.

"Your mind?"

He quirked his head at me in disgust. "No, silly. The drink! You just pour it back in, and it comes out different!"

So it had a magical component. Or more than one. "How much did this thing cost, exactly?" I asked. I hated to think that, interesting as it was, the Coffee Robo-Alimental could have cut into my annual bonus.

"Don't worry about the cost," Saga said suddenly, coming into the kitchen behind me.

I jumped. I guess I was more on edge than I'd thought.

"It's not coming out of your bonus," he leaned over to say to me in a stage whisper as he walked past.

"Ha ha ha," I said.

"And it wouldn't kill you to drink green tea once in a while instead of coffee. Any of you," he added. "In fact, quite the reverse."

"That reminds me," I said, ignoring the dig, "How much will the bonus be if I solve the Coro problem?"

He turned sharply away from the Coffee Robo-Alimental to face me, his cup only half-full of green tea. "What have you got?"

I shrugged. "Maybe nothing. We don't know yet what it might mean." I told him about the map as we each gathered our drinks and fixed them to our tastes. Trip asked for chai, and was inordinately excited to get it. I sipped my coffee gingerly. It was exceptional.

"Show me this map," Saga said, so we trooped back to my office, picking up Glaive on the way. Anna was out.

"If only we knew how this prophet's divination magic worked," Saga said. "This could be nothing, or it could be everything."

"What I don't understand," Trip complained, "is if the police knew about one of these messages, and they thought the message came from a Seer predicting a murder, why couldn't they stop the crime?"

Glaive shook his head. "In this case, no one even knew — or knows now for that matter — if the Murder Prophet really is a Seer or just a crackpot. And the police can only do so much, even if a Seer reports something like this. We all know Lumden's Ninth Law of Divination."

Trip cocked his head to the side inquiringly. "Eventually all intestines will hold omens to the future?" he said.

We stared at him. After a minute Glaive said, "Nooooo, that's not it. I was talking about 'Divination reveals hidden dynamics but does not pierce the veil of the future.'"

"Oh, that one," Trip said comfortably. "I always get those mixed up."

I stared at the goose for a moment longer, then turned back to Glaive. "So the police don't pay a whole lot of attention to Seers who see future crimes, because they're only *possibilities?*"

"That's about it." Glaive had worked some time on that side of the law, so he probably knew what he was talking about. "I mean, there's enough crime out there actually taking place to keep them busy — they don't have the officers to spend a lot of time trying to check out every divination report they get. And while a low-level Seer might get an inkling of a future crime, it takes a high-level ability to provide really concrete information. Much rarer. Sometimes if it's a high-level report and seems credible — and if they have a name — they'll let the possible perpetrator know that a Div report's come in on them — that might be enough to change the 'dynamics' so that the event doesn't happen. But there's just not enough time or manpower to take care of them all. And the reports are often vague — they don't name a particular potential offender."

"But with the Murder Prophet—I mean, he or she has been right about a murder eight times now," Kiku protested. "They should be paying attention to that!"

"They are—they did offer Mr. Coro protection," Saga reminded her. "But in these cases, no perpetrators were named, nor even details provided," Saga said. "Merely the warning—or however you wish to interpret it—to the victim. And as Glaive has pointed out, the police simply don't have the manpower to essentially start a murder investigation before there has even been a murder."

"Which puts us back to square one," Glaive said. "Finding the Murder Prophet."

"If I could do that," I said, "I'd sleep a lot better tonight."

"We all would," Trip said, swilling the last of his chai and wiping his bill with the back of his hand. "I'd better go practice my moves some more."

———◆———

Glaive had offered to drive me home that night, but I told him not to be silly. He wouldn't let it go, so in the end I just sneaked out the back door without telling him I was leaving. I said goodnight to Trip on my way through the kitchen and he actually looked up from the video game. On the screen, flying monkeys laid their ninja moves on some hapless humans.

"Are you sure you want to do that, Kit?" he asked, pushing the 'pause' button.

"I'm sure. Just don't tell Glaive you saw me, okay?"

He looked doubtful. "I don't know...what if he's right? What if you're in danger?"

I shook my head impatiently as I zipped up my jacket and made an effort not to yell at him. "I'll be fine. I'm a big girl. And the message only came today, anyway. Just don't tell him I'm gone."

He hesitated, the sides of his bill pulled down. "Glaive's kind of...you know, scary, sometimes."

"Oh, that's just his way. He's not going to hurt you. Promise you won't say anything!" I insisted.

He didn't look happy about it, but finally he nodded. "Okay. But be careful!"

"I will. Careful is my new middle name." I drew a finger in an exaggerated cross over my heart and made my escape as Trip turned back to his game and the monkeys flew into action again.

Yeah, maybe it was childish, but despite my nervousness, I hated feeling like I couldn't look after myself. After all, it wasn't even dark yet, and the streets would be full of people heading home from work.

I was almost home when I began to suspect I was being followed.

I'd been tempted to walk, but that would be taking my *I-can-look-after-myself* bravado too far, and I *had* promised to be careful. I caught a bus as I usually did. *Safety in numbers*, I thought, although as I looked around at my fellow passengers I hoped I wouldn't be calling on them to help keep me safe. Most of them looked either twelve or eighty. I doubted that any of them were armed, beyond the odd walking cane. There was one dog, sentient obviously since he was reading a newspaper, but he was only beagle-sized. He also looked over at me with that mix of doleful understanding and neediness that put him squarely in the "best friend" category, as opposed to "heart-of-a-Rottweiler".

However, the bus trip passed uneventfully. I stared out the window and thought about all those murders so distinctly removed from Aleshu Coro's neighborhood. I didn't have any epiphanies.

The walk from the bus stop to my apartment was only about three blocks, and it still wasn't dark, so I wasn't worried. I'd only gone a block when I had that prickly eyes-on-my-back feeling. My heart kicked into high gear as the adrenaline rushed through me. Fight or flight. I stuck out my chin, stopped walking, and turned around.

The street lay deserted behind me. Streetlights punched holes in the darkness at intervals, but no-one moved through them.

I turned and started walking again, hoping no one had seen my abrupt about-face. The adrenaline receded, leaving my arms and legs leaden. I was only a block from home when I felt it again. Eyes. Watching me.

For the second time I whirled to confront whoever it was. This time my hand slipped inside my jacket, to the LaserWaster in my shoulder holster.

Again, the street stretched empty and harmless-looking back to the corner where I'd left the bus.

By then I was so rattled by the chemicals awash in my body that I gave in to them. They demanded fight or flight. There was no one to fight, so I ran the rest of the way home, my feet pounding the sidewalk. The bright streetlight spots flashed past me and I silently thanked Phoebe for nagging me out for my run so many mornings.

I gained the outer door of the building, realized fleetingly that there was no sound of footsteps following me, and decided I didn't care. I took the stairs up three flights instead of waiting for the elevator, and slammed my key into the lock at my door. It turned smoothly and I practically fell inside when I pushed into the door and it opened.

As I slammed the door behind me and put my back against it, I knew that I absolutely had to find the Murder Prophet. And fast. Living like this was going to make me grey before my time. If I didn't run out of time first.

NINE

Never Argue With a Lady with a Gun

"Do we need assistance?" Phoebe asked tensely as I stood with my back against the door, panting slightly. "I can summon emergency responders."

"No, everything's fine," I answered.

"Kit, your heart rate and breathing are elevated," she said in a voice tinged with reproach. "*And* you slammed the door."

"It's my door, and how the hell do you know about my heart rate?" I snapped. I probably would have just shrugged it off if I hadn't already been in a state, but it was a good question.

After a moment of injured silence, she said, "I am programmed to monitor all aspects of your well-being and security, Kit."

"Well, you don't need to take it this far." I stomped out into the kitchen and yanked open the refrigerator. There wasn't much there, and I remembered that she had warned me we were low on supplies and made a list, but I hadn't gone shopping or told her to actually order them. That only made me more annoyed.

"Your job is dangerous, Kit. I've been worried about you for some time now—"

"I don't need a nanny, Phoebe. I could have your

programming changed, you know."

More silence met that threat, the air heavy with mute reproach. The silence was fine with me. I really didn't feel like fighting with my apartment AI again tonight. I flipped on the radio and began scrounging the cupboards. Phoebe didn't say anything more.

I didn't contact LemurCandy until after I'd stir-fried up some only slightly soggy vegetables and rice for supper, brewed myself a nice soothing cup of peppermint tea and had a hot shower. I also offered an apology to Phoebe, which she accepted graciously. By that time I felt calm enough to think about Aleshu Coro's case with some objectivity again.

When I sat down at the computer, I found something surprising. LemurCandy had left me five messages, and the second I signed on to Chatterz® he messaged me live, so he must have been watching for me. I sat back and took a deep breath before I answered him. I felt ridiculously excited *and* annoyed that he might be worried about me, and I certainly didn't want that to show.

<Hey,> I said casually, <Made any new progress on the case? >

<What took you so long to get home?>

I frowned. How would he know how long it took me to get home?

<How would you know how long it took me to get home?> I typed.

<I couldn't get you at the office,> he said, <so I talked to Kikufaax. She said you'd already left, alone. I thought Glaive was going to take you home?>

I scowled at the screen, even though I knew he couldn't see me. <Have you been talking to Glaive about me?>

The cursor blinked silently in place a dozen times before he answered. <*We're all a little worried about you, Kit,*> he said finally. <*You should be taking precautions.*>

<*I shared the ride home with a busload of people, and I do carry a gun,*> I typed. <*And I still don't know how you knew what time I got home.*>

After another pause, he typed, <*Phoebe told me.*>

For a moment I was too stunned to do anything but stare at the screen. Finally I typed, <*You hacked my apartment AI?!?*>

<*No!*> he typed hastily. <*I just queried her, and since she knows I'm a trusted user on your accounts, she told me.*>

And she was probably mad because I yelled at her, I thought, *so it was her way of getting back at me.* I was going to have to adjust her privacy protocols.

<*I'm starting to think I have to limit her upgrades,*> I typed. <*I don't know what she's doing half the time now. Or who she's talking to.*>

<*But she really helps us keep track of you,*> he protested.

<*Exactly what I mean.*>

<*I'm sorry,*> LemurCandy said. <*Like I said, we're all concerned about you.*>

I wasn't quite ready to give in. <*This is not exactly a desk job at the best of times, you know.*>

<*I know. But you don't always have a death threat hanging over you.*>

<*Well, thanks,*> I retorted. <*I feel much better now.*>

<*Okay, okay, we'll change the subject,*> he said. <*Kikufaax said you'd noticed something weird about the other murders.*>

I took a deep breath and counted to ten, then told him about the geographical anomaly and checked my mail through a few moments of silence while he laid out the same map.

<Very nice,> he said. *<So what do you think it means?>*

I hadn't told anyone in the office this, but I did have a theory. Somehow it was easier to tell LemurCandy. *<I think they were deliberately chosen because they were far away from Coro's house.>*

<For what reason?>

I shook my head, even though he couldn't see me. *<I'm not certain. Misdirection, maybe. I think it must mean something.>*

<Like what?>

<I guess I don't really know, yet. But I think it's significant.>

<Fair enough. I'll think about it, too.>

<Did you find out anything about Sandrine Coro? Or her husband's online time?>

<Heh. I did. Mrs. Coro has one username, 'SandrineC', which she uses for her mail and messages, and a few online shopping sites like MegaNetzMall.>

I grinned, strangely amused by the thought that both Trip and Sandrine Coro shopped at the same online venue.

<Apart from that,> Lemur continued, *<I can't find anything linked to her in any way. And I can't find any convergences of SandrineC with PsychoticMuslinCrayon.>*

<So whoever he's with when he's being that blond and well-muscled avatar, it isn't his wife.>

<Nope. But PsychoticMuslinCrayon and his blond avatar have a monthly tryst at one of the cheesy meat virtuals—Hook, Line, & Sinker—with someone called SereneQueen. They rent a private room every time and spend about an hour together.>

<One of the great unanswered questions of our time,> I said. *<Does having a virtual affair with someone amount to cheating on your spouse?>*

<Not unanswered for me,> LemurCandy said. *<I think it's cheating all the way.>*

Points for him. *<I agree,>* I said, *<but the courts can't seem to sort it out.>*

<Anyway, I haven't managed to track down this SereneQueen yet. She's somewhere out of the country and that just adds a whole lot of roadblocks for tracebacks.>

<Let me know what you find out,> I said. It hit me suddenly that I was really exhausted again. I guess being under a death threat can do that to you. My eyes were drooping even as I read the words on the screen. *<I think I'm going to call it a night.>*

<Not up for another trip outside the grid?> he asked, but he added a smiley face so I knew he was joking.

<Not tonight,> I said. *<But I'll take a rain check.>*

<Lock your doors,> he said.

I sighed. *<Already done. Quit worrying, Lemur.>*

<No promises,> he said. *<Have a good night, Kit.>*

And once I was in bed with the lights out and the covers pulled up, I let myself admit that his concern was touching. I just wondered if I'd ever be able to tell him that in real life.

————•————

When I got to the office the next morning, I found Glaive leaning against the doorframe of my office, wearing a look as black as his clothes and waiting to bawl me out. Saga sat in one of my chairs, arms folded reproachfully across his elegant black-and-gold jacket. I listened meekly while Glaive had his rant, which included words like "reckless" and "stupid." Then I said, "Glaive, do you remember the Hattenborough case?"

"What's that got to do with anything?" he almost shouted.

"Remember, you took a laser shot in the leg, and went down behind my car?

"Of course I do—"

"And do you remember that they got the bright idea to start shooting under the car at you, and that I opened the back door, hauled your sorry ass inside, and then took out both of them with my .368 while they were still trying to get a sight on you?"

"That was different—"

"And Saga," I said, turning to him, "do you remember when we were under that wharf, and the Delano nutcase wanted to turn us both into Swiss cheese?"

Saga merely nodded. He knew what was coming.

"And you couldn't get a straight shot off because of the angle of the boards, and I banked one off that yacht mirror and took him down?"

He nodded grudgingly.

I pulled the .368 out of my shoulder holster and looked at it. "Well, guess what, fellas? I've still got this," I said, "and I still know how to use it. And I still know my tai-ki-do. Just because someone has *possibly* threatened my life, doesn't mean I can't take care of myself."

Glaive pressed his lips together and Saga frowned, but I felt better. Maybe I'd needed to convince myself, too.

Suddenly Glaive shrugged. "Never argue with a lady with a gun," he said.

Saga stood up. "I know you are an independent thinker, Kitano," he said. "That's one of the things that makes you so valuable. But there is no weakness in knowing when to ask for help. That is also a strength. Just be certain *you* remember *that*."

I smiled at them both so they'd know I wasn't really angry. "I will. I just can't feel strong if you're making me feel weak, you know?"

They shared a glance that I read as "women!" but I let it go. It wasn't like I'd never shared one that said "men!" with Anna or Kikufaax.

Later that day I was doing some work online, when I began to get the feeling I was being followed there, too.

TEN

A Conspiracy of Secrets

Don't ask me how I knew—it wasn't anything overt. There was a sluggishness in my computer that I initially put down to not having cleaned up the directories lately, and a few times I thought I spotted the same avatar turning up in places I went. Not like that would tip anyone off, really. Lots of people use the same or similar avatars. It was just— like I said, I don't really know. Maybe something to do with my magic, although it had never worked that way before. It was just a feeling.

At first I suspected LemurCandy, although I had no idea what dangers he thought might lie in wait for me online— besides more Harmonized Divination Nexes, and I didn't think they were dangerous unless I was using my magic. But when I went looking for him, he didn't seem to be online at all. A while back, though, he'd given me a cool little piece of contraband software that let me search for instances of people searching for me or my usernames. Not public searches, anyone could do that, but more intimate, private and high-level ones. It was supposed to be government and Registry use only, and I didn't ask how Lemur had gotten his hands on it. I also didn't actually think I'd ever have a use for it, but now seemed like a good time.

What I found didn't make me feel any better. There were two distinct tracebacks working on me, one starting the day before I got the Murder Prophet message, and one that dated back longer than that—a few months.

The more recent one didn't bother me after I'd thought about it for a minute. It seemed like conclusive evidence that the message was really linked to my involvement in the Murder Prophet case, and wasn't a Seer divination of something destined to happen. Someone was trying to scare me, or get me off the case. That was fine. It was nothing that hadn't happened in the past, apart from the mystical element. I could shrug it off.

The other one caused me more concern. Who'd been interested in me for that length of time, and still was? And why? I had a moment of panic when I thought it might be something to do with...my secret. But if that was the case, why hadn't it come to anything before this? And why hadn't I picked up on it sooner? If I'd had the feeling of being followed today, it stood to reason that my inner alarms should have gone off some other time, too.

Glaive came to my office doorway and leaned against the frame again. "Feel like taking a little trip?"

"Back out to Alchemist's Ridge?"

He shook his head. "Nope. We're getting nowhere with any of Coro's business contacts, so Saga wants us to try the two ex-wives."

I frowned. "Do we know where they are?"

"Kiku's on the trail of number one; somewhere in Europe, looks like. We know where number two is. She's on a little island off the Fijis, apparently living in the lap of luxury."

"I hate her already," I said. "But going to visit her doesn't sound like too much of a hardship. When do we leave?"

"Fly out at three o'clock," he said. "If you can be ready by then?"

I gave him a look. "Pick me up in an hour," I said, and headed home to fetch my travel bag. I always keep one packed because in this job, you never know when you're going to have to catch a flight or a train on short notice. I took the bus home again, and once more I thought I could sense someone behind me once I was walking those three blocks to my house. It felt like they were getting longer. This time I didn't turn around. It was broad daylight. *It's nothing. You're imagining it.*

Phoebe was annoyed with me when I told her I was going out of town. "You told me to order groceries," she scolded. "Now the perishables might go to waste."

"Cancel the order," I told her, "And send it again when I get back."

She sighed, or at least that's what it sounded like. "The usual away message if anyone calls?"

I frowned. "No, maybe it'd be best not to say I'm out of town. Just say 'unavailable,' and that I'll call back."

"You might have given me a little more notice," she grumped. "And I don't think it's a safe time for you to be travelling."

"I only found out myself twenty minutes ago," I said, before I realized that I was arguing with an AI again. Then I realized what else she'd said.

"What do you mean, a safe time to be travelling? Did LemurCandy say something to you?" I demanded, although it's hard to be indignant with someone when there's no face to glare at. Apart from my little freakout the night before when I ran in and slammed the door, why would my apartment AI think anything unusual was going on?

But on that note, she went annoyingly silent, and wouldn't answer my question. "Sure," I muttered as I grabbed my toothbrush. "*Now* you decide to be quiet."

I kept glancing at my computer while I changed into a black pinstriped skirt and green blouse (more suitable for travel and interviews), checked through my bag to make sure everything was there—slippers, sleepshirt, emergency reading, spare running shoes and sweats, swimsuit, change of presentable clothes—and dashed on some makeup. I knew I should message LemurCandy to let him know what was going on. But even if I didn't, he'd find out quickly enough from someone else at the office. On the one hand, I didn't want him to think I was getting too dependent on keeping in contact with him. I mean, I didn't want him to have the wrong idea in case we ever met and the chemistry just wasn't there. On the other hand, he was definitely acting worried about me lately, and I didn't want to piss him off and mess up my chances in case we ever met and the chemistry *was* there.

In the end I messaged him just before I packed up my laptop to take with me. Why take a chance? I'd half-hoped he might be offline, but he messaged back right away.

He didn't like the idea. <*Why does it have to be you?*> he asked. <*Why can't Kikufaax go with Glaive?*>

<*Kikufaax is following up another lead.*>

<*But you could do that instead. Did you ask?*>

<*No. Anyway, I'm the only one who can tell if the ex-wife's lying when we interview her.*> Maybe I shouldn't have messaged him. He was taking this all too seriously. <*You're taking this all too seriously,*> I said.

<*Kit?*> he said, <*When you get back...*>

I waited, but he didn't finish the sentence. The cursor blinked cryptically. Finally I typed, *<What?>*

<I was thinking maybe we could get together and go over some of this data.> It sprang up on the screen so quickly I knew he must have had it all typed out and was just trying to decide whether to hit the 'send' button.

My heart thumped hard for a moment, and my throat went dry. I'll admit it, in that minute, I was more scared than I'd been when I'd seen the Murder Prophet's message in my inbox. More scared than when I'd thought someone was following me the other night. *What if I didn't like him in real life? And what if he didn't like me?*

But I knew I shouldn't wait too long to send a message back, or he might jump to all sorts of conclusions. It was just for work, after all, right?

<Sure, no problem,> I typed quickly. *<We'll set something up when I get back.>*

<Let me know you're there safely, and how it goes with the ex-Mrs. Coro,> he said.

<Sure.>

<Great. Take care,> he said, and then he was gone.

I stared at the screen for a minute, then shut the laptop down. I was sliding it into its case when Glaive sounded the horn from outside. I grabbed my bags and headed downstairs, wondering if I'd just made a huge mistake.

———•———

The flight to Fiji passed uneventfully, although I spent a lot of time deliberately not looking out of the window at the huge expanse of sparkling blue water below us. Magic-powered flight has been around for long enough now that it's the norm, but I always wonder how safe it can really be. All kinds of magic occasionally misfires or wears off before anyone expects it to. Ten thousand feet above the ocean would be an especially bad place for a spell to fail.

Fiji itself was only a stopover on the way to the little island the second Mrs. Coro called home. I understood that she hadn't kept his name after the divorce, which didn't seem to have been exactly amicable, so I made a mental note not to actually call her Mrs. Coro.

Our hotel was on the main island, Viti Levu, and as we checked in and found our rooms it was obvious what a difference a well-heeled client could make to expenses. The place wasn't extravagant, but with its perfectly matched white wicker furniture, tiki lights, sparkling tile floors and crisp room décor, it was a far cry from some of the fleabags I've had to bunk down in. Coro's expense account could stand the hit, and I didn't feel the least bit guilty as I took ten minutes to stand on the balcony and let the sea breeze ruffle my hair. I found myself thinking the Murder Prophet, whoever he or she was, would never find me here.

When I met up with Glaive again, he'd already put in a call and found out from Clarice Valencia's housekeeper that our quarry was out for the evening and never "available" until after noon, so we made an appointment to see her the following day. We spent an hour going over our lines of questioning, and then Glaive retired to his room for a nap and I succumbed to the inviting turquoise pool set just a stone's throw from the equally inviting pale sand beach.

We met up for dinner in the hotel restaurant, which was just as enjoyable as the rest of the hotel. Glaive had scallops in wine and I had tuna with wine, and then Glaive announced his intention to check out some of the local clubs. "Coming along?" he asked.

I shook my head. "Don't think so, thanks. Travelling always makes me tired. I'd rather relax than socialize with strangers."

He regarded me with narrowed eyes. "Are you sure? Because if you *are* going anywhere, we should go together."

"What do you mean?" Glaive had never shown more than a co-worker's or, at best, a brotherly interest in me. I couldn't imagine he was hitting on me now. And the look on his face was stern, not seductive.

"I mean, you still have to take precautions and stay safe."

I chuckled and shook my head. "You think the Murder Prophet is going to come after me here?" I looked around the restaurant, with its muted sconce lighting, crisp white tablecloths, and oases of exotic greenery. Muted conversations and laughter echoed around the room as well-heeled patrons enjoyed their meals, attended by quietly watchful wait staff. The restaurant curved around a section of the pool, now twinkling with underwater lights. "We're in a completely different part of the world! I've never felt safer."

He leaned back in his chair and crossed his arms. "You're not taking this seriously. You could still be in danger. We don't know enough about the case yet to make assumptions."

I sipped the last of my wine and set the glass down. "Well, I'm making an assumption. I'm assuming you're crazy."

He rolled his eyes and shook his head. "And you're reckless."

"I promise I won't do anything reckless," I said,

sketching a cross over my heart with deliberate exaggeration. "The most exciting thing I'm thinking about right now is a nice long sleep uninterrupted by Phoebe's early morning reveille. Give me the file on Clarice Valencia to look over if I get bored, and go have fun if you want. I won't be leaving my room once I'm in it."

He didn't continue the argument, but he did stay in the hallway outside our rooms until I was inside and he'd heard me lock the door.

"I locked the door," I called through it. "Go away now."

"See you in the morning," he said, and I assumed he left then, although the carpeting in the hallway was so thick I couldn't actually hear him walk away.

I wasn't bored, but Clarice's file did make good bedtime reading, when curled up under a magnificently puffy duvet with some soft music provided by the room AI. The AI had a soothing male voice and absolutely no desire to boss me around.

Apparently Clarice Valencia had been a technician at MageData, Inc., during the years of its climb to ascendancy in the magic data registry field. I hadn't realized in my initial glimpse at Aleshu Coro's life, though, that she'd actually worked at the MageData subsidiary where the magic ability-identification research was going on. I'd mentally placed her at the main company, although with no good reason. That made me wonder what her own talent might be, if any. I found it on the second page of her file. She was a Seer, with a minor talent in enchantments.

Interesting. How closely involved in the research had she been, and did her talent as a Mancer contribute to the marriage breakup? It always seemed to me that it could be uncomfortable being in a relationship with a Seer. I mean, how much fun is it to argue if you always know who's going to win ahead of time?

For that matter, how much fun would it be to be in a relationship with someone who always knew when you were lying? I'd found out the hard way that for a lot of people the answer to that question was, "not much."

I put that thought, and Clarice's file, away. I toyed briefly with the notion of going out somewhere just to be rebellious, but I'd promised Glaive—and the bed was far too comfortable to get out of it without an awfully compelling reason. Once I put the light out, sleep came swiftly. I breakfasted alone the next morning since Glaive didn't put in an appearance until it was time to catch the boat over to Clarice's island. I wasn't sure if he was piqued at me about last night, or worn out from his own activities, whatever they'd been. He wore a black t-shirt in deference to the heat, and matching dark circles under his eyes. He didn't say much, although he seemed to be in a good mood, and I wondered briefly how late he'd been out, but didn't dare ask.

We walked the short distance to the dock where Glaive had arranged for a boat to ferry us over to Clarice's island. It was a small, clean centre-console craft with a cheerful owner who introduced himself as Maru. He and Glaive spent the pleasant ride out to the island discussing the boat's specs. I spent the time musing that at least here, no-one was following me.

Clarice Valencia's island was an oval, tree-dotted paradise, the requisite white sand beach on one side sloping down into the turquoise waves. The house, fully glass-fronted to take advantage of the view, perched atop a small hill, and a winding path that looked just wide enough for something like a golf cart led up to it. A pale board dock extended out into the water and our boatman fetched up at it expertly.

Clarice Valencia did not come down to the dock to meet us, even though we were expected. She didn't come to door when we pulled up in front of her palatial home in the well-appointed and predictable golf cart she'd sent to meet us. In fact, she didn't come into the house or even get up off her *chaise longue*. Maybe, on reflection, it had been the housekeeper who sent the golf cart. A maid led us out to the poolside where Clarice lounged in a violet two-piece bathing suit that showed off her excellently preserved body to good effect.

She did deign to pull her designer sunglasses down to the tip of her nose and gaze up at us over the tops of them. Her eyes were a washed-out grey, but they were the only thing about her that verged on colorless. Her hair was an artful mix of dark and light blond highlights, with a shot of pure color, midnight blue, defining one chunk on the left side. Her skin was light bronze, even and taut. She gave me only a cursory glance, but gave Glaive a predatory once-over. I wondered if he noticed, and if so, if he minded. At any rate, she got the first word in.

"I don't really know what I could tell you about Aleshu," she drawled, as if we amused her. "We've been divorced for quite a while, now."

"We know that, ma'am," Glaive said smoothly. I couldn't tell if he was impressed with her bikini—or what was in it— or not. "We don't know what the motivation for this threat might be, so it could date back any length of time—to when you were together, or even before. We're just looking for any information that might help."

She pushed her glasses into place on her perfect nose and wriggled a bit on the lounger. "Well, you might as well both sit down, at least. I'll have Marguerite bring you some drinks." She pushed a button on the table beside her and requested the drinks cart.

Glaive and I pulled up two vacant beach chairs, and while we awaited the drinks I asked her, "Have you spoken with your ex-husband lately?"

She shook her head. "No, we don't really talk," she said with an enigmatic smile.

Marguerite arrived with the drinks. I accepted a small glass of wine and Glaive had lemon iced tea. Clarice had something pale pink and bubbly, complete with a red paper parasol and a thin slice of lime perched on the rim.

"Do you still receive support payments from him?" Glaive asked.

"No. We had a lump sum settlement. He's never had to make monthly payments." She nodded, seemingly to herself. "I thought I'd prefer it that way, a clean break as far as the money was concerned, and I was right. It was much better to have those messy details out of the way."

I'd taken my Maginox® after breakfast, so I didn't hesitate to apply a little Mancer talent. Her answer held the hint of a lie. Maybe she wasn't entirely happy with the financial outcome of the divorce, despite apparently having enough cash to fund an enviable lifestyle. "Do you know of anyone who would want to harm your ex-husband?"

She laughed then, displaying bright, perfect, white teeth. "I doubt that Aleshu has gone through life without making anyone dislike him," she said. "For a while I hated him, but I got over that long ago. I'm sure his first wife hated him, too, at least for a while. She certainly stuck it to him financially when they divorced. And there are lots of ways to make enemies when you're in a business as big as he is." She paused for a moment and then shook her head. "But no, honestly, I can't think of anyone in particular who'd want Aleshu dead."

"You don't see him at all, then?" I pressed, trying to follow up my first question.

"I've seen him in the media from time to time, but I know that's not what you're really asking." She smiled that sphinx-like smile again. "I haven't actually seen him since the divorce was finalized."

Having seen that smile twice, I wondered what it meant, so I turned on the magic. The reading was weird. It said she was lying, but it also said she wasn't lying. I kept my face still, but I didn't know what it meant. I was sure she was doing it deliberately. I wondered if there was any way she might know what my talent was, and was playing with me. I decided I'd check every word she said now, although it was almost certain to trigger the Maginox® headache even quicker than usual.

Glaive, however, had picked up on something else she'd said. "What do you mean about his first wife? The financial end of it, I mean."

Clarice shrugged elegantly. "It wasn't enough for her to take a money settlement; she wanted a part of the company, too. Her lawyer claimed she'd supported Aleshu during the years he was building it up, and in the end the judge said she had a right to shares in MageData. Aleshu was wild. Nothing he could do about it, though."

"Does she still have those shares? How big an interest in the company did she get?" Glaive tried to make the questions sound casual, but I knew by the way he leaned

112

forward with his elbows on his knees, head thrust out like a dog catching a scent, that he thought this was important.

"I have no idea," Clarice said, sipping from her drink with studied nonchalance before she answered. "But I certainly learned from her mistake. When Aleshu and I split up, I was happy to take a reasonable payment and walk away clean."

Sure you were, I thought. My magic suggested that she hadn't been at all happy about that. No doubt it was Coro who had learned his lesson and insisted on a pre-nuptial agreement with Clarice, taking MageData off the table if things didn't work out.

"Do you know if she tried to take an active part in the company after the divorce?" Glaive pressed.

"Well, she stopped working there around that time." Clarice's dark glasses still masked her eyes, but a note of irritation crept into her voice. "Then she went to board meetings for a while. I know that, because Aleshu would be terribly frustrated when he came home from them."

"They fought about things?"

She readjusted the brim of her hat and rearranged herself languidly on the chaise. "I suppose. She wanted to take the company in a different direction, or something. Change the focus of the research end, put resources into helping more people actually use their magic abilities. Eliminate the need for Maginox®, or find a better drug, one with fewer side effects." She shook her head. "Look, it didn't last long. She didn't have the support of the board. Eventually she moved away, and frankly, I was happy to see her go."

Well, according to my magic, that was the whole truth, and nothing but the truth. I felt the first twinges of the

113

expected Maginox® headache coming on, though.

"I don't know why you care at this point," she continued, her carefully bored monotone finally cracking to let annoyance through. "It's ancient history."

"The people who've been killed aren't ancient history. Neither is the message your ex-husband got," Glaive said.

Clarice snorted. "I doubt it came from *her*. She's too scattered to come up with something like that. She used to come up with these wildly elaborate ideas, but she had no practical planning skills. I heard she took up painting, and she's pretty good at it. That's more her style. I don't think she had a head for business, or much magic to speak of. Honestly, I always thought she didn't have the brains of a goose."

I was suddenly glad that Trip wasn't with us. The last thing we needed was him demonstrating his killer moves on Coro's ex-wife.

"Well, thank you for your time, Ms. Valencia," Glaive said smoothly, standing. We obviously weren't going to get much more from her. I stood up, too.

"If we need anything else, we'll contact you," he added, since she wasn't volunteering. She nodded, but her body language said that she didn't give a damn one way or the other.

I wished I could think of something pithy to say, but my brain wasn't doing pith at the moment, so I merely echoed Glaive's thanks and said goodbye. The maid who'd ushered us in appeared as if by magic of her own to escort us out.

Glaive waited until we were outside the mansion before asking me, "What did you think of that? Think the first wife needs a close look when Kiku tracks her down?"

"Maybe." I watched the driver with the golf cart

approach. "If she's still a shareholder, she might have something to gain if he were dead," I said, squinting against the bright sun. The water threw it back in diamond sparks that stabbed into my eyes, and there was so much water there was no escaping it. "But I have a wicked Maginox® headache coming on right now, and I don't want to have to concentrate on anything else until we're across this water and back on dry land again, okay?"

Glaive raised his eyebrows but said okay, and I kept my eyes closed as we jostled down to the dock and putted back across the channel, not even trying to untangle the twisted skein of truth and lies Clarice Valencia had handed me.

ELEVEN

Two Aspirins and a Shot of *Sprakele*

I drank two glasses of water while I changed for dinner, and it took the edge off the headache. Glaive and I met up again in the hotel restaurant. It was quieter tonight, and as I contemplated the tall, cool glass of *sprakele* on the table in front of me, I felt ready to consider what Clarice Valencia had told us.

"I called Kiku," Glaive said. "She traced Evangeline Coro to London, but she hasn't been able to pin down an address or specific contact username yet. I told her to get the shareholder information for MageData and see if Evangeline's still listed."

"She could have divested those shares ages ago."

"Sure, but what if she didn't?" Glaive said, picking up a menu. "If she had enough shares, she might be able to influence the board of directors if Coro was out of the way."

"But his shares would just go to someone else if he died," I said, opening a menu myself. It had changed since last night. The first thing listed was *kakoda* (raw fish marinated in lemon juice) and *ota* (a local seaweed). I closed the menu for a moment and signalled the waiter to bring another *sprakele*. I had a feeling I might need it. I took a healthy sip of the first one and enjoyed a pleasant shiver as it tingled its way down my throat.

"Yes, but if Evangeline knows other shareholders or some of the directors, she might be able to influence a majority of them. Some of them might switch their allegiance to her if Coro were gone. Some might sell out to her."

I shook my head. "Okay, but why? She hasn't appeared to have any interest in the company all these years. Why now? What would she even be trying to influence them about? Could she still want MageData to become a different kind of company?"

Glaive shrugged. "We'll have to wait until Kiku finds out more to be able to answer those questions. But I wouldn't be surprised if it just comes down to money in the end."

On that cheery note he went back to his menu, and decided to order the prime rib and cassava balls for dinner. I sipped sprakele while I perused all the choices this time, smoothly avoided the seafood and went with chicken fricassee and green pawpaw salad.

While we waited for the food to arrive he leaned back in his chair and laced his fingers behind his head. "If you're talking to LemurCandy later he might know something. I'll bet Kiku will get him to run a check on Evangeline. And when we get back, if Kiku hasn't beat us to it, we'll go see Aleshu Coro. He might be able to tell us something."

"Why do you think he didn't mention Evangeline owning shares in the company?"

Glaive shrugged. "Like you said, maybe she doesn't even have them anymore. Or for whatever reason, they're just not an issue."

"Yeah." I contemplated my two empty sprakele glasses in mild surprise, and signalled for another. "I guess we can't really figure out anything until we know more."

"You get anything else from what Clarice said?" Glaive asked.

I frowned. "There was a lot of stuff going on with her. Truth, lies, all kind of mixed up together." My drink arrived and I took a soothing gulp. "I think she wash...was lying about talking to Coro, but..." I shook my head, then closed my eyes since the head-shaking had made the room slosh around rather alarmingly. When I opened them, Glaive was staring at me with a strange expression on his face. "I can't sort it out right now," I said. "I think I'm having a worse reaction than ushu...usual to the Maginox®."

Glaive raised an eyebrow. "Yeah, the Maginox®, I'm sure that's it."

I sat up straighter in my chair. "You can't always predict how it will affect you."

"Right."

I thought Glaive looked too serious, so I tried to talk him into having a *sprakele* too, but he wouldn't hear of it. I know it's not exactly a manly drink, but I was thinking this case had been difficult for him so far. No one to beat up yet, much less kill, like in the old days. It had to be a strain on him. In the end he agreed to a beer, but I suspected that maybe he'd had his fill of those the night before, because he didn't seem to enjoy it all that much. We stopped talking about Clarice because of my headache.

Meanwhile, dinner arrived and I drank the third (and maybe a fourth) *sprakele* while we ate, and barely made it up to my room before I collapsed. Luckily, it was on the bed. My third-last thought before passing out was that like everything else, magic made things both easier and more difficult. Magic drinks could get you drunk without getting you addicted, but they worked so fast they took all the fun out of it. Especially when you'd been a good Mancer and taken your Maginox® as directed.

My second-last thought was that this trip would have been a lot more fun if LemurCandy had been here with me instead of stuffy old Glaive. It could have been a romantic paradise instead of just a work stopover.

My last thought was that LemurCandy was going to be mad that I hadn't contacted him like I promised, but before I could get back out of bed to send him a message, I was asleep.

———◆———

If he was mad he didn't show it, possibly because Glaive had contacted him and asked him to run the search on Clarice Valencia. It seemed Glaive had also let something slip about the way I couldn't hold my *sprakele*, because there was a message on my screen when I opened it up in the morning that said, "Two aspirins washed down with an ounce of *sprakele* does wonders for a hangover."

"Very funny," I muttered as I checked my other mail. I didn't have a hangover, anyway. Well, not exactly. The sun seemed awfully bright again, but we were in Fiji, right? I'll bet a lot of people think the same thing.

Our flight back home wasn't until just after noon, so we spent a busy morning making the rounds of the local police department, magic Registry, and a couple of spots that looked likely for local gossip, but we discovered nothing out of the ordinary about Clarice. Except that she really did seem to have the money to live the way she did. No legal troubles, no staffing troubles, no community troubles. It looked like she'd just figured out what she wanted to do with her life and had the means to do it.

Now I really hated her, and it wasn't just for giving me a headache.

We flew home, feeling like we'd wasted Saga and Anna's money. There was still the matter of following up with a visit to Coro, but neither of us expected it would amount to anything. Maybe because we felt guilty, we dropped off my bags and swung by Coro's office before we went back to our own. I downed a couple more Maginox® on the way. Might as well be able to make a full report, and headaches be damned.

MageData occupied its own stately high-rise in the industrial park on the outskirts of the city. The architect had avoided the tackier full-on medieval theme that some magic-related businesses went in for, and instead settled on a facade of concrete and glass that just hinted that somewhere in its ancestry, there might have been a castle.

Inside, the lobby was modern and spacious, dotted with elegant waiting chairs clustered around low tables, and punctuated by lush greenery. A bank of elevators ranged along the back wall, guarded by a semi-circular reception desk that somehow managed to look both welcoming and imposing. The auburn-haired receptionist was as thin, stylish, and perfectly-made-up as Kikufaax, and I was suddenly very aware that I'd just spent hours sitting, dozing, and fidgeting on an airplane.

Not surprisingly, Coro saw us right away. We travelled up in his personal elevator, after the receptionist unlocked it for us with some kind of password spell. I guess if you're in the magic database business, you know where to find the best people for every job.

The assistant (or maybe she was his personal Mancer, I

hear that's all the rage in the corporate world these days) who met us as we emerged from the elevator led us into an enormous space—not a corner office, more like half a floor of window-studded walls that gave on various panoramic views of New Kendrickson. Furniture of blond wood and burgundy leather populated strategic areas of the room, inviting you to use it for cozy chats or board meetings or impressing investors, depending on the mood or the circumstances. Plants—neatly contained in coordinating pots and suiting the ambiance of their various nooks and corners—added touches of green and color; the carpet was soft but not spongy underfoot; computer displays offered their services discreetly from desktops and wall mounts. The requisite bar, mirrored and polished, stood waiting to serve like a dignified butler.

The room was the epitome of elegance and function, and it was bigger than Darcko and Sadatake's entire workspace. I stayed close to the assistant as she ushered us in and over to Coro, so I wouldn't get lost.

It was sort of pathetic, the way he looked like a hopeful puppy in a pet store when he saw us, then had his hopes for any real progress on the case dashed away.

"We've been to see your ex-wife Clarice," I told him, after he'd conscientiously seated us and asked if we wanted anything to drink. I might have said 'no' a little quickly.

He didn't look terribly interested, but asked, "How is she?"

"She seems quite well," I said. I tried to phrase my question as close to the way I'd asked it of Clarice as possible. "Have you spoken with Clarice lately?"

Coro shook his head. "No, I haven't spoken with Clarice since...I don't know. Probably since the divorce."

Magic check. He was telling the absolute truth. No ambiguity whatsoever.

"Have you seen her at all?"

The answer came without hesitation. "I think I saw a photo of her once in relation to some charity event. But that's it. Our paths just don't cross."

Again, none of the ambiguity that had accompanied Clarice's answers to the same questions.

I looked at Glaive, passing the ball to him. "One thing she said interested us. Your ex-wife, Evangeline—does she still own shares in MageData?"

Coro frowned. "I believe so, although to be honest, I'd have to check." He nodded to the assistant, and she hurried away on silent feet across the plush carpet. "Why does that interest you?"

Glaive raised his eyebrows. "We're looking for reasons someone might want to harm you, sir—in fact, to remove you from the gameboard. An ex-wife with a financial interest in your company could be in that position."

Coro quirked a wry smile. "I suppose you're right, but not this particular ex-wife, I think. Evangeline hasn't taken an interest in the company in years. I'm sure she only holds on to the shares—if she does still have them—because they pay decent dividends. And she isn't a major shareholder. She has no real control."

As far as I could tell, he was telling the truth about that, too.

The secretary returned. "Evangeline Coro retains her original shares, sir, but she hasn't attended a shareholder meeting or voted on any issues for at least ten years."

Coro nodded. "As I suspected. I don't think Evangeline is plotting any kind of financial coup."

Glaive didn't look convinced, but he changed the subject. "Well, Mr. Coro, today marks a week since you got the message. Have you given any thought to leaving the country for a bit, or letting us put you in a safe house?"

Coro shook his head, frowning. "I don't want to run from this thing."

"You know the time mentioned in the message isn't an absolute," I said, taking Glaive's lead. "Whoever is behind this could come looking for you at any time."

"I know. But I have a feeling that I'm safe for now. I'd rather just carry on my life as usual."

Glaive gave me a look that plainly said, *famous last words*, and with a few brief pleasantries, we left Coro to his work.

It was raining again, and we sprinted to the Cloudwalker. Once we'd ducked inside, Glaive asked, "So?"

I shook my head. "He's being straight with us. He hasn't talked to Clarice, and he doesn't suspect Evangeline."

Glaive pulled out onto the highway that would take us back to the city centre "So, are we any further ahead?"

I looked out the window at the darkening, cloud-studded sky, hovering low over the city like a funeral pall. "If we are, I can't see it. Maybe someone else will have a different take on it."

By the time we got back to the office, however, the front door was locked and the only one there was Trip. He told us the others were all out working on various aspects of the other Murder Prophet cases, trying to unearth some connection that the police had overlooked. It was unusual to leave only Trip in the office, but it happened from time to time. He could answer the phone, after all.

I was tired and cranky from the travel and the hangover,

and I had a terrible taste like burnt onions in my mouth from taking Maginox® two days in a row, so I gave in and let Glaive drive me home. No one seemed to follow us. Phoebe said she was happy to see me home, and I told her in all honesty that I felt the same way. I didn't even open up my computer to check in with LemurCandy before I went to bed. Two aspirins and a shot of *sprakele*, huh? It would serve him right if he had to stay up all night wondering if I'd gotten home safely.

Of course he didn't, because Glaive got in touch to see what he'd found out about Clarice. I didn't find that out until the next morning, though, when he called me to say that Saga was missing.

TWELVE

Missing, Presumed...in Really Big Trouble

The phone woke me. I really dislike being woken by the phone, because I hate sounding like I was asleep when I answer it. I know that's crazy. If it's the middle of the night, how else would the caller expect to find me, other than asleep? But if it's morning, even early morning, I don't like to appear that I've been caught napping. So to speak.

"'lo?" I managed to croak, once I finally fumbled the receiver off the night table. I don't keep a vid model in the bedroom. Does anyone?

"Kit?" asked a tentative voice I didn't recognize.

It seemed like a nice voice, but it was odd that a caller I didn't know would be so familiar. I realized that I'd sounded extremely sleepy when I'd first answered, and cleared my throat as if maybe I'd just had a frog in it.

"Yes, this is Kit," I confirmed as brightly as I could manage. "Who's this?"

There was a pause. "Kit, it's...it's...LemurCandy. Saga seems to be missing."

My still-groggy brain struggled to assimilate the information it had just been given.

LemurCandy had phoned me. In real life.

Saga was missing.

He has a really nice voice, I found myself musing. Warm

125

and sweet, like melted caramel. And then, *Did I sound like an idiot when I answered?*

And then, *Saga's missing?*

Fortunately, this was the first of those musings that I actually said aloud. "Saga's missing? What do you mean?"

I heard him swallow. "He was working on one of the Murder Prophet files, but he didn't check in with Kikufaax last night."

We have a "buddy" system at the office. If we had to spread ourselves so thin that we couldn't travel with a partner, we all had someone with whom we had to check in regularly to report progress and let them know we were all right.

"And he didn't check in with you, either," I guessed. LemurCandy was everyone's backup contact, if we couldn't reach our assigned buddy.

"No, I've looked at everything. He didn't leave me any messages anywhere."

I hoped it wouldn't sound rude, but, "Why are you calling me, instead of Kiku?" I asked.

"They're all out searching already," he said. "I offered to call you since you weren't at the office yet..."

I glanced at the clock and stifled a yelp. Ten o'clock? How had I managed to sleep until ten o'clock? And at a time like this?

"I have to go," I babbled into the phone as I struggled to kick off the sheets. "I don't understand how I could do this...and Phoebe didn't wake me—"

"Take it easy, Kit," LemurCandy said, "You've been under a lot of stress lately, and after the other night...I mean, it's not surprising you're tired."

After the other night...did he mean my ill-advised third

126

glass of *sprakele?* Well, okay, it had probably been four glasses, but what did he think, I was some kind of lush?

"I'm not that stressed," I sort of...snapped. Okay, I admit it. This was the first time I'd ever spoken to the man I loved outside of the Netz, and I snapped at him. I was rattled, and embarrassed, and now he'd made me mad on top of it. "I have to get to the office."

"Okay," he said. "I'll be in touch. It was...nice talking to you, Kit."

"Thanks, bye," I said, and hung up, already halfway to the closet before I realized what I'd done. Now I'd *hung up on* LemurCandy the first time I'd ever gotten to speak to him. However, I thought suddenly, at least I knew for a fact now that LemurCandy *was* a "him."

It was nice talking to you, Kit, he'd said, and I'd hung up on him.

Nice going, I thought, as I threw clothes on the bed and rushed into the shower. "Phoebe!" I yelled, "Why didn't you wake me?"

"I knew you were tired, Kit. I thought it best to let you sleep."

"Since when do you get to make decisions like that?" I knew she could hear me over the rushing water.

"Concern with your well-being is part of my programming, Kit."

Bah. There was no point in arguing with her, or chastising her for making me look bad in front of LemurCandy. I had to look into these 'upgrades' she'd been getting, when I had a chance.

And then as I quickly towelled my hair I felt even worse, because here I was worrying about my personal life and letting it overshadow something that had never happened before in all the time I'd been at Darcko and Sadatake.

Saga was missing.

—————•—————

I said to hell with the expense and the fuzzy-headed feeling and caught a magicab to the office. It took me to within a block of the door and the fresh air cleared my head by the time I'd walked the rest of the way. The place was locked up tight, which was highly unusual, but I had my key and let myself in. To my surprise, Trip didn't come rushing out of the back room to see who it was. Even *he* wasn't there. I couldn't remember the last time I'd been in the office and entirely alone. It felt dreadful.

I sat down at the reception desk and paged Kikufaax. She answered immediately. "Is he there?" she asked without preamble.

I shook my head. "No, I just got in and the place is deserted. What's going on? Lemur called me but I didn't stay on the phone long." *Stupidly,* I thought.

Kiku punched up the vid. Worry lined her usually smooth, beautiful face. "He's never done this before. He was following up a lead on one of the other murders, and then he just didn't check in."

"Did he think he'd found a link to the Murder Prophet? Or Coro?"

"I don't know. Glaive's gone to Saga's apartment, Anna's at Magic Vehicles trying to get them to put a trace on his MedLev, and I'm on my way to the police station to get the access codes for the personal information in the file."

"Can't we just call them up on the database?"

She shook her head. "The guy has moved since the

murder, and his new address is protected. Stupid privacy thing. Saga was the only one who had the new data for that file. He got it as a favor from a contact he has in the department, but I don't know who that was."

I heard the creak of Trip's special door in the back, and he came waddling out to see me as soon as he heard my voice. "What should I do?" I asked Kiku.

"Sit tight, in case he calls in," she said. "We were worried about having no one there except Trip."

I glared at the goose over the phone. He hadn't even been here!

"All right," I told her. "Let me know the minute—"

"We will," she said. "See you later."

I pressed the disconnect and turned on the goose. "And where were you? There was no one here to even answer the phone if Saga called in!"

"I only went out for a second," he said defensively, putting up his hands. "And I had the phone forwarded to LemurCandy. It was important."

"As important as Saga being missing?"

"Geez, Kit, give me a break. I thought so. Are you okay?" he asked.

I pressed my fingers over my eyes. Despite the shower I still felt half-asleep and sick with worry. "No, I'm not okay," I said. "Do you know what case Saga was looking at?"

The goose considered. "I think it was the first Murder Prophet one. I'll be in the back if you want me," he added.

I shook my head. Couldn't he leave the video games alone for five minutes, at a time like this? As soon as I thought that, though, I relented. It was probably better for him to have something to do than just sit worrying. That's how I felt, too. I called up everything I could access on the case Saga had been working.

I hadn't gotten very far when the phone rang. I picked it up before the ring ended.

"Hello?"

"Kit, it's just me," said the voice that I immediately recognized from this morning. LemurCandy. "Have you heard from him yet?"

"Nothing yet. I was just going over the file for the case he was looking at. Everyone else is out following leads."

"What case was it?" he asked quickly.

"The first one with a Murder Prophet message," I said. "Why?"

He didn't answer right away, and I heard the faint ticking of keys in the background. I pictured him looking something up, the way he always did when we were chatting online. It was extremely weird to be talking to him in person instead. He hadn't turned on the vid, and neither did I. But the difference between talking to him online and talking to him this way—

I froze in place, still holding the phone to my ear. *Two* distinct ways of talking to LemurCandy, but I thought of them both as "talking." Could that be what Clarice Valencia and her coy little smiles had meant? She said she hadn't been talking to her ex-husband, but she had thought of it as a lie as well as the truth; if she'd been "talking" to him only online, and not in person the way I'd meant the question, that might account for the ambiguity. I hadn't seen it because I'd been distracted by the after-effects of magic and Maginox® and *sprakele* and the financial fallout of the two Coro divorces.

"Kit? Kit, are you still there?" I didn't know how long Lemur had been trying to get my attention, I'd been so lost in my epiphany about the oh-so-clever former Mrs. Coro.

"Yeah, I'm still here," I said slowly. "Did Glaive ask you to run a search on Coro's ex-wife, Clarice Valencia?"

"He did. I ran the trace last night, came up with a few usernames, but that was it. She spends a fair amount of time on the Netz. I suppose that's not surprising, since she lives in a kind of isolated spot."

Thinking back to the gorgeous, sunny island, I didn't think I'd be pining away for the rest of the world if I were living there.

"So there was nothing weird?"

He chuckled. It sounded nice, warm and real. I decided that we could never go back to communicating only online. "Depends on what you'd call weird. This is the Netz, Kit. It can get pretty weird."

"I'm just wondering if she ever gets in touch with Aleshu Coro that way," I said.

"Didn't you ask her that?"

I felt strangely shy telling him what my magic had read in Clarice's answers, but what the hell, he already knew about my talent. "I did, but her answers were ambiguous. She said she hadn't been 'talking' to Coro, but that seemed to be both a lie and the truth. When we asked him later, he flat-out said he hadn't been talking to her, and that was the truth. So then I wondered, maybe if she'd been 'talking' to him online—"

"With a username he didn't connect with her—"

"Exactly," I said. "That might explain the results I was getting."

"So you think they chatted, or his avatar met up with her avatar, but only she knew who she was really connecting with."

"That's what I wonder."

"That's brilliant," he said, and the admiration in his voice sounded sincere. I felt my face go hot and was glad, just for a second, that there was no one else in the office.

"Well, I don't even know if that's what happened, yet. But it seems to make sense. Maybe you already checked to see if there were any convergences of her usernames with Coro's, though?"

"No, I didn't. But I will. Do you want me to call you back?"

"Yes, please. I'm kind of going crazy here just waiting to hear from Saga."

"It'll be okay, Kit, I'm sure of it. I'll call you back soon."

"Thanks," I said, and we broke the connection.

Strangely, now that I'd heard LemurCandy's voice, it was inextricably linked to the avatar I'd seen him use last, the one with the short brown hair with a hint of a wave, the average build, and those knowing green eyes. They seemed, ridiculously, to fit together, although there was absolutely no reason to think that any particular avatar looked like he did in real life. If I hadn't been so worried about Saga I could have daydreamed about that voice, and a real-life version of that avatar, for the rest of the day.

But I was worried. And the phone wasn't ringing, no emails or messages were popping up on my computer, and my cell phone was absolutely still. So I got back to the file I'd been looking at when LemurCandy called.

This was the first murder where the victim was known to have received a message from the Murder Prophet, about six months ago. The file held no personal information, just the outline of the case. Kiku was after the access codes for the rest.

The text of the message was what I'd now come to think of as predictable—a verse quotation mentioning (albeit ambiguously) both a time frame and impending death:

> *The wind of death that softly blows*
> *The last warm petal from the rose,*
> *The last dry leaf from off the tree,*
> *To-night has come to breathe on me.*[3]

The female recipient, one Harriet Fingard, had thought it was spam and disregarded it. Then she'd been murdered on the last day of fall, and the police found the message on her computer. In retrospect, it made sense.

The prime suspect, not necessarily for the message but for the murder, had initially been her husband, Brad Fingard, but he had an alibi that held water with the police, and he invoked his right not to be questioned about a crime with a lie-detecting Psych present. I still think that's a ridiculous law, but civil liberties won that one. Anyway, I guess Saga wondered if that water-tight alibi might start to drip if someone poked at it, and in that case, if the murderer knew anything about the Murder Prophet. There had been no other leads apart from the husband, so the case was still open on the books.

A message popped up on my Chatterz®, from LemurCandy. I felt an instant disappointment that he hadn't phoned so I could hear his voice again. *<Did Kiku get those access codes yet?>*

<I haven't heard from her,> I said. *<Why?>*

<I've got them,> he said simply, and my computer beeped to signal a file transfer in progress. *<Call her back and tell her not to waste time at the police department.>*

<But how?> These were supposed to be secure files. I couldn't believe, even with his Netz talents, that Lemur could get his hands on them.

<Never mind,> he said. <Better if you don't know. But maybe you and Kiku can move faster now.>

<Thank you so much,> I typed quickly.

<No prob. Later,> he said, and was gone.

I called Kikufaax right away, but her line was occupied. I sent her a text to drop what she was doing and come back to the office. I tried Anna next and got her.

"I'm in the Vehicles office, finally," she said in a low voice, so I concluded that she wasn't alone. "A tech is running the trace for me now. Keep trying Kiku, or get Glaive. I'll call you for the details when I'm done here."

I shook my head in frustration. If I didn't get one of the others soon, I was going to take the information LemurCandy had unlocked and head over to the address myself. I half-stood up to do just that, but sat down to try Glaive. I'd catch double hell for going off on my own when one of us had already gotten into trouble that way.

Glaive's phone rang and rang. No one picked up. This was starting to feel scary. I texted him and waited a full minute, watching the seconds tick off on my watch. No reply.

Then the office phone rang, startling me. I grabbed it and breathed "Hello?"

I did not expect to hear Nana Nina's voice, troubled and low. "Oh, Kit, I'm glad it's you. This might sound strange, but is someone you work with in trouble?"

I blinked. Huh? "Ye—yes," I stammered. "Saga's gone missing. How did you know?"

She took a deep breath, loud enough that I heard it over

the line. "I...I can't go into that now, Kit, but you need to find him fast. He's going to end up dead if you don't."

THIRTEEN

Losings, Findings, and Revelations

"It's urgent that you find him," Nana said.

"We're trying, but we only have a few leads. I just got an address that might be connected."

"You'd better hurry. You might not have much time."

How could she know this? "We're going to talk about this later," I told her, checking my .368 as I said it. I punched in the access codes that LemurCandy had sent me and got the address for the suspect in the case.

"I know," she said with a sigh. "Be careful, Kit."

"I will, Nana," I said. "I have to go find him now."

"Kit? One more thing—"

"What?"

"Don't be afraid to...to just do whatever is necessary to stay safe, okay?"

"Okay, Nana. Thanks for calling."

"*Whatever* is necessary, Kit," she repeated. She didn't say goodbye, just hung up.

What did she mean by that? But I didn't have time to ponder it. "Trip!" I yelled.

The goose scuttled out of the back room and dropped into his guard stance. "What? What is it?"

I sighed. "No one's attacking us, don't worry. I might know where Saga is and I'm going after him. He's in danger."

"You're not going alone?"

"I have to. I can't reach anyone else and I can't wait around trying." I threw my jacket over my shoulders.

"I'll come with you."

I shook my head. "No, you stay here in case anyone calls in. Keep trying to get Glaive or Kiku. If you get them, tell them this address." I pointed to it on the screen.

"We can call them from your mobile," he protested, stretching his neck up and flapping his wings in agitation. "You shouldn't go alone!"

"I don't have time to call them. You have to do it. And I'll be fine." I couldn't count how many times I'd said that to people over the last few days.

"Kit—" he began, but I opened the door. Rain and wind lashed in.

"Just keep trying them," I ordered, and left. The rain sheeted down, the wind whipping and snapping the awnings outside the businesses that lined the street, so I sprinted for the nearest magicab box. I'd charge the ride to the company. I didn't think Saga or Anna would mind.

When I got there, of course there was a lineup. I stood fuming and dripping, wishing for the thousandth time that I'd gone ahead and spent the money on a car last year. In the end I'd decided that it was easy enough to get around the city between walking, magicabs, and the bus, and enough of my friends had their own cars, too. Now I wanted to be under my own power. When time was of the essence, these other methods fell woefully short.

Finally it was my turn. As I stepped into the box, I had that being-watched feeling again, for a fleeting second. I glanced down the street and didn't see anyone suspicious-looking, just people running to get out of the weather, so I shrugged it off. No one could follow me through a magicab anyway.

The familiar fuzzy-headedness fogged my brain as I stepped out of the magicab on the other end, but the howling wind and rain brought me back to earth quickly. The street was all but deserted. The cab had deposited me about four blocks from the address LemurCandy had sent. I didn't want to run and attract attention, but I figured no one would think anything of someone walking fast in this weather. I turned up my collar and headed down the street.

I must have developed some kind of sixth sense. Despite the weather, when I was about halfway there I knew someone was tailing me.

"*Phash*," I muttered. I don't swear often, but the last thing I needed on a rescue mission was someone else mucking things up for me. I kept walking, hoping I was wrong. Then I heard a splash, just a faint one. It removed any doubt from my mind.

Blame it on the stress, blame it on the fact that I was sick of this game. I forgot that I was trying not to attract attention. I stopped, turned, and hauled the .368 out of my shoulder holster, pointing it down the street and steadying it in both hands.

"Show yourself," I yelled over the noise of the wind. "I've had it with this! Come out or I'm coming to find you!"

For a minute nothing happened. A door had opened across the street, but it quietly closed again, as if someone had been coming out and then thought better of it. Considering what I must have looked like, I can hardly blame them.

"Last chance!" I yelled again. "Then I'm coming looking

for you!"

Trip stepped out of an alleyway, looking as dejected as a cold, wet, feather-flattened goose can look.

My grip on the gun faltered. "Trip? What the—?"

He waddled up to me. "I'm sorry," he said miserably. "I've just been worried about you."

It took a second for me to realize what he was saying. "*You're* the one who's been following me?"

He nodded, water beading and running slickly down his feathers. "I was just keeping an eye on you. In case you ran into trouble."

"You know you had me scared half to death?"

He fidgeted, scraping a webbed orange foot along the sidewalk and wringing his hands. "I'm sorry. That's where I was when you got to the office this morning. LemurCandy called to say you were on your way in, so I went to watch out for you."

I glared at him. "Did LemurCandy put you up to this? Or Glaive? Or Saga?"

"No. It was my idea. Nobody else even knew."

"But you've all been keeping tabs on me."

He hesitated, then nodded, not meeting my eyes.

A thought occurred to me. "How did you get here so fast? I took a magicab."

"I know, I watched you get in. I flew."

I stared at him. "I thought domesticated geese couldn't fly?"

He shrugged. "I was really scared for you, and I had a tail wind. I can do it, in short bursts. It's just not easy."

"How'd you know where to go?"

He smiled, a little. "You showed me the address on the computer screen."

I just stared at him. *I couldn't spot a big white goose following me?* Some detective I was.

"Anyway," he said, "that's not important now. We have to get Saga."

I frowned. Much as he annoyed me sometimes, I didn't want him waddling into danger behind me. "*I'm* going to get Saga. You're either going home or waiting here."

Surprisingly, he lifted his chin. Er...bill. "No, I'm coming with you, because I can help."

"Look, I know your moves are good—"

"It's not that. Kit, I'm a Finder. Just a little, it's weak. But if I'm in the same building..."

I just stared at him for a moment. A *Finder*? That meant he had a magical talent for, well, finding things. Things, or *people*. "How does it work?"

He hunched his back, which qualifies as shrugging when you don't really have anything to call 'shoulders.' "I don't really know...I mean, if it's someone I know, I just concentrate on them, and I get a feeling for where they are —as long as they're pretty close by. Lost items have a sort of —I don't know, an *aura* of lost-ness. I can feel it if I get close enough to them, or touch them. Like your puzzle book!"

"Wow. And Kiku's earring." I'd never known a Finder, but this sounded like the real thing. "Anything else?"

"Yeah," he said, sounding kind of excited now to talk about it. "I can sense magic sometimes, if it's strong enough."

I stared at him. "You mean you can tell if someone has magic?" No-one could do that, as far as I knew. If the government found out he could do that—

"No, not like that," he said quickly. "I mean, if someone is using it, I can tell, sometimes. Not what kind of magic or what they're doing with it. Just that it's there."

"Wow," I said again, but it suddenly made sense. No wonder it was always Trip who found all the lost items around the office. It wasn't just because he was close to the ground and had a different perspective. It was magic. I couldn't believe we'd never put two and two together. "Why'd you never say anything?"

He looked at the ground and shuffled one orange foot. "I don't know of many animals who got sentience *and* magic," he said. "And I already stand out with these." He waggled his fingers at me. "I don't want people to think I'm a freak."

I stifled a smile, but I could understand where he was coming from. "Okay, you really think you can sense Saga if we get close enough?"

Solemnly he nodded and crossed his white-feathered breast with his index finger. It was one of the weirdest things I've ever seen. "I really do. I want to help, Kit."

"Come on, then," I said, and together we hurried down the street.

The address wasn't much to look at, when we arrived. A battered duplex, with horribly mismatched paint jobs on the two sides, and a ragged postage-stamp yard outside. I was not in any mood to be subtle. I marched up to the side where the murder had taken place and pounded on the door.

No answer.

I knelt down beside Trip, who had climbed up the three rickety steps behind me. "Is he in there?"

Trip closed his eyes, concentrating. He swayed back and forth just slightly. I didn't know if using the magic made him sick, or if it was just the wind. Actually, I didn't know if animals with magic were subject to the same side effects as humans, or not. Trip was right, they were rare, so I'd never thought about it.

Finally he opened his eyes and looked at me. "I think so," he said. "It's hard to tell, with this weather and not being inside, but...I think so."

"Good enough for me," I said, and kicked the door in.

I do not go around indiscriminately kicking in doors. In all honesty, this was probably only the second door to which I'd ever administered such treatment—okay, maybe the third. But I was stressed, I was worried, I'd already had to pull my gun once today. I just wasn't Taking Any More.

No one screamed or ran or yelled or anything else when the door burst open. I had my .368 out, but I was really hoping that I wouldn't have to use it. Trip leaped through the door past me, and landed with a quiet slap of wet webbed feet on linoleum. He bobbed slightly in place, hands up to guard as he scoped the place out. If the situation hadn't been so serious I would have laughed.

"Is he here?" I asked again, now that we were inside.

Trip didn't close his eyes this time, just narrowed them in concentration. After a few seconds he nodded. "Downstairs."

First we had to find the way to get downstairs, which necessitated a quick but careful search of the main floor. The furniture was thrift-store, and not the chic variety. Stained wallpaper hugged the walls, not so tightly in some places. The whole thing smelled of cabbage with a faint underlying note of old urine. Not at all a pleasant place to hang out. We made a good team, I have to admit, taking turns on point and watching each other's backs. Not that I know what Trip would have done if we'd been attacked or ambushed. Tried those killer moves, I guess. In any case, it was strangely comforting that he was there with me.

The door to the basement, when we found it, was locked. We still hadn't seen anyone else inside the house. I got ready to kick it open, (which would have been a record, two in one day) but Trip motioned to a little nail in the doorframe and the key that hung from it. It was probably his finder magic that let him see it, I told myself as I took it down. I mean, surely I hadn't just missed it.

The key turned easily in the lock, tumblers falling into place with a soft click. I opened the door. It creaked like a rotted floorboard in a haunted house. Luckily, there didn't seem to be anyone around to hear it. The steps leading down looked rickety, the stairwell dark. Since the door had been locked from this side, presumably no one lay in wait for us down there, but it pays to take precautions. I didn't step on the first step until I'd found the switch and flooded the basement with light.

Okay, not so much a flood. What actually happened was that a single, faint bulb switched on, throwing just enough illumination for me to see to walk down the stairs. Which I did, cautiously, the .368 held out in front of me and steadied with both hands. Trip followed me, hopping quietly from step to step.

Saga sat at the far side of the cluttered basement, bound to a wobbly chair and gagged with a strip of incongruously colorful red duct tape. Judging by the fire in his eyes, he was certainly all right. My heart leapt with relief. I swept a look around the basement to be certain we were alone, then knelt in front of him and set the .368 down so I could carefully peel the tape from his mouth. He grimaced as it pulled away from his skin, but then he smiled.

"I hoped someone would come looking for me before

too long," he said. That was Saga, king of the understatement.

"You can thank Trip, and LemurCandy," I said, moving quickly to work on the knotted, dirty ropes that bound his arms and legs. "LemurCandy found the house for us, and then Trip found you."

"Thank you both," Saga said gravely. "I will have to send LemurCandy a message as soon as—"

The shadow that loomed suddenly on the stairs took us all by surprise. I couldn't believe a man that big could move so soundlessly. The floor above hadn't creaked at all, which didn't seem at all fair. The gun he had trained on us looked equally gigantic.

My eyes went immediately to the .368 lying on the floor beside Saga's feet, but the man said in a gravelly voice, "Nope."

Then, unbelievably, I saw his finger start to tighten on the trigger. He wasn't going to talk about this at all. He was just going to shoot us. Me first, it looked like.

Trip must have seen the same thing, because he screamed "*Hiii-yahhhhhh!*" and launched himself at the man, wings and hands and feet flying in the complex dance of his "killer moves."

The man hesitated just a fraction of a second, presumably torn between shooting me, or taking out the crazed goose first. I took that fraction of a second, and did the only thing I could. I couldn't worry about secrets, repercussions, or not having taken my Maginox®.

I used my long-denied *other* magic ability and transmuted the man into another goose.

The huge frame shrank and twisted, smoothing out as white feathers took the place of clothing. His face elongated, ears and hair disappearing, a beak stretching out from what used to be chin and nose. It took about a second, far less time than it takes to describe it.

This goose had no hands, naturally, so the gun dropped to the floor with a heavy clunk. So did Trip, come to think of it, when his intended target suddenly disappeared from his trajectory, and he sailed over the man-turned-goose's head.

The nausea hit me so hard and fast that I barely had time to turn my head to the side before I retched horribly and threw up. When I turned back, both Saga and Trip stared at me, wide-eyed and open-mouthed. A second wave of nausea hit and the ill-lit basement blurred and disappeared behind a shower of stars sparking in my darkened vision. My legs went wobbly under me and started to buckle. I managed to catch myself as I fell, so I eased down to the hard-packed dirt floor instead of hitting it face-first.

Just before I passed out I heard Trip say in an awe-struck whisper, "Oh. Wow. *Killer*."

FOURTEEN

Keeping It In The Family

It seemed like Trip didn't stop talking for a long time after I came to. If I could have stayed unconscious longer, I would have missed most of it, but Saga said I was only out for thirty seconds or so. Trip paced around the basement waving his wings menacingly, ostensibly keeping an eye on the other goose. Who seemed to be too stunned to do anything but sit on the floor, staring straight ahead dazedly, so he didn't need much watching anyway.

"Kit's a *Transmute*, Saga! Did you see that? I can't believe she's a Transmute and she never told us! *Zap!* Just like that! Kit, I can't believe you're a Transmute and you never *told* us! Why'd you turn him into a *goose*, anyway, Kit?"

I'd managed to sit up at this point. Saga couldn't help me because I hadn't achieved much untying before the man with the gun showed up. I cocked an eyebrow at Trip. "I don't know. For some reason, geese were on my mind. Now why don't you help me get Saga free?"

He did, but he chattered non-stop as we finished untying the knots. Saga and I shared a "what now?" kind of look. Finally Saga turned to the goose—*our* goose, that is—and said gently, "Now, Trip, I know this is all very exciting, but this has to be our secret for a while, all right? If Kit didn't tell us, she must have had a reason, and we're going to respect that, aren't we?"

There might have been a hint of reproach in Saga's voice.

Trip stared at us. "We're going to tell Glaive and Anna and Kiku, aren't we? We can't keep this a secret from *them*!"

Saga looked at me. I licked my lips. "If we have to tell them, we'll tell them," I said slowly, "But I'd rather do it on my own schedule. You know, Trip, like what we were talking about earlier?"

The goose's face showed realization. He'd only told me about his Finder ability when he had to. He nodded. "Yeah, I get it."

LemurCandy's name hadn't come up, but I really, really didn't want him to know. Not yet, at least. *Oh, why had I had to do that?* I felt sick every time I looked at the other goose, but it was a different kind of sick from the magic nausea. It made my chest tight and my throat dry.

"He really was the murderer, wasn't he?" I asked Saga, who nodded gravely.

"The police hadn't checked the alibi quite diligently enough, I'm afraid," he said. "But the...perpetrator," he said, looking at the silent goose, "Realized what I was doing—I believe a friend tipped him off. He surprised me, I'm sorry to say, and brought me back here." Saga was obviously uncomfortable about being caught off-guard, so I didn't ask for any details.

"We were all so worried—" I said, but broke off. "Oh my goodness, I have to call the others and let them know you're okay!" I fumbled my mobile out of my pocket and tried Anna first. She picked up on the first ring.

"He's safe, I have him," I said immediately, and her sigh of relief came through loud and clear. "Anna, can you call

147

the others, and we'll meet you back at the office?"

She didn't waste time with further questions, just agreed, and I broke the connection and turned to Saga. "So," I said.

"So," he agreed.

"What now?"

"If we call the police, there will be questions about unregistered magic abilities," Saga said slowly.

I nodded. "And it's completely illegal to use Transmute powers—even registered ones—on another human being."

"Completely, yes." He stared intently at the goose for a while. "It is permanent?" he asked me.

"Yep. Until I change him back, or some other Transmute does."

"He is a murderer," Saga mused. "I don't imagine any punishment is too severe."

For a second I didn't understand what he was saying. "You mean, just leave him like this?"

The goose obviously understood our conversation, because at that he struggled up on wobbly orange feet and honked in alarm.

Saga shrugged. "There is a certain elegant justice about it. He's as good as incarcerated, but costs the government nothing. I wonder that the justice system hasn't thought of something like this before now."

I looked at the goose, considering. "We can't just leave him here, though," I said. "He'd starve."

"I have friends with a farm outside the city," Saga said. "They'd take him in. Of course I'd have to give strict instructions that he was once a pet or something, and that I wouldn't want him ending up on the dinner table."

The goose gave another strangled honk and began to

run around the basement in panicked little circles, beating his wings and stumbling now again on his unaccustomed feet, but I felt strangely little concern for him. He'd been about to shoot us, after all. Me first.

So it was settled. We gathered up the protesting goose, collected Saga's car, and drove the creature out to the farm. For a while it squawked and flapped, then settled into a sullen silence. The only downside was that Saga had never had the chance to question him about the Murder Prophet, but we discussed it and came to the conclusion that there was likely no connection.

I suppose I *could* have offered to change him back so we could question him, then turn him back into a goose, but I didn't volunteer to do it and Saga didn't ask. What I'd done was illegal, certainly, even if it was self-defense and I considered it moral justice in hindsight. In the moment of crisis, I'd used my ability reflexively, but I doubted I could do it with cold-blooded deliberation. Even tempering the physical effects by taking Maginox® wouldn't change the emotional effects. I'd spent so long denying the ability and hiding it, that it felt a bit...repulsive, to use it.

I tried to explain my feelings to Saga on the drive back into the city. "It's just been so long." I kept my eyes on the road ahead as I talked. "I kept quiet about it initially because...well, that wasn't the life I wanted. The scheduling, the medication, the responsibility, I guess. And then, the longer you keep the secret, the more of a secret it becomes. If you know what I mean."

Saga nodded. "I do."

"I'm just not ready to talk about it with everyone yet. It's more than trying to avoid the attention of the Registry." I thought of LemurCandy's chuckle over Aleshu Coro's talent. How long would I keep the secret from someone I really cared about, if it ever became an issue?

Saga nodded again. "However you wish to handle the matter, it is your business, Kitano," he said. "Trip and I shall say nothing to the others—will we, Trip?"

Trip snorted in the back seat. He'd sat as far away from the other goose as he could, and spent most of the drive glaring at him. "Not if you don't want us to," he agreed grudgingly. "It just makes such a great story. I mean, the guy's about to shoot us, and I go after him with my moves, and then when I've got him distracted, Kit hauls off and—"

"We know, we know," Saga said soothingly. "*Zap!* He's a goose."

I stifled a grin. "At least there's no chance we'll leave the wrong goose out here," I said to Saga, "Although it might be quieter..."

"Very funny," Trip retorted. "Maybe I'd like a little vacation on a farm. A vacation from snooty Transmutes, anyway." But I could tell he wasn't really mad.

The delivery of the transmuted goose went smoothly, and if Saga's friends thought it odd that he would suddenly deliver them a goose for safekeeping, they didn't let it show. Maybe being friends with Saga, you learned to expect the unexpected. The goose honked in protest a few more times, but then settled down and waddled despondently off toward a nearby pond. He might have had time to consider the alternative—police, trial, incarceration—and decided to make the best of it.

When we arrived back at the offices of Darcko and Sadatake, everyone had gathered and were ready for a celebration. Chinese takeout boxes waited on the lunchroom table, and after hugs all around when we walked in, they made us sit down and tell the whole story, first Saga's adventure, and then the big rescue. In the version we shared with them, the man had never come home, and we quietly sneaked out with Saga once we'd freed him. Not nearly as exciting, but not nearly as complicated to explain, either.

Saga merely said he'd become convinced that while the man was probably the murderer, it would be difficult to prove, and he didn't think there was any connection to the Coro case. We invented a trip to the police station to report Saga's findings by way of explaining the delay in our arrival. Since we weren't being paid to solve that particular murder, no one had much of a problem letting it go. They were willing to take Saga's word on it, which made me feel a bit guilty. It was my secret he was lying to cover up.

By the time I headed for home I was mentally exhausted, and I wished I could call LemurCandy up and tell him the whole thing. I pushed that thought away. I couldn't go getting all dependent on him, when I'd still never even met the guy. At least, I thought as I walked the last block to home, I could stop worrying about being followed. I'd had a talk with Trip and he promised to stop following me around "for protection." I thanked him for his concern, and told him that I'd be sure to take him along any time I thought I needed a partner to watch my back. He seemed satisfied with that.

As I unlocked my door I could have sworn someone ducked into an alleyway half a block back, but I chalked it up to my imagination. I didn't slam the door behind me this time. Since she'd overheard my conversation with Lemur that morning, Phoebe had enough questions about where I'd been without adding to her concerns. It wasn't that I didn't want her to worry—I just didn't know if I could stand it.

———•———

After a long, hot shower and a bowl of French Vanilla ice cream smothered in chocolate and caramel sauce, I started to feel normal again. Curled up on the sofa with one of Nana Nina's hand-crocheted blankets over my legs, I called her. It rang so many times I was beginning to think she wasn't home, but then she picked up, vid and all.

"Hello, Kit," she said breathlessly. Stray wisps of silvery hair stuck out at odd angles around her head and bouncy music pounded away in the background, so I figured she'd been working out. I run to relieve stress; Nana Nina does dance workouts. "Is everything okay?"

"Saga's safe, if that's what you mean," I told her. "Thank you. I got to him just in time, and I wouldn't have hurried so much if you hadn't called."

"Oh, I'm glad to hear it, honey," she said. "He's a nice man, that Mr. Sadatake. Did I ever tell you about the time he—"

I cut her off, as nicely as I could, and fixed her with my best interrogatory stare over the vidscreen. "Nana, how did you know Saga was in trouble?"

She glanced away from the phone, not meeting my eyes, and didn't answer right away. "Why do you even ask me, Kit?" she said finally. "You must know."

"You're a Seer."

She nodded.

"Even though you've always denied it."

She shrugged gracefully. "You could have used your

magic on me, you know, even though I appreciated the fact that you didn't. We all have secrets, Kit. Things *we have our own reasons for keeping quiet about*? But when it becomes necessary..." She looked back at the vid then, her blue eyes piercing as they met mine.

She knows, I thought suddenly. *She knows about me.*

I shook the thought away. That was impossible. Until today I'd never told anyone about my ability. Never. And it hadn't manifested until I was a teenager, so my parents had never known. But her words from this morning echoed in my ears. *Do whatever is necessary to stay safe.*

Was that what she'd meant?

I felt an uncomfortable urge to get off the phone. She'd turned the tables on me. Damn grandmothers. You can't trust them at all. "Well, everything turned out all right, anyway. I just wanted to say thank you."

She continued to look at me intently. "Are you all right, Kit?"

I faked a yawn. "Just tired, that's all. It's been a long day."

"How's your friend, WeaselTreats?"

I shook my head, grinning. "LemurCandy. He's fine."

"You should go out more, Kitano," Nana Nina said, abruptly changing the subject. Or was she? "You need a little more fun in your life."

"Fun takes energy, Nana, and tonight I just don't have any. I'll talk to you soon, okay?"

She smiled. "I'm glad your friend is safe. Love you, Kitty-cat."

I smiled back. She hadn't called me that since I was little. "Love you, Nana."

I went to sleep vaguely wishing I'd talked to Lemur

again before the day ended. Ugh, so sappy. I was really going to have to work on that.

FIFTEEN

Stalkers, Stakeouts and Screwups

I woke up the next morning with one thought: it was now a week and a day since Aleshu Coro had first phoned the office, and we didn't seem to be getting any further ahead with the case. It was also almost a week since my own Murder Prophet message had arrived, and the brighter morning and insistent birdsong outside my window told me that the first day of spring was fast approaching.

I didn't even wait to get to the office—I logged onto my Chatterz® at home and went looking for LemurCandy. Yes, I could have retrieved his number from my phone and called him (and I would have loved to hear his voice again), but this was more comfortable. Yesterday had been an emergency. This was business as usual.

Anyway, he answered me right away. <*Hey,*> I said. <*Thanks so much for...yesterday.*> I didn't want to mention the access codes directly, since what he'd done had been on the questionable side of legal. Highly questionable.

<*I'm just glad I could help, and that Saga's all right,*> he said. <*But I didn't get any of the details.*>

I sat looking at the screen for a minute. <*Not much to tell,*> I typed finally. <*Saga was there, right at the address you gave me. I managed to get him out before we ran into any other trouble.*>

<*You make it sound so easy,*> he said.

I crossed my fingers for the lie, then said, <*Well, it was. Oh, and I found out that it was only Trip stalking me all along.*>

<*Stalking you????*>

Oh, *phash.* I hadn't told LemurCandy about the whole being-followed thing.

<*It was nothing,*> I lied. <*I just thought maybe someone was following me the last few days. It turned out to be Trip, thinking he had to take care of me or something. It was kind of funny.*>

There was silence on the screen. The cursor seemed to blink at me accusingly. <*Hello?*> I typed.

<*I think you have to start being a little more careful, Kit,*> he said. <*After that message...I mean, it could have really been someone. You should have told me about that. Or Glaive. You could be in real danger, but it's like you won't admit it.*>

I filled my lungs with air and blew it out slowly. <*I know. I will. Be more careful. But if I start tiptoeing around, that'll make me even more scared.*>

<*Just make sure one of us always knows where you are, okay?*>

<*I'll try,*> I said, but that was as far as I'd go. LemurCandy didn't know it, but I always had my secret transmutation weapon I could pull out. Maybe that's why I wasn't more worried in the first place, although it hadn't been a conscious thing before. The thought of using it still made me feel sick, but intellectually I knew it was there as a last resort if I needed it.

He must have realized it was time to change the subject, because he said, <*Nothing on Clarice Valencia's usernames, yet, but I've got a possible lead on something else linked to Coro.*>

<*What is it?*>

<*Business deal that went bad. Coro bailed, and I'm not*

certain how the other side took it. They may be holding a grudge.>

<When was this?>

<Six months or so ago,> he said. *<Coro didn't mention it to anyone there?>*

<Not that I know of. I'll ask them when I go in to the office,> I said.

<I'm digging for the details now, so I'll keep you posted. Take care,> he said.

<See you later,> I typed, and logged off.

"Was that LemurCandy?" Phoebe asked cheerily.

I jumped, startled, because I'd sort of forgotten Phoebe was there. "Yes, why?"

"You should invite him over for dinner sometime, Kit," she suggested. "I could get some recipes from the Netz and help you with them."

"You weren't monitoring my conversation, were you?" I snapped.

She made a sound like a sigh. "If I were, I wouldn't have had to ask who you were conversing with, would I? I am programmed to monitor all aspects of your well-being and security, Kit. However, your privacy is always paramount."

"Hmmm. I seem to remember finding out just the other day that you told LemurCandy what time I'd come home."

"I wasn't aware that was a secret," she said in a tone of icy affront. "Shall I annotate that as private information in the future?"

I got up from the computer and headed for the shower. You can't really win an argument with an apartment AI. "Never mind. Just stop disparaging my cooking skills, okay? And let me set my own social schedule?"

She had nothing to say to that, for which I was profoundly grateful.

———•———

The weather had finally cleared, so I walked to work that morning. I didn't think anyone would mind if I was a little late—it wasn't the kind of office where you have to punch a time clock. Half the city seemed to be out and about as people poked their heads out after yesterday's rain, so I had no worries about anyone following me with malicious intent, no matter what LemurCandy had said. Personally, I thought he was taking it all too seriously. Here, outside, in the bright morning sunshine, the possibility that anyone would want to hurt me seemed remote and absurd.

When I walked into the office, Kikufaax practically barked at me. "Where were you?"

"Um, walking to work?"

She shook her head in annoyance, her long black hair swishing. "You have to let someone know when you're going to be late," she said. "Phoebe said you left long ago. We were starting to worry."

I mimed pulling out my hair. "Phoebe? You too? This is nuts!" I said. I stipulate that I did not shout. "No one's even come near me since I got that message! The only one stalking me was Trip! I'm starting to think you're all insane, and you're going to drive me onto the crazy train, too!"

I stomped into my office and shut the door, then pressed my palms together and did deep breathing for a few minutes. I hadn't meant to go off on Kiku like that, but coming on the heels of LemurCandy's over-solicitous chastisements it was just too much.

When I was calm again I opened the door. "Has LemurCandy been in touch?" I asked in a completely normal tone. "He said this morning he might have a new lead on something to do with Coro."

I don't know if Kiku was expecting an apology, but she didn't give any sign that she was. She didn't give me one, either, but that was fine. I knew it was just because they cared—but that didn't make it any less annoying. Glaive stood beside her desk, dressed entirely in his usual hit-man black from mock turtleneck to polished loafers, studying something on her screen.

She nodded. "I'm checking out the people in the other firm, while he tries to get a handle on exactly what the deal was. I'm surprised Coro didn't mention this to anybody."

"He didn't say anything that first day, with Anna and Saga." I moved over to sit on the side of Kiku's desk, so I could see the screen, too.

"And not when we asked him about his second wife, either," Glaive added.

"Has anyone else been talking to him?"

Anna walked out of her office just then, wearing a gorgeous tangerine dress and jacket ensemble. Gold hoop earrings swayed almost to her shoulders and matched the chunky gold and citrine necklace at her throat. "I was. I dropped into his office one day to ask him more details about the staff at his home and his employees. He didn't mention anything about this deal then."

Glaive frowned. "Doesn't it seem like the kind of thing that would stick in a person's mind? You piss someone off to the tune of millions of dollars and then six months later someone wants you dead? Wouldn't you make the connection? Or at least think there might be one?"

Anna shrugged. "I don't know. Maybe we're reading more into it than was actually there. Maybe it was more amicable than we're imagining, or it wasn't worth that much money. This kind of thing could happen all the time in Coro's world."

"I guess we'll know more once LemurCandy gets back to us," I said.

"I'm going to check into the situation surrounding the last Murder Prophet message before Coro's," Anna said. "It hasn't been solved yet, and I want to get the access codes for all the details, just so we can be sure there's no connection."

"Mind if I tag along?" asked Glaive. He grinned. "I don't want you pulling a Saga on me and disappearing."

"Har-de-har," Anna said. "I'm quite sure I'll be safe at the police station." She made a show of inspecting him from head to toe. "However, you look acceptable today, so I suppose you can tag along."

Glaive grinned in response, since he looked exactly the same as he did every day. They left and I went back into my office, but I couldn't settle into anything. I was contemplating the awful possibility that I would have to clean my desk when a phone call rescued me.

The call came in, and Kikufaax answered it in her usual cheery tone. Turned out to be a client who'd asked us to do a little tailing for him a month back, then called and changed his mind before he'd actually laid any money on the table. He thought an employee was stealing from him, but then started to doubt his suspicions.

Seemed like those suspicions had caught fire again and he wanted the guy tailed—right now. He'd instant-transfer the money over the Netz if we'd send someone to track the employee when he left the store.

"I'll go," I mouthed to her over the top of her screen. I could hear both ends of the conversation since he was using vid and audio and Kiku had the speaker on. I went to the door and pulled my light jacket on over my turtleneck to conceal the shoulder holster.

She couldn't make a face at me since the client was looking straight at her, so she told him we'd have someone there within half an hour, got the funds transfer straightened out, and broke the connection. Then she could frown at me, and did.

"Are you sure? I don't know if you should be going alone..."

"Look, it's nothing at all to do with the Coro case," I said. "And keep your voice down before Trip hears you, or he'll be demanding to come along as my bodyguard."

She pressed her lips into a straight line and tugged at a silvery earring. Saga hadn't come in today, and with Anna and Glaive gone it was either me or her. I'd volunteered, and she couldn't pull rank and tell me I couldn't go. Except for Saga and Anna, there were no ranks. "I should tell Trip exactly what you're doing. That would teach you."

"Haha. You say a word to him and I'll tell Glaive you have a secret hankering for men who wear black."

"Very funny." She shrugged. "Oh well, I guess I can't stop you."

"That's exactly right," I agreed, grinning. "Show me this guy's mug."

———•———

The thing you tend to forget about tailing someone, if you haven't done it for a while, is how deadly boring most of it is. I found the business with no problem, slipped on my dark glasses, and glanced inside to see if my mark was there. He was, standing behind a cash register and backed by a wall of computer equipment, rocking slightly from foot to foot. He checked his watch a couple of times, and I figured the boss had managed to keep him there long enough for me to arrive.

I went across the street to a little cafe, ditched the glasses, reversed my jacket in the ladies' room, pulled my hair back into a twist, and ordered coffee and two oatmeal cookies. A grey tabby cat came in and ordered straight cream, but she wanted it to go so I didn't have to extricate myself from potential conversation. Magic-sapient cats are more chatty than I ever imagined they'd be. I took a tiny table next to the window. Here I was directly across from the door of the business, and if I squinted, I could make out my mark behind the counter inside.

While I sipped coffee and nibbled at the cookies, I wondered idly why the client was going about things this way. I mean, if he really thought the guy was stealing, why not hire a lie-detector Mancer (like me) and just ask him straight out? Why not install vidcams? Really, if I thought about it, there were quite a number of easier ways to catch an inside crook, without hiring someone like me to follow him home. What was I supposed to see, anyway?

But those lines of thought don't get you anywhere, because the only real answer lies with the client, and he wasn't here to ask. Once I'd come to that conclusion, my mind drifted toward LemurCandy and the way our relationship seemed to be evolving—but in what direction, I wasn't sure. I didn't get to dwell on it for long. The guy I was watching came out and locked up the door behind him, pulling on a blue windbreaker. That should make him easy to keep in sight.

I got up from the table and strolled out, standing in front of the cafe for a minute as if wondering which way to walk. My mark had already set out on foot heading east, toward the downtown. Casually I started in that direction, glancing in windows stuffed with sale items as I went and generally trying to give off an air of going nowhere in particular.

We'd gone about a block when, even though I had most of my attention focused on the mark, I had that feeling again. The feeling that someone, probably equally casually, was following me.

Damn that Trip, I thought, *If it's him again...*

Now I had to do two things without being observed — keep my own guy in sight, and try to catch a glimpse of my own follower. I managed the first, but the second was impossible. Whoever was tailing me, if indeed someone was, they were good.

My own mark seemed oblivious to the possibility of being followed. He walked with purpose but didn't hurry, and didn't glance back once. He wasn't heading home, though; he passed the cross-street that would take him quickest to his apartment. I'd retrieved that address from Kikufaax before I'd left the office.

At one point I ducked into an entryway and switched my jacket back to the other fabric, donned the glasses, and let my hair down again. I didn't want the mark to realize I was following him, and I didn't care if my follower learned my tricks.

The mark walked on until he'd passed through the downtown and out the other side, into an area populated mostly by apartment buildings and small hotels. He turned in at one of these and I ducked into a deli across the street and ordered a ham and cheese sandwich on whole wheat. I was puzzled. Had he tagged me? I didn't think so. Was he meeting someone here to pass off whatever he might have stolen from work? That also seemed unlikely, but just in case, I set up my minicam on the table beside a tall glass of WizWater® and my sandwich, and took pics of everyone entering and leaving the hotel for the next little while. I'm certain the deli owner, a tall, thin man with saturnine features and dark, world-weary eyes, knew what I was doing, but he didn't say a thing. I expect if you own any sort of eating establishment across the road from a hotel you get used to seeing things like this. On the upside, the sandwich was excellent.

I had no idea where my own follower might be now, assuming I hadn't imagined him into existence. For all I knew, he was across the street in the hotel lobby, surreptitiously taking pictures of anyone who entered the deli in case they were coming to meet me.

After about an hour and half, my mark came out of the hotel and started back the way he'd come. I slipped out of the deli, leaving a nice tip behind me on the table, and fell in behind him. He didn't look back, so he either had no notion that I was there, or didn't care. This time he did take the cross-street that led to his apartment building, a functional but uninspired crackerbox, walked to it, and went inside. I stopped in the shadows of an awning-covered doorway and waited a while to see if he was coming back out, but it didn't look like it. He was probably in for the night.

With that thought I realized that full dark had descended on the city. The street was far from deserted, though, so I started back the way I'd come. Vague annoyance settled over me, as I wondered if this little escapade had accomplished anything for the client. I'd jumped at the chance to get out of the office and have something to do, but in retrospect it seemed like a pretty silly assignment. Ah, well, I had a bunch of pictures and I'd eaten a great sandwich at the deli. Sometimes you just have to make the best of things.

The hairs on the back of my neck twitched in response to some subliminal trigger. My follower had stuck with the program, and was behind me again.

I wasn't utterly vulnerable with other pedestrians around, but the creepy feeling prickling my neck was hateful. I wondered suddenly if marks felt this way when I was tailing them. They never seemed to show it, if they did.

At the bus stop I waited with a small clutch of folks heading home late from work. While we stood, united in the discomfort of trying not to make small talk, I glanced casually down the street a couple of times. No one. Maybe I'd been wrong? Maybe whoever it was had given up and gone home?

At any rate I felt ridiculously relieved when the bus pulled up and we all boarded. No one had arrived at the stop after me, so my supposed stalker couldn't be among my fellow passengers. I took a window seat and tried to peer outside past the reflections as we drove through the brightly-lit streets. This unsettled feeling every time I went somewhere alone was really starting to bug me. I'd thought, once Trip confessed, that it was all over, but apparently I was wrong.

No one else got off at my stop. The three blocks to my house stretched out long and lonely ahead of me as I left the fluorescent warmth of the bus and set out alone. I didn't sense anyone behind me, but my legs throbbed with the urge to run. I fought it down. I couldn't give in every time I felt nervous. I couldn't let this change me.

My apartment block loomed within sight as I rounded the corner onto my quiet street. A figure, shadowy and indistinct, hovered near the entrance to my building. Just a resident, I told myself, waiting for a drive, or perhaps someone waiting for a resident to come down. My stride slowed as I assessed the situation, and I was so focused on the figure that I stupidly didn't hear the guy come up behind me.

He wasn't a professional, or not a very good one, because instead of just taking me out with a sap to the back of the head, he grabbed me, one hand sliding over my mouth and one going around my waist. That left him open for an elbow to the solar plexus, which I delivered with pleasure and a great rush of adrenaline.

He grunted, but he was tough and didn't let go. His hand over my mouth smelled of cheap aftershave and the chili dog he'd had for lunch. I almost gagged. Instead I tried to bite him, while I grabbed for his lower arm. If I could get a good grip I might be able to throw him.

His hand brushed my breast and for an absurd second I thought he was trying to grope me, until I realized he was looking for the gun in my shoulder holster. That meant he knew exactly who I was. Still struggling, I briefly considered transmuting him. The taboo against that was pretty strongly ingrained, though, and the unpleasantness of the last time I'd done it, especially *sans* Maginox®, fresh in my mind. I didn't feel like puking my guts up again just now. That would be a last resort.

I got both hands on his arm and threw my weight to the

side to flip him, when I heard a sickening, fleshy impact and he fell away from me, suddenly limp. I stumbled, off-balance, and another hand grabbed my arm, steadying me and spinning me around to face my rescuer. The man panted as if he'd just been running, and although I'd never seen them in real life, the green eyes staring into mine from a mere six inches away seemed awfully familiar.

"Kit! Are you all right?" LemurCandy gasped.

I nodded, dumbstruck. The only thought in my head was, *He looks just like his avatar.*

SIXTEEN

Conversation and Mocha Insanity

So there we are, me and LemurCandy, in the flesh, face to face, on a dark street where he's just come to my rescue, and he looks gorgeous and I'm thinking *in real life he's 'way more good-looking than that Aleshu Coro avatar* ever *was*, and what do I say to him?

"I could have taken him myself." I heard the words emerge from my mouth with a sense of disbelief. Not *thank you*, or *kiss me, you fool*, but *I could have taken him myself.*

Lemur dropped my arms and took a step backward. "Of course you could have," he said off-handedly. "I just thought I might as well lend a hand...since...since I was here."

I snapped back to my sense and started babbling. "Oh, absolutely! And thank you, thanks...I'm grateful, really! I wonder who he is and why he was following me? And...and...so this is really you! Just like your avatar, only—"

I'd been going to say "cuter" but I bit the word off just in time. I realized that what was coming out of my mouth should not have anything to do with what was going on in my head. "—only, in real life," I finished lamely.

Fortunately LemurCandy didn't seem to notice as he knelt down beside the unconscious thug. He looked up at

168

me. "What do we do with this?"

I took a deep breath and tried to cudgel my brain into some sort of composure. "I don't want to leave him here without knowing why he was following me."

"Should we just call the police?"

The police! "That's probably the best idea," I said, pulling out my mobile. Surprisingly, they were on the spot before the guy woke up, more businesslike and efficient than I would have thought possible. They frisked him, took our statements, put him in their blue-and-black wagon and left, asking us to come down to the station in the morning and sort out anything else. I figured one of them had a talent similar to mine, so he knew our story was true. I guess that's one place that magic has definitely made people's lives easier. Unless your talent is undetectable lying, you'd better not decide to live a life of crime.

However, with the police gone from the scene, it left me and LemurCandy standing uncomfortably on the darkened sidewalk near my apartment, neither one of us apparently knowing what to say to the other. Streetlights splotched patches of brightness here and there in either direction, but few pedestrians moved through them. The night air tickled my face, crisp and cool.

"So," I said finally. "What are you doing here, anyway?"

He glanced up at the nearest streetlight. "I thought...I'd just pop by and see...when you wanted to get together and go over that data."

It didn't take magic to know he was lying. Why even try that with me? Unless he'd forgotten about my talent. Or maybe he didn't understand how it worked.

"Really?" I asked, looking him straight in the eyes. I hadn't taken any Maginox®, but maybe I could bluff him.

Might as well give him a chance to come clean.

"Well...not really," he admitted with a rueful smile. "Look, I was worried about you, so I thought I'd just make sure you got home okay. Kiku told me you'd gone on a stakeout alone and—"

"Do you want to go for a coffee?" I interrupted. "There's a good place not far from here." I didn't want another lecture on how to avoid getting into trouble. It never seemed to do me any good to hear it, anyway. And I really didn't want to get ticked off and snap at him.

He seemed to relax, shoving his hands into his pockets. "That would be great," he said, and we headed down the street. He didn't attempt to hold my hand, as his avatar had the night we went off the grid. I found that unreasonably disappointing. However, the night seemed much less menacing with him walking beside me.

"Anything come out of that Coro business deal you were looking into?" I asked, to break the silence and stop myself from drifting off into an unrealistic daydream. He was chatty enough online, but so far, in real life, he was pretty quiet. I guess I couldn't blame him. He might not even have been planning to show himself to me, and now here he was, on the front lines, you might say.

"I'm not sure yet. Still waiting for some details."

The coffee shop showed welcoming lights at all the windows, and LemurCandy held the door for me as we slipped out of the chilly spring air into the warm scents of coffee and pastries. One of the baristas who works there lives in my building, and we're—not friends exactly, but friend-ish. Diamanta evaluated Lemur with one practised glance, and threw me a wink and a nod when he had his back turned pulling out a chair. I winked back and was grinning when Lemur turned and sat down.

"What?"

"Oh, nothing," I said. "That's a friend of mine at the counter, that's all."

I ordered a large coffee with cream and sugar, and Lemur had a Mocha Insanity. I shuddered when it came. "You like that stuff?" I asked. An inch of thick froth, studded with bits of chocolate, obscured any sight of the coffee that lay underneath.

He shrugged and smiled. "I like my sugar with a shot of caffeine," he said.

Finally, now that we were sitting down like two civilized people in a half-empty coffee shop, not dealing with thugs and policemen on a dark street, I could actually look at him. He had definitely modelled that avatar on himself, probably left the faceskin input pretty much untouched, the way I did. The brown hair, the green eyes, the same lean but muscular build—it was him exactly. I felt a twinge of self-consciousness about the...adjustments I'd made to my own avatar. How noticeable were they?

"I was thinking I should do some more background work on the folks at MageData," he said, looking up from his drink. "I feel like it's got to be someone close to Coro."

"Not the business deal, then?"

He shrugged. "I don't know. There doesn't seem to be much there. And would you really kill someone over something like that?"

"I don't know," I said. "I've never thought about what might make me want to kill someone."

"Well, nothing, I hope," he said with a grin.

"You're probably right. Except for self-defence," I said, considering the man with the gun in that dark basement. If

I'd still had the .368 in my hand, and had the option of killing him or transmuting him, which one would I have chosen? I shuddered. I honestly didn't know.

"So you think there might be answers inside Coro's company, then," I prodded.

"Maybe. I doubt you can run a business that large, for as long as he has, without getting some people mad at you."

Diamanta sashayed over to see if we'd like anything else, although I think it was a ruse to get another close-up look at Lemur. She managed to talk us into a couple of fresh Danish, apple-walnut for me and chocolate for LemurCandy. She threw me another wink and an approving smile as she turned away.

"It would be great if you could even pinpoint someone we should talk to," I said. "The company's too big to question everyone in the time we have."

"Does Coro get along okay with the Board of Directors?" LemurCandy asked. "That's who he has the closest contact with, I guess, and the most opportunities to butt heads."

"I think so. I asked him about that, and I didn't think he was lying when he said there was no conflict there."

"How does that work, anyway?" he asked, leaning forward with his elbows on the table. "Your talent, I mean." His hands were square and tanned and strong, not what you might expect from someone who spent that much time at the computer. I knew they were strong because of the way he'd held my arms outside on the street earlier.

"It's not an 'always on' thing," I said, fiddling with some grains of spilled sugar that had escaped Diamanta's cleaning cloth. "I have to concentrate on what the person is saying and deliberately try to analyze it. And if I haven't taken Maginox® it makes me kind of sick. Usually nothing serious, but uncomfortable."

He nodded as if he knew exactly what I meant. I itched to ask him if he had any magic, but it wasn't a polite question, and I didn't get the chance anyway.

Diamanta brought the pastries. LemurCandy bit into his and chewed reflectively.

"I think by tomorrow I'll have the results for Clarice Valencia's usernames."

"I guess a search like that isn't easy if she doesn't want one to be found," I said.

He shook his head. "No, but it's easier to trace from a person to a username than from a username to a person. Most of the blocks work better one-way."

"Really?" I tried the apple-walnut. It was delectable, although pastry flakes showered the table.

"Oh, yes. If I just met someone named *Kitano Kick-ass* online, it would be pretty much impossible to find the real you from that. But knowing Kit Stablefield, I can go in the other direction pretty easily."

"I thought you had checked Clarice Valencia out already, though," I said.

"Well, I did, but now I'm digging deeper. There are levels. I set up a matrix of Coro's usernames and all the ones he's had contact with, then started working outward along the grid. At the same time, I started with her name and set the 'bots tracing the grid in that direction, too. Then when they start hitting convergent nexus traces—"

I put a hand to my temple and shook my head. "Never mind, I'm not going to understand it. I'm sure whatever you're doing will work." I grinned. "Just watch out for those harmonized divination whatchamacallits."

Lemur stopped with his chocolate Danish halfway to his

mouth, looking suddenly grave, his green eyes darkening. "You haven't had any more messages, have you?"

"Of course not." He seemed so downcast that I hated myself for mentioning it.

"I still feel terrible about that," he said in a low voice.

"Oh, forget it. I'm not worried about it, so you shouldn't be, either."

What followed that was an awkward silence, and I finished the last few sips of my coffee and nibbles of Danish to cover it up.

"I'd better get you home," Lemur said, and drained the dregs of his Mocha Insanity. I shuddered again. He stood up. "It's been a long day."

I couldn't argue with that. Lemur adroitly picked up the tab and we left the coffee shop and walked back to my building in relative silence, although it wasn't uncomfortable. He didn't hesitate outside the door. "I'll be in touch tomorrow, Kit" he said, smiling and turning away almost immediately.

"Sure," I said, trying to act just as nonchalant. "Good hunting!" I went into the building without a backward glance, then raced up the stairs and unlocked my door in a rush to see if I could catch a glimpse of him from one of my windows before he disappeared into the night. I couldn't. He was gone without a trace.

"Kit, where have you been?" Phoebe asked in a voice that sounded strangely breathless, for an AI. "You left the office hours ago!"

I rounded on her. Well, I would have rounded on her if she'd actually had a physical presence. As it was, I sort of whirled around ineffectually. "Do not tell me that you told anyone from the office I wasn't home yet!"

"No," she admitted, "But I was about to! You know that your well-being and security—"

"I know, I know, it's in your programming. Well, if you must know, I was with LemurCandy, so I was perfectly safe," I told her, shucking my jacket and shoulder holster.

She sounded immediately more cheerful. "I thought that was him waiting outside earlier. Did you have a date?"

"No, I wasn't expecting him at all. We just went for coffee on the spur of the moment." No way was I going to tell Phoebe about the guy who'd jumped me. Then I realized what she'd said. "And how do you know what he even looks like?"

"I've seen his avatar, Kit," Phoebe said patiently, as if I were a little kid.

Again I questioned whether all these software upgrades and integrated Netz access had been such a good idea after all. However, I wasn't going to fight about it right now.

I sat down on my bed, then kicked off my shoes and flopped back on the colorful quilt Nana Nina had made for me when I was a little girl. I hovered on some weird emotional balance board between elation and depression. On the up side, I'd finally met LemurCandy, and he was just as, well, wonderful as I thought he'd be. He'd been concerned about my safety. He'd come to my rescue. He was handsome and sweet and who cared if he liked to drink Mocha Insanity? I was definitely in love with the guy.

On the down side, his feelings about me were...ambiguous, to say the least. He hadn't sent any clear signals that I'd picked up on, in either real life or the virtual one.

I fought down a sudden urge to smack myself in the head. I hadn't even found out what his real name was. And really, I couldn't imagine kissing someone I knew only as LemurCandy. I'm as modern as the next girl, but that would be asking just a bit much.

I crawled into bed and swore that I'd ask him the next time I saw him.

Unfortunately, it didn't turn out quite that way.

SEVENTEEN

Family Ties and Netz Lies

In the morning I caught a bus down to the police station to file a formal account of the attack on me the night before and see what they'd found out about the guy. Turned out I just missed LemurCandy, which was a huge disappointment, because I'd spent some time lying in bed picturing how we'd meet up at the station and I'd ask him his real name and then we'd go for coffee again and spend the day walking in the park...

Okay, okay. I have a healthy imagination. At this point in my imaginings I realized that he was already committed to a lot of Netz research today and if I wanted to run into him at all I'd better get my butt down to the station. I missed him anyway.

The thug who'd attacked me was not a fount of information. All the police could squeeze out of him was that he'd been approached online by an anonymous "client" to "terrorize" me a bit. He'd been paid through an untraceable cash-based PayMate® account. They'd sent him all my relevant information and he was not to really hurt me, just, well, terrorize me. Apparently this kind of activity was his main source of income.

Wow, the career choices that my high school counsellors had never mentioned.

I asked the police to forward any data they confiscated from the guy's computer over to LemurCandy, and surprisingly, they agreed. I think they were just as happy to hand off the scutwork, but that was fine with me. I knew Lemur would do a better job than any police hacker.

Lemur, Lemur. I felt much freer knowing that the thug was behind bars, so I walked the rest of the way to work, even whistling erratically in the fresh morning air. The scheduled overnight rain had scoured everything clean, and I noticed trees furred with the first pale hints of green. Spring was drawing closer.

I shuddered and turned my thoughts back to Lemur and my stupidity in not asking him his real name. Yes, I was obsessing over it. But I really hate it when I do something that stupid. Could I ask him over the Netz, I wondered? I didn't think it was proper etiquette, for some reason. I mean, he had his reasons for dealing with everyone (or practically everyone) from behind the shadow of his usernames. Granted, he was using an avatar that looked exactly like him, so how zealous was he really about guarding his identity?

This debate wound around and around in my head and brought me all the way to work. I'd come to the decision, regretfully, that I couldn't ask him over the Netz. It wasn't much, but at least I felt better for having answered one question.

Kikufaax was stationed at the reception desk when I arrived at the office, fingers skimming in a blur over the keyboard. Her outfit today was oddly subdued for the time of year, a navy sleeveless shell and plain gold chains. I wondered if she was deliberately not dressing in her usual bright spring colors out of consideration for my feelings.

That would be nice of her. Not that I wasn't already acutely aware of just how close we were to the first day of spring.

At any rate, she didn't bark at me as I stepped in the door this morning, which was also nice. She didn't ask me anything about the night before, like "How was your night?" so that I could tell her all the exciting and wonderful things that had happened, which was disappointing. Instead she said, "Morning, Kit. LemurCandy wants you to contact him right away, okay?"

"Okay," I said. I felt kind of disappointed at not having anyone to sit and chat about it with, but then I remembered Kiku's absolute truth rule and that I couldn't trust her to cover me if she knew how I felt about Lemur. Yeah, best to keep that one close to my chest. And although I knew I'd have to tell everyone in the office all about the attack eventually since it might be important to the case, I didn't mind putting it off a little. It was probably only going to trigger a whole new round of be-careful admonitions. And hadn't I done just that? Sure, LemurCandy had helped, but as I'd so ungraciously told him, I could have taken the guy myself.

In my office, I logged in and messaged Lemur, and he answered almost immediately. *<Hey, Kitano, you were right!>*

Now, those were words that I didn't get to hear nearly often enough. *<Right about what?>* I sent back.

<The ex-Mrs. Coro,> he said. *<Remember your hunch about usernames?>*

<You found her?>

<I did. Remember PsychoticMuslinCrayon and SereneQueen and their monthly tryst?>

I stared at the screen for a minute. *<You're kidding!>*

<Go virtual,> he typed, and an icon flashed on the screen.

I slipped on my faceskin and clicked the icon, and the Netz whisked me into LemurCandy's "office."

I'd been here a couple of times before, reviewing data for one case or another. He had recreated an old hard-boiled detective's office, from the wood and black leather desk chair to the pinup girl calendar on the wall and green-shaded banker's lamp on the desk. Dust motes sparkled as they drifted lazily through the beam of lamplight. He sat in the chair wearing his brown-haired, green-eyed avatar, a black fedora tipped low over one twinkling eye.

I laughed and sat in the "client's" chair, a wing-backed, red leather affair. *<You're pretty pleased with yourself,>* I teased.

<It took me some major hacking,> he said. *<She didn't want to be found, I can tell you that.>*

I shook my avatar's head. *<You really think Coro doesn't know?>*

He shrugged. *<He doesn't know unless she wants him to know, that's for sure. He couldn't have found out on his own who she really is.>*

To say that LemurCandy was confident about his Netz skills was a vast understatement. Was he *really* that good, I wondered?

<And judging by what your magic told you when you spoke to them both...>

<That's true,> I said. *<I didn't get any feeling from him that he'd been talking to her in any sense of the word. He certainly didn't think he was lying about it.>*

LemurCandy's avatar leaned back and put his feet up on the desk, lacing those square, strong hands behind his head. *<What's she playing at, do you think?>*

<I don't know.> I pursed my lips and thought for a

minute. *<Do you think it's just some kind of sick revenge? For him divorcing her?>*

<That's way beyond me,> he said. *<What's more important, do you think she has anything to do with the message?>*

I leaned back in my chair, and my avatar did the same in the big red leather one. *<You know, I don't think so,>* I said, *<but it's really only a feeling. She's a registered Seer, and that should make her even more suspect. You didn't find anything to link her to the Murder Prophet?>*

<Not a thing,> he said. *<And I looked, believe me.>*

<If this is revenge, it's probably enough for her,> I said, putting the thoughts together as I typed them. *<I can't see her actually wanting him dead. She struck me as the type of person who'd enjoy this more—she's got the money, lots of it, and she's got a piece of him, even if Sandrine Coro has the rest. And sending all those other messages? I doubt she'd bother. Too much work. She seems to value her relaxation time.>*

<We'll have to be sure, though.>

<Oh, definitely. I'm not as confident in my ability to read people as you are in your ability to track them on the Netz,> I told him with a grin. *<Do you want me to let Saga know?>*

He nodded. *<Sure, you tell him, and I'll send him my report. If he wants me to dig further, I will, but whatever she's been playing at with Coro, I don't think Clarice Valencia is the Murder Prophet.>*

<Neither do I,> I told him. *<Talk to you later.>*

———•———

Saga and Anna were definitely interested in the news, and they didn't buy Clarice as the Murder Prophet, either. Anna got through to her at home and told her we had obtained some information and wanted her to speak with a registered Psych on the line (at this point Anna raised her eyebrows at me and I ducked into the bathroom to wash down a couple of Maginox®). Clarice protested a little, but Anna reminded her, with the quiet authority that Anna does so well, that if she refused she could be obstructing an investigation into the misuse of magic, which was the one thing international law had finally gotten right and penalized stringently. Not surprisingly, the ex-Mrs. Coro eventually gave in.

Besides the threat of prosecution, I knew what would be going through her mind. Refusing to talk to me would make her look guilty, without providing any information about what she was guilty of. We'd jump to our own conclusions then, and likely they'd be worse than the truth, and we'd start digging—really digging—into her life, and only she knew what was there to be found. So in the end she showed up on my vid, blonde hair dark and wet and slicked back from the pool or the beach or the shower. She looked pouty, bundled up in an expensive-looking white robe.

"Hello again, Ms. Valencia, I'll make this brief," I said, as pleasantly as I could. "Are you connected to an online Netz avatar known as SereneQueen?"

She pressed her lips together in a thin line for a moment, then said, "Yes."

"And that avatar has in recent months been meeting regularly with an avatar whose username is PsychoticMuslinCrayon?"

Again, just the "Yes." Her washed-out eyes had gone steely, but they never flickered away from the vid.

"And you are aware that PsychoticMuslinCrayon is a

username registered to and used by your ex-husband, Aleshu Coro?"

She nodded.

"Verbally, please," I said cheerfully.

"Yes."

So far she'd been totally up-front. "Ms. Valencia," I said, "Does Mr. Coro know that SereneQueen is you?"

She pursed her lips, then couldn't seem to stop them pulling back into a self-satisfied smirk. "No, not to my knowledge" she admitted. "Are you going to tell him?"

"One more question, first. Are you, or are you in any way associated with, the person known as the Murder Prophet, or anyone sending the messages that have been associated with someone known as the Murder Prophet?"

"NO!" She looked horrified. "No," she repeated in a calmer tone. "I don't really wish Aleshu any harm. I just..." She shrugged her shoulders under the soft white terrycloth robe and ran a hand over her wet hair. "I just wanted something else. I can't really put a name on it."

If she was lying, she was good, and had some magic talent we didn't know about that allowed her to trump mine. As far as my magic was concerned, she was telling the absolute truth. "Thank you, Ms. Valencia. I don't think we'll need to tell Mr. Coro about this, unless it comes to have a bearing on his case, which I don't anticipate."

She sighed. I thought probably it wouldn't be an issue after this anyway. The fun would have gone out of it for her now. "Well, thank you for that. Goodbye, Miss Stablefield," she said, and closed the connection.

"One lead down the tubes," I said to Saga and Anna, who'd been watching and listening from the other side of the room.

Anna rose from her chair, the clutch of gold bangles on her wrist clanging like wind chimes. Today she looked serene in a pale, leaf-green pantsuit that shimmered faintly when the light caught it just right. "Thank you, Kit. Nicely done, as usual."

Saga sighed deeply and shifted in his chair. "It is always both satisfying, and a heavy disappointment, when a suspect is exonerated," he said with a wry smile.

"Truer words," I agreed. "We'll have to see if LemurCandy comes up with anything else."

That afternoon I sat at my desk, staring at that geographical map of the Murder Prophet murders and waiting for inspiration to strike. I'd already downloaded the hotel pictures from my camera so that yesterday's client could have a look at them. I sent them to Saga's computer and left him in charge of contacting the client. Now I couldn't think of anything else to do except try and lose myself in some Anagrammatic puzzles, but it seemed there should be some more productive way to spend my time. Luckily, just then I heard the front door open and someone come in.

"Hey, you!" Kikufaax said, sounding delighted, "Long time, no see!"

I glanced up, wondering who Kiku's long-lost friend was, and saw a face and form that I recognized only too well. LemurCandy? Here in the office? I'd never seen that before—didn't know it had ever *happened* before, and certainly not in the year I'd been here.

Now, LemurCandy had been part of the team at Darcko and Sadatake before I'd come on the scene, but I'd had the impression that no one in the firm knew him any way other than virtually. As I sat at my desk, slightly stunned, watching him lean over the desk to kiss... *kiss*...Kiku's cheek, I wracked my brains to see if I'd just missed or misunderstood something. He'd certainly never been in the office when I was present in the past year. He didn't come in person to the holiday parties, although he'd "attended" twice as an on-screen avatar. I had just assumed that his identity was as secret from everyone else as it was from me.

Apparently not. Well, I thought, shaking myself out of my stupor, at least I'd find out his real name this way. I slicked a hand over my hair and plastered on a smile just in time. He caught sight of me through the door and waved.

"Hey, Kit," he said.

"Hey...there," I answered brightly. "What brings you to this neck of the woods?"

"The Coro case," he said. He turned back to Kikufaax. "Are Anna and Saga in?"

"Sure thing," she said, then glanced at me with a puzzled frown. "But wait a second...have you two met already?"

I braced myself for the long explanation that was about to ensue, but Lemur must have realized that I hadn't told anyone about last night yet. "Sure we have," he said smoothly, and I heard Saga's office door open at just the same time. Saved!

"Saga!" LemurCandy said, his voice warm.

I strained to listen.

"If it isn't the cagiest Lemur on the Netz," Saga joked, crossing to meet LemurCandy at the desk. They shook hands and half-embraced as well, doing that male pounding-each-other-on-the-back thing. But Saga didn't call him by name. *Damn.*

I decided I might as well come out of my office and join the party. No one seemed to mind.

"I had to run downtown, so I thought I'd come in person to talk this one through," LemurCandy said.

Anna was the next one out of her office. Whatever she called LemurCandy I missed, because she only spoke while she hugged him, so her voice was muffled against his leather-jacketed shoulder and the gold bangles on her wrist clanged loud enough to drown out anything she said anyway. Glaive buzzed out from his office just then to ask what was going on.

"Come and see who's here," Kiku told him.

"We might as well all be in on this, but we can't really use the boardroom; not enough chairs," Anna said. "Lock the door there, Kit, and we'll make ourselves comfortable out here." Glaive came out of his office as I was doing it, and called LemurCandy some kind of street slang like "camigo" or something as they shared an intricate fist-bumping, mirror-gestured handshake. Trip bounded in from the back room, shedding feathers, and called him LemurCandy. Mentally I shook my head. Was anyone ever going to call LemurCandy by another name? Maybe they didn't know it? How could that be?

Anyway, we all got settled in chairs and Kiku brought coffee, tea, and even a Mocha Insanity for LemurCandy, courtesy of the Coffee Robo-Alimental. It was totally weird seeing LemurCandy sitting there in a worn brown leather chair, drinking out of Anna's big "Chick with Attitude" mug, instead of moving around as a tiny figure on the computer screen or manifesting just as a line of text. The coffee shop encounter still had a dreamlike quality, but here in the office his presence was very real.

He did look a little uncomfortable, I thought, even though he apparently knew everyone better than I knew him. It was a strange world, I thought, where people could be friends and colleagues and yet strangers at the same time.

Eyes twinkling, Saga asked, "So, the Coro case. I'm glad we got involved, just to enjoy this unusual pleasure."

LemurCandy squirmed a little in his chair. "I know, I know, I don't get in here often enough. But you know how it is. The Netz is a big place now. Monitoring and searching it—"

Saga held up a hand. "No need to explain. We all appreciate the work you do, and how time-consuming it is. What have you found of interest to us?"

Lemur leaned forward in his chair, both hands around his mug of super-sweet coffee. "Six months ago, MageData was poised to merge with one of the big magic database companies in the UK. Not a takeover either way, from what I can learn, but a fundamentally friendly merger that would benefit both sides. Apparently it fell through when Coro saw the books for the other company, and didn't like what he saw. Coro had the final say, and I guess his say was "no." The other company took a big financial hit when the deal went sour, and their stock prices plunged. They may be holding a grudge."

"When you say 'they,'" Glaive asked, "Do you mean someone in particular?"

LemurCandy shrugged. He'd hung his leather jacket on the coat rack and wore a blue-and-grey striped sweater that showed a nicely-muscled upper body. I tried to concentrate on what he was saying. "It's a private company, same as

MageData. MagicBase UK. The woman at the top is Anzai Namiko."

Saga shook his head. "Never heard of her," he said. "What do we know about her?"

"She's not known in the business world for her subtlety, but she's grown her company into something with the same kind of stature as MageData," LemurCandy said. "I've seen the words 'ruthless' and 'cold-hearted' bandied about, but only in a business context."

"What if she thought that taking out Aleshu Coro was 'just business?'" Kiku mused. "If she thought the future of her company was at stake, she might be inclined to be ruthless in other ways, I suppose."

"She might," Lemur said hesitantly, "But from what Kit has been telling me, there's a link—or there appears to be— between all the Murder Prophet cases. I can't see Namiko getting that involved in something so far away, just to get at Coro. It would take too much time away from her business, which seems to be her ultimate concern."

"We haven't really hashed out that theory. Do we have any more thoughts about what the link between the cases might be?" Glaive asked languidly. His dark eyes were half-closed, giving an impression of sleepiness. I knew it meant quite the opposite.

All eyes turned to me. I felt my face flush. "Okay, I've been thinking about it some more," I said. "Kiku, could you bring that file up on your screen? The one we were looking at together?"

She nodded and hit a few keys, then swivelled her screen around to face the room. The red dots for all the Murder Prophet messages except Coro's and mine clustered in one area like flies on a piece of meat. "It strikes me as suspicious that all the others were so far removed from Aleshu Coro," I said, crossing to the screen to point to them. "I mean, in all other respects they appeared to be random, right?"

"Removed geographically, you mean, Kit?" Saga asked, peering at the screen.

I nodded. "You can see, they're clustered generally in the southeast of the city, about as far from Alchemist's Ridge as you could get. But when I looked at the distribution of all the murders in the city over the same time period, there was no correlation."

"What about your message?" LemurCandy asked. "How does it fit in with the scheme of the others?"

I shook my head. "It doesn't. I'm in the west of the city, well outside the original cluster, too." I pointed to the general area of my apartment.

Glaive frowned. "But what does any of that mean?"

I spoke quickly, all the vague ideas I'd had coming together as I put them into words. "What if the other messages were some kind of smokescreen for the one to Coro? If you didn't want anyone to make a connection, you might subconsciously choose ones that were far away. You'd be trying to make them all look random, but you'd be laying a pattern, a different kind of pattern, one that you wouldn't realize you were creating."

Saga held up a peremptory hand. "Wait a minute, Kit, let me understand. You're saying that perhaps all of the other murders were motivated by the Coro case in some way?"

I shook my head. "Not the murders themselves. Just the *messages*. That's why no one has been able to uncover anything that links the murders—there's nothing to find. The murders would have happened anyway, and it seems pretty clear that they had no link to Coro. Only the messages did, and the motivation could have been to create a smokescreen, to draw attention away from the Coro murder—the only one that really mattered to the person we're calling the Murder Prophet."

"So the others were simply chosen at random, from events that the Murder Prophet could foresee with his or her Seer abilities," Anna mused.

"Right. But even though they were supposed to be random, the Murder Prophet subconsciously chose ones that were geographically removed from the one that was really of interest, because he or she wanted the attention to be elsewhere. And it worked, until you look at them all this way. Then it has the opposite effect to what they intended."

"What about the message you got?" LemurCandy asked, looking at me.

"That's the one that really supports my theory," I said, nodding. My palms felt sweaty, but I didn't want to obviously wipe them on my jeans. "No one else investigating any of the other murders has ever received a message themselves—not until now. I think the message to me was a panic move on the part of the Murder Prophet, because the Coro message is the important one, and I'm messing around in that case."

Kikufaax leaned back in her chair. "So the Murder Prophet foresaw the murders and let them happen, sent those cryptic messages instead of informing anyone like the police of exactly what was going to happen, because this way they would make Coro's murder seem like part of something else. The messages were a false clue. A red herring. They used the murders as a cover for their own intended crime, instead of trying to save the victims."

I shuddered slightly at Kiku's words, the sweat on my palms going cold. "Right. The Murder Prophet could have prevented those murders, but chose not to because having them happen suited his or her purpose. It's pretty damn cold-blooded."

Glaive shrugged. "The police might not have followed up on them anyway, you know that. Remember we talked about that before. The police don't always take these warnings seriously, and even if they do, they don't always have the resources to deal with them.

Anna looked thoughtful and tapped a pearly-tipped finger against her lips. "It's not like we have a lot of suspects. The CEO of MagicBase is across the ocean, and Seer magic doesn't work at those distances. She'd have to be travelling here regularly to be able to foresee the murders. It seems like a lot of time and money, and it might only make her look more suspicious if someone noticed it."

"Unless she had an accomplice here," Kiku said. "They could just feed her the information."

"True, although every time you add an accomplice your chances of getting caught multiply." Anna sighed. "So it still comes back to having to find the Murder Prophet and figure out his or her true motivation." She turned to LemurCandy again. "We're doing what we can from this end, but you're the only one who's got a chance of getting anything from the Netz."

Lemur nodded. "I'll keep at it. Here's something strange. There doesn't seem to be any doubt that the Murder Prophet messages came from the same source, right?"

"That was my understanding," Saga said. "There was no publicity about the first two, yet they and the third followed the same style and were signed in the same way. It would have been too much of a coincidence if they'd been completely independent of each other. Then the third got a lot of publicity, and it's been wide open since then."

"Okay, but I've linked some of the messages to four different usernames. The first three messages all came from different usernames, although they are in the same format."

"What were the usernames?" Kiku asked.

LemurCandy pulled a small coil-bound notebook from the back pocket of his jeans. "They're interesting, to say the least," he said with a grin. "SurlyHypnoticMoccasin51, Artsy_Symphonic_Council, and my personal favorite, Loony#Pushcart%Cynicism."

Okay, I admit I had to turn my face away a little to hide a smile. A guy named LemurCandy thought they were "interesting"? Now that was funny.

"Well, they are similar since they all use three words," Kikufaax said. "That could point to them all being the same person, couldn't it?"

LemurCandy shrugged. "Maybe. There are a lot of username generators that will give you results like this, if you can't be bothered thinking up a name yourself."

I resisted the urge to ask him if that's how he'd come up with 'LemurCandy.'

"Didn't you say there were four usernames?" Anna asked.

"Oh yes," Lemur said. "Those were the first three. They've repeated, and then the last one was different. This time it came from MushyNonsocialCryptic."

"What about the one that I got?" I asked, trying to make my voice as casual and matter-of-fact as possible.

"SurlyHypnoticMoccasin51," LemurCandy said.

"Do you think there's any significance in the usernames

each message came from?" Glaive asked.

"I have no idea," LemurCandy said, and he sounded, for the first time, tired.

I don't know if Saga picked up on that, too, or if we were all just weary of talking over the same ground, or someone realized it was almost suppertime. The meeting broke up shortly after that, and I swear that even saying goodbye, no one called LemurCandy by his real name, not that I heard, anyway. I couldn't believe it. I almost asked him myself when I said goodbye, but it just seemed like a ridiculous time to bring it up.

We all parted ways out on the street, and no one offered to walk me to the bus stop. I should have been happy that they were starting to respect my wishes, and it wasn't even dark yet, but I felt perversely disappointed about it. Of course I'd been hoping LemurCandy would ask, but when he didn't I felt mad at the rest of them, too. With a pang of guilt I realized I'd gone the entire day without telling anyone about last night's attacker. However, it was obviously too late to bring it up now. Tomorrow would do.

I spent the evening on the sofa, watching my vids of *Quantum Task Force Gauss Rangers* and *Supreme Neon Ultra Force Weather Five*, working Anagrammatics puzzles, feeling grumpy and resisting Phoebe's various attempts to cheer me up or pump me for information about what I was working on. I didn't even sign on to the Netz to see if Lemur had left any messages for me, because I felt it served him right if I didn't get them.

Yeah, I know it was stupid, but everyone's entitled to a little bit of stupidity now and then. Unfortunately, that wasn't the thing that ultimately got me into trouble.

EIGHTEEN

Invitations and Conversations

I should have checked my messages the night before, because once again there was an urgent "contact me" from Lemur blinking on my screen when I got to the office. So I logged in to Chatterz®, sent him a message, and waited. He was there almost immediately. <*Kit, we need to talk.*>

I was about to say *Sure, where and when?* but he continued, <*Can you go virtual and meet me at Bitz 'n Bytz?*>

My soaring expectations took a nose dive into a pool of icewater. <*No problem,*> I said. <*Be there in a sec.*>

I got up and closed my office door. I knew that no one would deliberately interrupt me, but I dislike being on display when I'm wearing a faceskin. I slipped on the skin as I sat back down at the computer, and sent my avatar over to the mind virtual LemurCandy had mentioned.

Once there I found him easily enough, although now that I'd met him in person his avatar was a pale imitation of the real thing. He said <*Private, okay?*> right away, and when I nodded he pulled us both into a private room. No fancy bedroom décor this time, though. Just a blue-furnished sitting room, but he didn't sit.

His avatar crossed to mine and even through the virtual interface, I could tell he wasn't happy. <*I'm figuring you didn't know this, Kit, which is why I came to you first. I have to give it to Saga, because when it comes down to it, he's my boss. I just didn't want you to be blindsided.>*

I couldn't imagine what he was talking about, so I just said nothing and nodded.

<I was going through the MageData database last night.>

<You said you were going to do that.>

<I found an employee—from a long time ago—that I didn't expect.>

I was even more confused. *<Well? Who was it? Does it have something to do with the case?>*

He looked really uncomfortable, his av shifting its weight from foot to foot. *<I don't think it has anything to do with the case, but I...I can't be sure.>*

He didn't say anything else so I asked again, *<Who?>* I wanted to grab him by the arms and shake it out of him, but I refrained.

Finally the words appeared. *<Your grandmother, Kit. Nina Morow used to work for MageData.>*

I hadn't taken my Maginox® that morning but I risked the nausea anyway. I didn't have to worry. It didn't take much magic to know that LemurCandy was telling the truth.

———•———

Saga frowned, that tiny crease bisecting his otherwise smooth brow. The mouth corners turned down, too. He sat up straight behind his desk, the fingers of his right hand drumming almost silently on the polished rosewood. "You didn't know your grandmother used to work for MageData?" he asked.

I shrugged. "She had a lot of different jobs, and I was

just a kid. I wasn't paying attention."

"Did you tell her Aleshu Coro is our client?"

I leaned my head against the chair's high back and cast my mind over our conversations, the night I'd gone over to dinner, and later, on the phone. What had I said, exactly? "I don't think so...no, I'm sure I didn't. I told her we were looking into a Murder Prophet case, but I didn't mention any names."

"What kind of work would she have done for MageData?" Anna asked. She sat in the other big wing chair in Saga's office, fingers steepled. I rose and paced.

I shook my head. "No idea. She was never much for using magic at all—I remember asking her once if she was a mundane, but she laughed and said no, she was just a Talent."

"What branch of magic?"

I hesitated. Nana Nina had always professed to be a Shielder, at the talent level. I knew, since Saga's recent trouble, that she was also a Seer, but obviously she'd gone to great lengths to keep that secret. I was torn. I didn't want to say too much until I'd talked to Nana, because I had to admit that this could look bad. We were looking for someone with Seer abilities and a connection to MageData, and there was Nana, filling both requirements.

But I owed it to her to talk to her first. I pretended I'd been wracking my memory, shook my head again, and said carefully, "I only remember her saying that she was a Shielder. But you can check the Registry. Like I said, I wasn't aware of her using magic much at all." It wasn't even a lie, although as far as I knew, neither Anna nor Saga could detect lies anyway. That's why they kept me around the place.

"Would you mind going to see her, find out if she can shed any light on the Coro case?" Saga asked politely. "I know we like to keep business and family separate, but in this case it seems they're already connected. She may have information that could help us immensely."

I blinked. I'd thought he was going to be suspicious of my seeming ignorance about my own family, but he seemed to have accepted my word. Now I felt guilty. Damn, sometimes I hate having a conscience.

"No, I don't mind," I said. "I can head over there right now, as a matter of fact."

"That would be perfect. One more thing, though," Saga said. "Are you busy tomorrow night?"

"I can't think of anything," I said warily. Was this going to be another stakeout? I'd forgotten just how boring they really were.

Saga slid an envelope across his immaculate desk to me. Gilt glittered along the edges of creamy parchment paper. Looked pretty fancy.

"Our client is taking his 'carry on life as usual' attitude to what I consider a dangerous extreme," he said, frowning again. The tiny crease deepened, so I knew this was serious. "MageData is hosting a charity fund-raiser tomorrow night, and Coro plans to be in attendance, front and centre"

"What?" I squawked, sitting down again in the other wing chair. "Isn't tomorrow the thirteenth day since he got his message? I thought he'd finally be ready to go into hiding by now."

"Quite the opposite," Anna said, shaking her head sharply. "He sent over an invitation because he admits to being 'a bit nervous' about the event—he'll be out in the open with hundreds of people around, many of them strangers. But he also seems to think that will afford him some measure of protection. He sent the invitation to us 'just to be on the safe side,' he says. And he doesn't want a big show of protection. There'll be security at the doors, checking invitations, of course, and he wants just a couple of us, who can blend in with the crowd and keep an eye on things." She sighed. "Honestly, I wish he wouldn't. But he's stubborn, too, and he's a man accustomed to getting his way."

I hadn't picked up the envelope yet. I felt as if once I touched it, I'd be committed. "Well, why aren't you two going?"

"We thought your abilities might come in handy, for one thing," Anna said. "But if you and Saga went as a couple, you'd be conspicuous."

I almost grinned. That was probably true. I was six inches taller than Saga and he was a good twenty years older.

"And I already have plans for tomorrow night," she added. "We thought Glaive might go with you."

"What's the attire?" I asked, picking up the envelope and sliding the invitation out. It didn't sound too bad. More creamy paper, deckle edges and fancy fonts.

"Black-tie formal," Saga said.

"And you think Glaive will go? Fat chance," I said. "Black, he can do, but I think I might have seen him in a sport coat once. *Once.*"

"Shall we ask him?" Saga beeped him on the inter-office com. "Glaive?"

"Right here."

"Would you be interested in attending an event that would require a tuxedo?"

"Not if I'd have to wear it," Glaive said without hesitation.

"Come on, Glaive," I said, leaning toward the com so he could hear me. "They come in your favorite color—black."

He ignored me. "Tuxedos make me look soft."

"Thank you," Saga said, and closed the connection.

"Then who do you suggest?" Anna asked. "It's business, so I wouldn't want to involve anyone who couldn't...take care of themselves, if there happened to be an event."

That was Anna, always good with the euphemisms. An 'event'—such as an attempt on the life of Aleshu Coro. The two weeks weren't up until the day after tomorrow, but the other murders had made it clear that the time frame was more an approximation. And it was damn close now at any rate.

"I could check with LemurCandy," I blurted, before I could think about it.

Saga raised an eyebrow. "I was thinking of an actual escort, not a virtual one. He doesn't make many appearances outside the Netz, you know. Yesterday might have been it for a while."

It was the perfect time to tell them about me and Lemur and the guy who'd "terrorized" me outside my apartment, but I really wasn't up for another be-careful speech, so I just said, "Well, it's worth a shot. I'll ask him and let you know what he says, okay?" Then I changed the subject and asked Saga if the client I'd done the tailing for had come in to look at the pictures.

"Yes," Saga said in a disgusted voice. "He recognized someone in one of them. His wife."

Apparently the whole theft story had been a cover to see if his wife was having an affair with the employee. I had no doubt that Saga had dealt with the man harshly after being duped into taking on that kind of case.

I excused myself to ask LemurCandy about tomorrow night and then head over to Nana Nina's. I went into my office and shut the door. Suddenly nerves took hold of me, dancing in my stomach and making my palms hot and clammy. I had agreed—no, I had *offered*—to call up LemurCandy and ask him for a date.

Was I out of my mind?

I decided that I couldn't possibly call him on the phone. Even if I retrieved his number from my phone, I still didn't know his real name. How was I supposed to ask for him if someone else answered? No, it would have to be online. And I wouldn't make it sound like a date. Strictly business.

I logged on and messaged him through Chatterz®. Got an offline auto-response. *Damn.* I left him a note to get in touch with me and logged back out. I'd have to have my conversation with Nana Nina and try him again later.

I decided to walk to her apartment. After all, it was a beautiful spring day, and the sun was doing its best to warm up every shadowy corner. It wasn't that I was trying to put off getting there. Okay, maybe I was. I wasn't looking forward to asking intimate questions about her past. If she'd never talked about her magic with me, she must have had her reasons, right? And now I had to go poking into them. I hated it.

But even walking (with a detour into the park to see how the ducks were enjoying the new fountain the city had installed), I got there eventually. She answered the bell right away and buzzed me in.

"What a surprise!" she said, opening the door and pulling me into our usual hug. "Do you want some coffee?"

"Sure," I said, immediately suspecting that it was not such a surprise after all. She rarely drank coffee except when I visited, or so she'd said once. "Sorry to drop in so early, and without calling first."

She chuckled. "That's okay, Kit. It's not like I have a whole lot to do, you know."

However, her easel stood in the morning light near the window, and her pastels and pencils littered the nearby taboret. She'd lain down a field of blue and green and pink strokes as the beginning of a colorful abstract, but I couldn't tell at a glance what was inspiring it. She poured dark, fragrant coffee into oversized stoneware mugs.

"I'm sort of here on business," I said hesitantly.

She raised her eyebrows as she passed me a steaming mug. "Oh, really? Something I can help with? Although I can't imagine what."

"I don't know if you can help or not," I said. "That's what I need to find out. You want to sit in the living room?"

"How mysterious," she said, smiling. She didn't seem at all apprehensive about our conversation.

We took our mugs into the cozy room and settled into facing chairs. "Well?" she asked. She looked, as always, completely serene and innocent. Her silver hair curled smoothly and close around her head and her blue eyes regarded me brightly.

I sighed. "Remember the other day, when I told you we were looking into a Murder Prophet case?"

She sipped coffee. "Mm-hmmm."

"Our client is Aleshu Coro."

"Ah." She nodded, pursing her lips for a moment, then frowned. "He's not dead? I'm sure I would have heard that."

I shook my head. "No, he's fine. For now. He got a

message, though. We're trying to make sure he *stays* fine."

"And your very competent friend, SquirrelCookies—"

"LemurCandy."

"LemurCandy, has dug up the fact that I used to work for MageData."

I took a deep breath. "Exactly."

She smiled and tilted her head at me like an inquisitive puppy. "You didn't have to be afraid to come and talk to me about that, you know."

I squirmed a little in the bright green armchair. "You never talked about it. I didn't know why."

"Well, I'm sorry if it took you by surprise. I didn't expect it would be an issue this long after the fact," she said.

"Saga and Anna wondered if you might be able to help us figure out who might want Coro dead—and why."

She settled back more comfortably in her chair and tucked tiny, slippered feet up under her. Wrapping both hands around her mug as if to warm them, she said, "Did you take your Maginox® this morning, dear?"

"No, I—hey! I wasn't going to use my magic on you!"

"Just checking," she said with a grin. "It doesn't matter, because I'm going to tell you the truth. About everything," she added, and that sounded more than a little ominous.

NINETEEN

Nana Nina Comes Clean

"First of all, I don't know if any of this is going to help your case," she warned. "It's a long time since I was at MageData, and for the most part, it was a pretty harmonious place to work back then."

"What did you do there?" I asked.

She took a deep breath. The sunlight slanted across her face, making her look almost ethereal. "I was involved in the magic ability-detection research."

I almost choked on my coffee. "Really? How?"

Nana Nina shrugged. "I'm a Spellquick. They thought we had the best chance of figuring out how to make detection work."

That time I almost *dropped* my coffee. My grandmother, who had rarely exhibited any magic around me or the rest of the family and seemed indifferent to it, was one of that group of rarest, less-than-one-percent of individuals in the world who had major magical abilities in *all* the realms of magic?

"No," I said flatly, shaking my head. "I don't believe it."

She chuckled. "I've got some Maginox® in the bathroom cabinet if you want to take some and see if I'm lying. It's prescription strength, though, so be careful. You'll have an unbelievable headache later."

"You can't be a Spellquick," I protested, still unbelieving. "I would have known!"

"I haven't used the magic much in years," she said. "Do you know why?"

I shook my head mutely.

"Because it worked," she said.

"What worked?"

"There were three of us at MageData," she said, shifting in her chair to get more comfortable. "Three Spellquicks. And we figured out how to detect—and identify—magical ability in others."

"But—" I sputtered, "But—it can't be done! I mean, if it could, why isn't anyone—the Registry—"

"Why is there no formalized testing? Because the government doesn't *know* we figured it out," she said easily. "We didn't tell anyone, because we decided that everyone was better off the way things were. In fact, as far as I know, you're the only non-Spellquick who knows even now."

I felt like sputtering again, but I sat quietly until I knew what I wanted to say. Nana sipped calmly from her coffee mug, looking serene and grandmotherly. The light filtering down from the skylight now almost made it look like she had a halo, and I wondered cynically if she could have set that up on purpose.

I took a deep breath again. "So, to be sure I understand: the Spellquicks figured out a way to detect magic ability in others, decided it would be better to keep that knowledge to themselves, and no one else has figured it out since then? That must have been twenty years ago!"

"Yes, it must be, almost. You were fourteen or so about that time."

"I don't understand how you could keep something like

this a secret," I protested.

"Well, remember," she said, "only Spellquicks can do it. We have a...a network, I suppose you could call it, and all new Spellquicks become members. They're sworn to secrecy about this."

"But how do you—oh, right," I said, shaking my head in wonder. "You just use the ability to detect new Spellquicks, so you can bring them into the club."

She grinned. "I always said you were a genius, dear."

I sat back in my chair, shaking my head. "The world is secretly controlled by powerful magic-users and a conspiracy of silence," I said. "It's like something out of a cheap holovid."

Nana laughed out loud then. "I wouldn't say we control the world, Kit. We very carefully control one piece of information."

"But isn't there always a chance that one of the companies will start up the research again—I mean, MageData tried it when you worked there. Surely someone else might want to try again?"

She sipped her coffee and winked at me. "Okay, I suppose there's a teeny bit of a conspiracy. The Spellquicks make sure we're major shareholders—and sometimes members of the Boards—of any relevant company. It's one way we can quietly make sure the secret stays secret."

"Like MageData, I suppose."

She nodded. "Naturally. I have a holding company for my own shares there."

I don't know what look was on my face, but she must have seen something there, and *tsked* at me.

"Don't look like that, honey. It's for the good of everyone, remember."

I took a sip of coffee and thought about what I wanted to say next. I felt slightly stunned by the magnitude of these revelations. "Are you sure it's for the good of everyone?" I asked slowly.

"I think so. I certainly think it was better for you, wouldn't you agree?" Her blue eyes twinkled.

My heart skittered in my chest. *She knew.*

"When did you know about me?" I demanded.

She shrugged. "Right about the time you were figuring it out yourself. I wasn't prying, Kit, I want you to believe that." She tilted her head to one side, considering. "At least, I suppose I was, but I didn't mean it in a personal way. At that time it was new, and we were curious about how the spells would work. Especially whether the subjects would know we were 'looking' at them. I knew something was up with you—either you were about to have your first period or a new magical ability was blossoming." She shrugged again. "I checked to see if I could figure out which it was."

"So you knew all along that I was a...Transmute?" Years of habit kicked in, still making it hard for me to say it out loud.

"Yes. And I knew that you were horrified at the prospect of having to go and work in an energy factory somewhere. I wasn't surprised when you kept it to yourself. Your situation helped me feel certain that we were right in keeping quiet. That you should have the right to make that choice yourself."

I sat in silence for a bit. We both did, sipping coffee that was starting to go cold. Nana Nina made a face and sketched a little nod in the direction of my cup and hers. The mug warmed under my fingers and I realized with a start that she'd used magic to heat up the coffee. If she wasn't going to hide her abilities from me any more, things were going to be interesting.

"So," I said finally, "what does this have to do with Aleshu Coro?"

Nana chuckled, her mouth quirking into a wry smile. "Nothing, probably. I was just tired of keeping it secret from you. Seemed like as good a time as any to get it off my chest."

I grinned and shook my head. That innocent, white-haired old grandmother act sure had me fooled for a long time. Anyway, I still had to ask her about the Coro case. "Okay, so back to the reason I'm actually here. Things were good at MageData when you worked there?"

"It was an exciting time, because the main company, the database end, was growing fast, which meant more funding for the research department. They had a lot of projects, not just the Spellquick stuff that I was involved in, but I don't know much about the rest."

"Coro was getting divorced from his first wife about that time, wasn't he?"

She paused, remembering. "Yes, he was. You know, that was probably the only black spot on that time. Not that I'd forgotten about it."

"It wasn't amicable?"

"Whoo-whee, no sir," she said. "It was downright nasty, and I knew all about it—everyone did—because of course *she* worked there, too. Clarice Valencia, who became Coro's second wife."

"I've met her," I said. "She didn't seem like my kind of person."

"Mine, neither. She made a blatant play for Aleshu Coro, and did everything she could to cut Evangeline out of the picture." Nana sipped her now-hot coffee. "Do you think Evangeline could be involved in what's happening now? The threat to Coro?"

I shrugged. "Probably not. Kiku ran a check early on, because of some things Clarice Valencia said about the divorce settlements. But although Evangeline still has shares in MageData, she doesn't seem particularly interested in them, or in leveraging her interests. She's been living overseas for years and years. And the divorce was so long ago—I didn't think it was likely to be linked to the case now."

She raised her eyebrows at me. "You'd be surprised. Sometimes the past casts long shadows."

"Are you saying we missed something? You think Evangeline Coro could have something to do with this?"

"She went back to her maiden name, Harrington, after the divorce. And I wouldn't go so far as to say that," Nana said cautiously, pulling a deep sigh. "But...it could be." She fell silent for a long moment, and I thought she was contemplating whether or not to say more.

"What?" I prodded.

She licked her lips. "I really, really hate to talk about this, Kit," she said, "but if there's any chance...well, I couldn't live with myself."

"What is it?"

"Evangeline—I knew her well. Really well. She was one of the other two Spellquicks at MageData."

"Huh," I said. "Clarice Valencia could have mentioned that." A sudden thought struck me. "Don't tell me Clarice was the third Spellquick?"

Nana Nina shook her head. "No, and I don't expect you'd get Clarice to even say Evangeline's name, unless you asked her point-blank. She probably doesn't even know about Evangeline's abilities, unless Aleshu told her himself. Anyway, I know for a fact that Evangeline was in touch with Aleshu Coro less than a year ago."

"Really? What for?" I mentally kicked myself for not looking harder at Evangeline already. But she'd seemed like a long shot.

"She wanted Aleshu and MageData to fund some big art initiative she was organizing. I know, because she contacted me about being a part of it, too. I begged off, since I'm just dabbling now." She nodded to her easel and implements over by the window. What she considered "dabbling" was more beautiful than anything I could ever create, but she was always modest about her art.

She went on. "She seemed excited about it, but Evangeline was always excitable. And maybe a bit neurotic. She hasn't been active in the Spellquick network over the last fifteen years. Too wrapped up in her own projects. It's almost as if magic was a hobby for a while, but she got tired of it."

"What did she think about keeping the magic-detection ability a secret from Coro?" I asked.

"Huh. At that point the marriage was already going down the drain. She wasn't exactly broken up about having him look like a failure in the research department," Nana Nina said.

"Did she push for the decision to keep it quiet? Influence the others, or try to?"

Nana shook her head. "No, I think we all felt that was the way it had to be. She had fewer misgivings than the rest of us—or if she had any at all, maybe it was easier for her to put them aside."

"But now—you don't think she still holds a grudge, do you?" My coffee cup was empty, so I set it on the table.

Nana wrinkled her nose. "I doubt it. Evangeline was always rather high-strung, although a very creative thinker, especially with magic. She could come up with the most intricate spells and applications—but someone else always had to take care of the practical side. I think in the end she got tired of seeing her elaborate ideas crash and burn because the logistics wouldn't work. And the divorce soured her relationship with the company. But still—a grudge after twenty years? I know some people like their revenge served cold, but that is a hell of a long time to cool off."

I looked at my watch; it was almost lunchtime. I figured I'd better get moving if I was going to get LemurCandy invited to the fundraiser tomorrow night before he made other plans. I got up and crossed the room to lean down and give Nana Nina a hug and a kiss. Then I knelt beside her chair. "So you don't think I should have just come clean about my ability and gone to work for the government like a good little citizen?"

Her blue eyes twinkled into mine. "Do you think you would have been happy doing that?"

"No. Not from where I'm standing—or kneeling—I wouldn't."

She smiled and patted my hand. "Then you did exactly the right thing. Now, do you think *I* did the right thing?"

"I think you did. Still are doing it, I guess." I stood up and grinned. "My Nana, part of the secret cabal of Spellquicks."

She laughed. "Just don't go spreading it around, okay?"

"No worries," I said, and hurried off to try and get a date

for the following night.

TWENTY

See You 'Round the Netz

I stopped back at the office to see if LemurCandy was online. He'd answered my message, and I got him live in Chatterz® after a second.

<What's up?> he typed.

I took a deep breath. *<Got any plans for tomorrow night?>*

<No, what do you have in mind?>

<Saga has a 'mission' for us,> I said. He didn't need to know that it was my idea to take him along.

<What's involved? Is it real or virtual?>

<Real, and you'll need a tuxedo,> I said. I wondered how long he would take to answer. I was a little surprised when his reply popped up on the screen almost immediately.

<No problem,> he said. *<What time and where?>*

Well, he didn't have a problem with tuxedos, and he didn't have a problem going with me to a place that required them. That was promising.

<It's a charity event at MageData, babysitting Aleshu Coro,> I told him.

<That sounds like a bad idea for him, going out in public at this point,> he said.

<I agree, but apparently you can't tell Coro that. Anna and Saga already tried, and if they can't convince him, you and I don't stand a chance. So maybe we should think of it as

'bodyguarding' rather than babysitting. You want to swing by my building at seven o'clock, or meet me there?>

<*I'll pick you up,*> he said, and that was that.

I breathed a sigh of relief as I logged off and sat back in my chair, trying to slow down the breakneck speed of my heartbeat. Now all I had to do was come to terms with my Nana's secret identity and figure out a way to tell Saga and Anna that she was a Seer without making them look at her with suspicion. I didn't want to lie to them outright, but I had to keep some of Nana's secrets or I'd have a pack of Spellquicks mad at me, and that would definitely be more than I wanted to tackle.

Kiku had come to my office doorway while I messaged LemurCandy, and mimed that she was going out for a bit, so I put off going to talk to Anna and Saga by installing myself behind the empty reception desk. I fielded calls, but my mind was elsewhere. On Evangeline Coro, to be precise. My conversation with Nana Nina had made me want to rethink her status as a suspect.

I sorted through my memories of the various conversations any of us had had with Aleshu Coro, trying to recall whether or not his first wife had come up. Glaive and I had spoken to him about wife number two, Clarice, but I didn't think I'd mentioned Evangeline.

In the first interview we'd had, just Coro and Anna and Saga, with me in the corner watching for lies, we hadn't really covered any personal ground. And I didn't remember anyone else mentioning her, either. Maybe her presence in Coro's distant past had made it easy for us to assume she was out of the picture. But if she'd been in touch with him as recently as last year, then maybe we'd all been wrong.

And why hadn't Coro mentioned that interaction to us?

My Netz skills couldn't come close to LemurCandy's expertise, but I could do a search on a person I knew existed and come up with a fair amount of data. I found Evangeline Coro (née Harrington) without difficulty and cruised around the Netz for a while, collecting, sifting, and assessing.

Her interest in art had developed into a passion since she and Aleshu Coro had divorced. She ran, organized, or supported half a dozen different artist's organizations and art cooperatives, and was very vocal on the merits and necessity of art in civil society. A foundation she supported —perhaps had founded, but that wasn't completely clear— appeared to marry the interests of art and magic, but their website didn't really clarify how they attempted to do that. She'd moved to the UK shortly after the divorce and carried on her activities from there. I couldn't find anything to corroborate Nana Nina's assertion that Evangeline had been in touch with Coro any time recently.

At this point I figured I'd done all I could on my own, and messaged LemurCandy to request further investigation. I'd done some of the groundwork for him, but he'd have to take it from there.

Surprisingly, he wasn't online. I wondered if he was out somewhere frantically shopping for a tuxedo, and smiled. I doubted it, though. There'd been no hesitation when I'd mentioned his needing one for tomorrow night.

The unanswered message stared at me from the screen and I sighed. This dead end was frustrating, now that I'd started. I still had no idea if Evangeline Coro could seriously be considered a suspect, but I'd gone through everything I could find on the upper levels of the Netz. If more information lurked out there somewhere, it would take some poking around deeper in the Netz to uncover it. And just when I needed him, LemurCandy wasn't there.

Luckily for me, Kiku came back after I'd grumbled my way through a few more phone calls. I gladly relinquished the front desk to her and went back to my own office with an idea. I shut the door and slipped on my faceskin, sliding into the world of the virtuals. If I could just remember how LemurCandy had arrived at the Library building he'd taken me to on the night we'd met FallenElfGeek, maybe I could dig up something else useful on Evangeline Coro.

I soon realized it was impossible. I didn't know how to move around outside the grid the way LemurCandy had done, and although I could glimpse the "pathways," they all looked equally ominous and uninviting, a multi-colored tangle I couldn't begin to navigate. I had no idea which way to go. It looked like I couldn't do it on my own after all, and Lemur still hadn't come online.

On a whim, I tried messaging FallenElfGeek. I doubted I'd get through to him, but to my surprise a text-only reply popped up almost right away.

<Hey, it's Kitano Kick-Ass,> he said, *<LemurCandy's ladyfriend. What can I do for you today?>*

<Hey, FEG,> I answered, *<Nice to see you. I have a question for you.>*

<Shoot>

<Before we visited you that time, Lemur took me to a sort of library outside the grid. I need to get back there. Can you help?>

<Sure, let me bring you inside,> he said, and I braced myself. Vertigo swept me and I pressed my hands against the desktop to counter the falling sensation, and then my avatar stood outside FallenElfGeek's building. I recognized it right away. FEG stood on the sidewalk outside, so there

wasn't much guesswork involved.

<Right this way,> he said, and his avatar took my avatar's hand. This flight along the glowing data pathways held a different feeling than when I'd travelled them with LemurCandy. Now it was as if an aura surrounded us, a field of something...not a color, or a scent, or a sound...something I could feel but not see or touch, even in Netz terms. I'd almost call it a *taste*, although I'm sure that would make no sense at all to anyone who'd never experienced it, or even gone outside the grid. But I had the distinct impression that FEG was using *magic*.

As soon as I'd had the thought I immediately pushed the notion away. Magic in real life was bad enough, but I'd already gotten in trouble once by messing with magic in the Netz. And the idea of that spooky ambient magic possibly hovering out here somewhere unnerved me; I didn't know what kind of mess we might inadvertently cause. So I concentrated more on the surroundings and less on the sensations. *I'm only going to do some research*, I reminded myself. *Just like that first time with LemurCandy*. To my surprise, I recognized a few of the routes and pathways I'd taken with him. *I could do this*, I thought. *With a little coaching, I could find my way around in here.*

Okay, a lot of coaching. I decided to ask LemurCandy to teach me. And if he wouldn't, then maybe my good friend FEG would.

Suddenly the front of the library building resolved, rising up in front of us as if it were sprouting out of the virtual ground. FEG brought us to a stop on the sidewalk at the bottom of the steps.

<You okay from here?> FEG asked me.

<Perfect,> I told him. *<Thank you so much.>*

<No problem, anytime,> he said with a grin. *<We could use more intelligent women in here.>* And then he was gone.

I sprinted up the steps to the library and crossed confidently to one of the floating terminals. In seconds I'd keyed in the search parameters on Evangeline Coro and was watching the data fly past, just the way LemurCandy had shown me that first time. As I accumulated data, I instinctively started discarding any items that were false or rumor-based or felt questionable. It was only after I'd amassed a tidy pile of facts and forwarded them to my email inbox that I stopped dead, my avatar's hands still resting on the keyboard.

What was I doing?

I'd started off just as I'd intended, straight research, and then without realizing it had brought the magic into play. This was exactly what had landed me in trouble before, using my magic to sift the truth out of items on the Netz. Sweat prickled my flesh under the faceskin, warm and sticky. I could be exposing myself to one of those same harmonized divination whatsis things, because I'd never really found out what they were, let alone how to check for one. And I'd blithely done the same thing just as unguardedly as before. If Saga and LemurCandy found out, they wouldn't be happy, and I'd be on the receiving end of another lecture.

Another realization struck me then. I didn't feel the least bit sickly back in my corporeal form, despite the fact that I hadn't thought to take any Maginox® before I'd started this venture. Yet I'd been using my lie-detecting ability freely in assessing the data on Evangeline Coro. LemurCandy's words came back to me suddenly: *Do you know, if all the power in the world shut down, the Netz would still continue to function? It would run on the ambient magic that's been absorbed by the datastreams. Your apartment could be completely dark, but your computer would still run if it was hooked into the Netz.*

Was there something about this ambient magic in the Netz that I'd somehow hooked into and used to power my own magic? Was that why I wasn't getting sick?

Reflexively, I glanced back over my shoulder as if the Netz magic were an ominous presence looming behind me, but all there was to see was the virtual library and all the avatars unconcernedly using the terminals. I couldn't shake a sudden trepidation, though, so I blanked the residual search data, logged out, and pulled off the faceskin. It stuck to my face unpleasantly, glued there by the spreading perspiration on my skin, and I had to carefully pry it away. An involuntary tremble in my hands didn't help. I sat back in my chair, breathing deeply, trying to ground myself back in the real world and let the virtual one slip away. That had been weird. Too weird. And I still had the taste of magic in my throat. That was not a sentence I could imagine actually saying to anyone.

I went out to the kitchen and pulled a huge mug of coffee from the Coffee Robo-Alimental. The heady aroma helped clear my mind even before I'd taken a sip. Trip came in just as I was adding cream and sugar. Although the machine could do that for me, I still liked to fix it myself.

"Watch this, Kit," he said, and leapt into a twisting, swirling, orange-and-white whirlwind of wings and hands and feathers and feet, punctuated by grunts and fearsome yells. He fetched up in front of me, feathers rumpled.

"Now that," I said, "Would scare me if I weren't expecting it."

"Really?" he asked excitedly.

"Oh, yeah," I said, "Because I am terrified of animals who appear to have rabies."

"Ha ha. Very funny." His bill twisted into a mournful moue. "Remember how I went after that guy with the gun, when we were rescuing Saga? I could have taken him, too, if you hadn't trans—"

"Hey, Glaive," I said loudly, as he came into the room. "Want some coffee?"

He surveyed us with narrowed, suspicious eyes for a moment, but didn't say anything except, "Sure, that's what I was after anyway. Hey, Kit, I hear you got Clarice Valencia to spill."

I shrugged. "It didn't take much. As soon as she knew the game was up she didn't even try to lie. Guess we can cross her off the list, anyway."

Glaive shook his head as he pulled dark, aromatic coffee from the Alimental. "I don't even know who's still on the list," he said. "Maybe that Namiko woman, but she doesn't sound very likely."

"I know." I debated telling him some of what I'd learned about Evangeline Coro, but something made me keep quiet about it. Maybe it was because I hadn't really thought through how to reveal what I knew about her and still keep Nana Nina's secrets, or maybe it was just that I wanted first crack at finding out about her without any interference from anyone else. At any rate, I went back to my desk with my coffee, turned my attention to some old paperwork, and studiously ignored the faceskin lying like a crumpled Halloween mask next to the keyboard.

———•———

The remainder of the day was quiet, and by the time the sky outside the windows was reluctantly letting go of the light, I had a tidy stack of caught-up files on my desk. I forwarded all my information on Evangeline Coro to my home computer, thought about the ambient Netz magic again with a shudder, and shut down my office computer and unplugged it from the Netz before I left. There was just something about the idea of it staying on by itself, powered by magic that had somehow acquired an existence of its own, that made me feel squirmy.

I treated myself to Chinese takeout for supper. When I came in the door with it, Phoebe said, "That smells wonderful, Kit!"

Her comment didn't really register until I was at the kitchen counter pouring up some milk to drink with my almond soo guy. "Phoebe, how can you possibly smell anything?"

The pause before she answered was brief but noticeable. "Oh, I can't really smell it, Kit, but I saw it on the cam and thought that was an appropriate and polite conversational remark."

Hmmm. Phoebe had never been very concerned with making either appropriate or polite conversational remarks before.

"What's gotten into you lately, Phoebe?" I asked her as I took my meal into the living room and settled myself on the sofa. "Have you had another program upgrade?"

"That's it exactly!" she said in a chipper voice. "It was an automatic upgrade from Live-a-Tronic."

Well, that made sense. The company that sold the home AI suite offered auto-upgrades for the first five years, and I'd had Phoebe for almost four. But geez, upgrades again?

How buggy was the software if they had to fix it this often? It was getting ridiculous.

I ate in silence for a bit, still mulling over Evangeline Coro, and then Phoebe asked, "How is the Coro case going, Kit?"

I shrugged. "Still nothing really concrete, we're all looking into different aspects of it. Today I was trying to find out about one of his ex-wives. I've got some stuff to go over later, too."

"I think you might be working too hard," she said in a disapproving tone. "Do you really have to bring work home with you?"

"Time is kind of important in this—wait a second," I said, dropping my fork into the takeout box and sitting up on the edge of the sofa. At times like this I really wished Phoebe had a physical manifestation—even just a screen— that I could look at when I talked to her. Maybe I'd send Live-a-Tronic some feedback on that. "How do you know our client is Aleshu Coro?"

After a pause in which I imagined Phoebe virtually shrugging, she said, "You must have mentioned it at some point."

"I don't remember that, Phoebe. Have you been eavesdropping on my conversations? Reading my messages?"

"Not at all, Kit, although you know your safety and security are my primary concerns."

"I thought your primary concerns were getting me up on time and keeping the fridge stocked," I muttered.

"My programming covers a wide range of services," she said stiffly. "As to the Coro case, perhaps you mentioned it during a phone conversation. I can hear your end of those, you know, and I don't consider that eavesdropping. It's not my problem if you forget I'm here."

"If only," I mouthed, rolling my eyes, but I didn't actually say it out loud. "Okay, forget it, Phoebe. I guess I'm wrong." I wasn't convinced, but it was, as usual, pointless to argue with her.

I finished up the takeout (obviously prepared by an Alimental and suitably delicious), did some light housework to clear my mind (because there's nothing like mindless work for that, if you just concentrate on what you're doing—it's mindless, right?), and then settled in front of my home terminal. I called up Evangeline Coro's files and retrieved everything I'd sent myself from the Netz library earlier, determined to ferret out any important detail that might be there. Five minutes into it, LemurCandy messaged me in Chatterz® to ask what I was doing.

I told him, and also mentioned that FallenElfGeek had helped me out.

<Oh, so I guess you won't be needing me around anymore,> he joked.

<You could still prove your usefulness,> I told him. *<If you could uncover some details on Aleshu Coro's personal correspondence for me.>*

<Hmmm...of course that kind of thing is private.>

<Well, yes,> I said. *<But you have your secret Netz powers...>*

<LOL> he laughed. *<What did you want to know?>*

So I told him I was looking for correspondence between Coro and Evangeline about a year ago, regarding a charity art event she wanted him to fund. It was a long shot, but he might be able to find it. I was beginning to think that if a thing existed in electronic form anywhere within the vast grid of the Netz, Lemur could uncover it.

<I'll get back to you,> he said.

So I finished sorting my Evangeline Coro data into nice little electronic piles. I hadn't, unfortunately, been able to find any pictures of her, except for one of her wedding to Aleshu Coro, so that was pretty far out of date. There was absolutely no mention anywhere of her being a Spellquick. Of course she was linked to some work in the research department of MageData, at the same time as Nana Nina was there, but unsurprisingly her actual role wasn't mentioned, since that had all been top-secret, according to Nana. Her connections to the various art charities were all well-documented.

But there was one thing I noticed that hadn't leapt out at me when I tagged it—the company registry for MagicBase UK listed her as a partner. That was Anzai Namiko's firm, the one involved in the failed merger with MageData. Publicly, it was a one-woman business, but the corporate documents said differently. I stared at the screen for a long few minutes. That couldn't be simply coincidence. And it gave Evangeline another reason for being ticked off at Aleshu Coro.

Aside from that, she was a member of some online artist communities, and some of her work was really good, even to my untutored eye.

But there was nothing, nothing, nothing else, to link her to MageData or Coro since the time they'd divorced. I rubbed my hands over my face. The question was, did a long-ago divorce and a failed business venture add up to murder? Maybe, for a crazy person, but there were so many arguments against it—including the fact that she didn't even live on the same continent anymore—that I couldn't make it make sense.

Night had enveloped the apartment building as I worked, folding darkness into every corner of the room. Only the blue-white glow from my monitor illuminated the tiny island of my desk. I got up from the computer and switched on a few lights. Facts and possibilities rattled around like bumper cars inside my head, banging noisily into each other and then hurtling off in opposite directions. I went into the bathroom, splashed my face with cold water, and slapped a headache spell-patch on the side of my neck. I blinked blearily at myself in the mirror, my eyes red-rimmed and scratchy-feeling from too much time in front of the screen.

Time. All the time we were looking for answers, it kept ticking away for both Aleshu Coro and me. I didn't believe we were any closer to figuring out who the Murder Prophet was than we were the day Coro had first called the office and I'd picked up the phone.

"Kit, are you feeling well?" Phoebe asked solicitously.

Startled, I glanced over my shoulder reflexively, although I knew it was only Phoebe. "I'm fine," I lied, switching off the bathroom light and mentally scolding myself. I should not be that jumpy in my own apartment. And how long had I been standing there, for Phoebe to notice? I wondered if her "upgrade" now allowed her to see my reflection in the bathroom mirror or something. I didn't want to be paranoid, but I might have to start putting a towel over it to get a shower.

She didn't say anything else. I curled up on the sofa with one of Nana Nina's colorful hand-knit blankets wrapped around my shoulders, and worked Anagrammatics again. This was getting to be a habit. Not one that seemed to have much of a future.

The incoming Chatterz® chime sounded from the computer and despite my red eyes, I left the comfort of the sofa (although I took the blanket with me) and sat down at my desk again. It was LemurCandy. *<Heya. Got anything?>* I asked.

<Well, I found the correspondence,> he said, *<but I don't know if it amounts to anything much.>*

I didn't ask him where he'd "found" the files.

<Evangeline contacted Coro about a year ago to ask him to donate a million dollars to founding an artist's colony on a remote tropical island,> he said.

I blinked. *<A million dollars? Geez.>*

<I know. That's quite a contribution. Coro's got it, though. He turned her down—nicely—and said that he was overcommitted for charitable donations for the year. She didn't write back, and that was the end of it.>

Damn. *<Doesn't sound like the kind of thing you kill someone over a year later, does it?>* I asked.

<Nope.>

<There wasn't anything else?>

<Sorry,> he said. *<Unless she contacted him in person, or by phone. There wouldn't be any electronic record of that.>*

I had a sudden thought. *<Hey, what's her username on the correspondence?>*

There was a pause as he checked. *<Would you believe, "MysticalPsychoUnicorn_245?">* he said. *<Geez, where do people come up with these things?>*

You're a fine one to ask that, I thought. *<Could you do one of those special username searches on her?>* I asked. *<Just to see if she goes by anything else?>*

<Sure thing. And I could do a Netz search on her myself,> he

offered.

I shook my head and then realized he couldn't see me since we weren't in virtual. <*No, thanks anyway. Just the usernames will be fine. I think I was pretty thorough.*>

<*You want 'pretty thorough,' you have to go to FallenElfGeek,*> he said. <*He's better than I am. But I'll bet you did a good job, at that.*>

It seemed like a rather backhanded compliment, but I decided to be gracious. After all, I was in love with the guy.

TWENTY-ONE

A Dress and A Mess

I woke up next morning to thin sunlight straggling in through my window, and Evangeline Coro still on my mind. Phoebe verbally nudged me out the door for my run and I banished the case from my thoughts as I navigated dew-wet streets and rain-freshened parks, but once I got home I let the first ex-Mrs. Coro have my attention again. I sat at the kitchen table with a bowl of strawberry yogurt and granola and seriously considered her as a suspect.

Had she followed up her million-dollar pitch to her ex-husband with a personal contact, leaving no electronic record for LemurCandy or anyone else to find? Only Coro himself would be able to answer that one. And how had she become involved with MagicBase? According to Nana Nina, Evangeline hadn't been very active in the Spellquick network in recent years—could she be changing her mind about the decision she'd made years ago at MageData? Was she now working with a rival company on the same research? It seemed like that would get her into trouble with the other Spellquicks, but maybe she no longer cared. If that was the case, she really was crazy.

Phoebe was uncharacteristically quiet as I quickly dressed in jeans and a sleeveless black tank. I pulled a bulky camel-colored sweater over it to hide the shoulder holster, but as the warm weather approached it would become harder and harder to hide. Summer is difficult in my line of work—so many fewer options for easily concealing weapons. I knotted a colorful, hand-dyed silk scarf around my neck (one of Nana Nina's creations) and pulled my hair back, twisting it into a knot. I dusted on a smattering of makeup, since I was planning to make a professional call. Also, if LemurCandy could show up unannounced at the office once, he could do it again, and I wanted to look at least decent.

Instead of heading straight for the office, though, I called in to see if I was needed right away.

"No," Kikufaax said, a bit suspiciously. We weren't in vid, but I could hear the touch of a frown in her voice. "What are you doing?"

"Don't worry, it's nothing dangerous," I told her. "I just thought I'd drop out to MageData and see if Coro's around."

"Do you want some company?"

"No, I'm fine. I'll take a magicab there and back to the office. It'll be quick and safe. See you in a bit!" I hung up before she had a chance to argue with me. In truth, I didn't know what might come up in my conversation with Coro, and I didn't want to be hindered by things—like Nana Nina's past history and current secrets—that I'd want to keep from anyone else. I phoned out to MageData and the smoothly polished secretary assured me Coro would be available, so I told her I'd be there in fifteen minutes.

True to my word, I took a magicab that put me within a block of the building. Coro's expense budget could handle it. For once, I didn't feel woozy coming out of the box. The sunlight, which had remained pale and dusty during my run, had now turned up the wattage and was doing a fine job of drying up last night's rain. I had to squint against the reflection it cast off the many windows of the MageData edifice.

The interior of the MageData building bustled with activity as the first floor was readied for tonight's fundraiser. Overall-clad workers dragged furniture around, and a caterer's truck parked out front disgorged boxes, baskets, and coolers. Decorators balanced atop ladders, hanging lights and drifts of tulle. I was happy to duck into the elevator to be whisked up to Coro's office.

Coro, sleek and professional in a shark-grey suit and red power tie, welcomed me graciously, although his palm was moist when we shook hands and his strained smile didn't go all the way to his eyes. I guess he didn't expect I was there bearing wonderful news. Saga or Anna would have been delivering that and accepting a nice fat cheque in exchange.

Seated in a supremely comfortable burgundy leather transform chair in one of the "cozy chat" corners of the office, I accepted a small glass of water and felt guilty that I was about to put him on the spot. But it was to try and save his life, after all. "I want to ask you a few questions about your first wife, Evangeline," I said.

Coro sighed and leaned back in his chair. "We were quite young when we got married," he said, and shrugged. "It didn't last. A familiar story."

"And you haven't had much contact with her over the years," I said.

He shook his head. "No. It was a pretty clean break. No children, the lawyers handled everything else. She didn't even stay in North America."

The wall clock ticked off a few seconds while I waited to see if he was going to volunteer anything else, but when he didn't, I said, "She worked in the research branch of MageData before the breakup."

He looked at me levelly. "That's right. I suppose the old employment records are still floating around out there somewhere."

I half-smiled. "Mr. Coro, *everything* is still floating around out there somewhere. Between magic and the Netz, it's almost impossible to keep secrets."

"I suppose so. Yes, Evangeline worked here. She was in a confidential research group."

I took a little sip of the water. It was ice-cold and held a faint sweetness. "I know," I said. I figured I might as well come clean. "Mr. Coro, Nina Morow is my grandmother."

His usual composure slipped for a moment then, and emotions scrolled across his face—confusion, realization, apprehension, acceptance—as he processed this information.

"So there are very few secrets from you, either, Miss Stablefield," he said finally.

I sighed and held up a palm. "I'm really just trying to put things together, not make trouble for anyone or betray any secrets. And I want you to know that my grandmother didn't tell me anything about her work at MageData until it seemed that it might have a bearing on this case, and on your safety."

He nodded, and a faint smile hovered around his mouth. "I know Nina Morow well enough to believe that," he said.

I leaned forward in my chair. "My grandmother told me that she and her colleagues were working on a method for reliably identifying magic ability, and that they were unsuccessful. I also know that Evangeline is involved with MagicBase UK, the company MageData was supposed to merge with a short time ago. And that she was in touch with you about a charitable donation, which you weren't able to assist her with. What I don't know is how these things fit together, if they do at all."

"Evangeline is with MagicBase? I didn't know that," Coro said, frowning. "Since when? And doing what?"

"I don't know when or exactly what, I'm afraid, at least not yet. Her involvement doesn't seem to have been very public, so I'm assuming she's a silent partner, maybe just a financial backer. You didn't come across her name when the merger was in the works?"

He shook his head. "Either she wasn't involved at that time, or they went to great lengths to keep it secret."

"So her involvement didn't cause the merger's failure."

He frowned and shook his head again, running a hand over his hair. "No. I didn't know she was connected to the company at all—if she even was at that time. I wasn't satisfied with the bookkeeping on their end, that's what sank the merger."

"After you turned down Evangeline's request for the funding for her artist colony project, did she get in touch with you any more?" I asked. "Call you, or visit, to press her case?"

Coro looked away from me for a moment, out one of the massive windows. I didn't think he was actually looking at the pleasant blue sky, though. "Yes, she called me, on the vidphone," he said. "It wasn't...a pleasant conversation. I was rather taken aback. She struck me as a bit unbalanced."

"She didn't...threaten you, did she?"

Coro rose abruptly from his chair, as if he couldn't stand to sit still any longer. His composure hadn't returned and he paced between the chair and the window, his shoes silent on the soft carpet, hands clasped lightly behind his back, fingers twitching nervously.

"Not—no. Not personally. She said some things about MageData that didn't really make sense to me at the time, but maybe she thought she could use her connection with MagicBase to...I don't know...get back at me somehow?"

"By damaging MageData?"

"I really have no idea."

"Well, what did she say?"

He frowned and turned his attention out the window again, took a deep breath and blew it out slowly. "Things like, she knew more about my own company than I did. Secrets that could ruin me if they came out. But she didn't elaborate." He turned to me and spread his hands in obvious bewilderment. "As I said, she wasn't making sense. I don't know what she could be talking about, especially since it's so many years since she even worked here."

I nodded, and I didn't need my magic to tell that he wasn't lying. He really didn't know what she meant. I was one up on him. I knew what one of those secrets was—the success of the Spellquick research—but I didn't think it would ruin Coro if it suddenly came out. It could be embarrassing, but that would be about it. Maybe he was right, and Evangeline was simply coming unhinged.

"If the merger with MagicBase had gone through, would one company have been absorbed into the other?"

"Not really," Coro answered. "It would have been more of a paperwork deal than any kind of physical restructuring or anything like that. We already exchange data, and each company would have retained its own name and profile. We're on different continents, after all. It just would have made some things more convenient, and possibly increased profits."

It was frustrating. I was no further ahead, and the hunch that had brought me out here first thing in the morning seemed to have been based on thin air. I stood up. "Well, I'm sorry to have taken up your time. I guess maybe I'm on the wrong track with this."

He stood too, and shook my hand. "Not at all. I feel privileged that you're all trying so hard to solve this for me."

Neither of us said a word about how quickly the time was passing, but I knew he must be thinking about it, just as I was. I left and caught a bus back to the office, staring moodily out the window all the way, and wondering what the hell it all meant.

———◆———

Back in my own office, I shut the door to muffle the video-game sounds coming from the back room, then printed out copies of all the Murder Prophet messages and laid them out in a row on my desk. I felt like an English prof getting ready to grade student papers as I began to compare them. They had enough in common to all have come from the same person, certainly. The lines of poetry, the references to death and time, the signature, "A Friend," handwritten in a spiky, genderless hand. That signature made me angry. Whoever was sending these messages wasn't anyone's friend.

I also looked up the data from LemurCandy (damn it,

what was his real name?) and printed the username of the sender at the top of each Murder Prophet message. The first eight messages had alternated between four distinct names: SurlyHypnoticMoccasin51, Artsy_Symphonic_Council, MushyNonsocialCryptic, and the oddly evocative Loony#Pushcart%Cynicism. Coro's had been from MushyNonsocialCryptic, and mine, finally, had come from SurlyHypnoticMoccasin51. They ranged from short, four lines like the first one and one other:

> *April is the cruellest month, breeding*
> *Lilacs out of the dead land, mixing*
> *Memory and desire, stirring*
> *Dull roots with spring rain.*[4]

to the longest, at eight lines:

> *How wonderful is Death,*
> *Death, and his brother Sleep!*
> *One, pale as yonder waning moon*
> *With lips of lurid blue;*
> *The other, rosy as the morn*
> *When throned on ocean's wave*
> *It blushes o'er the world;*
> *Yet both so passing wonderful!*[5]

Sometimes they mentioned a period of time, as in Coro's fortnight, some a date, like my first day of spring or a month, like April, some another pinpoint in time, like the waning moon. Some were easier to interpret than others, although they all made sense in hindsight, after the murder had occurred.

But looking at them all laid out here, I had the strongest feeling that they had to be from the same person. A person with very strange ideas about usernames. They made "LemurCandy" look quite normal.

I messaged LemurCandy on Chatterz® and he said, *<Hello again!>*

<Hey,> I said. *<I'm looking at these usernames again. Did you have any luck linking anything else to Evangeline Coro?>*

<Not yet. You're getting kind of fixated on this woman, aren't you?>

<I don't know,> I typed, trying to come up with a way to explain why I thought she was important. *<This case is full of threads that don't seem to lead anywhere. She seems to have more threads than anyone else.>*

<Well, the only username I can link to her is the one from her letter to Coro, MysticalPsychoUnicorn_245. Don't know what else to tell you.>

<What about that woman from the other company, Anzai Namiko? Any of the names link up to her?>

<Don't you think I would have told you if they did?> he asked.

<Yeah, sorry.> I thought hard for a moment. *<Did you ask FallenElfGeek to help you track down the owners of those usernames?>*

There was a pause before he answered. *<No, why? I do know my way around the Netz, you know.>*

I expected that if he was using an avatar right now, it would be pouting. *<I know that,>* I said, to soothe his ego. *<But I had the weirdest impression yesterday when I was with FEG— —does he have any magic ability that he uses on the Netz? >*

There was an even longer pause this time, and then he

typed, <*Yes, he does. He's a Netzer. But I didn't know it was that obvious.*>

<*It wasn't before, but I thought I picked up on something then. Just...call it a hunch,*> I said. <*Ask him to look into those, would you? And maybe see if you can link any other usernames to Anzai Namiko, like you did for Clarice Valencia.*>

<*I will,*> he said. <*See you tonight if I don't talk to you before then.*>

<*Okay!*> I typed, but my heart suddenly lurched and a cold sweat prickled my skin. Tonight! What was I going to wear?

I looked up from my screen. Kikufaax stood in my doorway, grinning. As usual, she looked stunning, today in a burnt-orange tank dress, countless oversized tassels dangling from the skirt. I would have looked like some kind of giant dusting mitt in it.

"What?" I asked.

"What are you going to wear tonight?"

"Help?" I said, and she laughed.

"Don't worry, we're going shopping."

"You're a life saver."

"And," she added, as she steered me out into the street, "Saga approved a budget."

"Really?" It wasn't like Saga to spring for expenses that he didn't think were absolutely necessary.

She grinned. "It's not a huge budget, but it'll do. I think it might be a touch of payback for saving his life."

"I'll take it," I said gratefully, and surrendered myself to Kiku's expertise.

———•———

Four hours and the entire budget later we were back at the office, although I'd only dropped in to see if there were any last-minute instructions for tonight. Kikufaax had totally come through, finding the perfect dress in one of her "secret" shopping spots after an hour or so. It was a deep mauve satin gown sewn with silver knotwork at the hems of the sleeves and skirt. The sleeves nipped in close at the shoulder but were wide and trailing at the wrist, and the skirt was a straight sheath that fell to just below my knees in the front, and flowed out into a short train in the back.

"Perfect if you have to run anywhere," Kiku told me. I hoped it wouldn't come to that. Intricate silver beadwork traced the front of the skirt. The dress fit me perfectly, making my curves look more like the ones I'd given my avatar than my usual endowments. We'd taken it straight to my apartment, and it now hung, safely encased in protective plastic, in my closet.

Kiku had also taken me to get my hair "done" in a downtown hair boutique so pink it made my eyes water. That translated into an hour and a half during which her stylist combed and straightened, trimmed and twisted and pinned until I was in a torpor brought on by too much gossip and hairspray and the fumes from glossy magazines.

Glaive cat-called me from his office as I walked past, and that was just for the hair and makeup. I stuck my tongue out at him, secretly pleased. If Glaive thought I looked good, chances were that LemurCandy would, too.

Disaster struck about a minute later. Saga emerged from his office wearing a more-solemn-than-usual face and beckoned me toward the boardroom. Anna, sombre today in a grey wool dress that looked so soft it made you want to pet it like a kitten, followed right behind us.

"What's wrong?" I asked as soon as the door shut.

Saga regarded me gravely and clasped his hands behind his back. He had a sort of parental 'I'm not angry just disappointed' look on his face. "A police officer called here this afternoon, wishing to follow up with you about an 'incident' the other night." He raised an eyebrow a quarter of an inch. "You forgot to mention this incident, Kitano?"

Phash. I really had forgotten it, for a while. I tried to play it cool, leaned against the embossed wallpaper and shrugged. "It wasn't anything really—I did forget to tell you about it. I handled it, and the guy's in jail. Nothing to worry about."

Anna shook her head, her eyes dark. The looped golden chains on her earrings tinkled their own disappointment. "Kit! We looked up the report, and it's *absolutely* something to worry about! It doesn't matter that we don't know who hired the man, it must have been triggered by the Murder Prophet case. It's the only big thing the firm is working on right now. And we already know you're a target, because of your message." She began to pace the small room, her heels ticking anxiously across the hardwood. "I can't believe you left us out of the loop on this."

"Okay, I'm sorry," I said, guilt descending on me like a hungry wolf. "I admit I put off telling you at first. I didn't want you to over-react, like you are now. And then it slipped my mind. It really did."

"It is not an over-reaction to try and make sure that our employees stay safe," Saga told me sadly. The tiny frown line was back. I opened my mouth but he held up a hand. "I know what you are going to say, Kitano, that this is a dangerous profession. That is very true. Which makes it all the more important that we avoid danger when we can."

I sighed. "Okay. I agree. I should have told you. I'll be more careful from now on. Now I really have to get going, or I'm going to be late—"

"Anna and I have decided that Glaive is taking you to the safe house, where you will stay for the next few days," Saga said, interrupting me.

For a moment I couldn't even speak. "What?" I finally sputtered. "I have to go to MageData tonight!"

He shook his head. "Kiku can go. You could be putting yourself in imminent danger if you were to go, and I can't allow that."

I turned to Anna. She had stopped pacing and sat in one of Saga's big armchairs, fingers tented in front of her, fingertips tapping slowly together. Surely she would be more reasonable. "I'm not in any real danger, you know that. The real danger is to Coro. The message to me was just a scare tactic."

She stopped tapping her fingers. "Perhaps. But you're an important part of our team here, Kit. I won't expose you to danger unnecessarily. The safe house is really the best idea."

I turned back to Saga and gave him a meaningful look. "You know I can take care of myself," I said, hoping he would remember that my transmutation magic made me much less vulnerable than a person without that ability.

"I do know that." He nodded imperturbably. He knew what I was talking about. "But it does not alleviate my responsibility to also take care of you. We do not know what resources this person has at his or her disposal."

"It's for your safety, Kit," Anna said in a soothing voice, but underneath it ran that ribbon of steel that I knew meant the decision was already made. No more discussion.

"We have already told LemurCandy to pick up Kikufaax

instead, and briefed him on the situation," Saga said. "Glaive will take you to your apartment to collect whatever you might need."

And that was that. Unless I wanted to quit, I didn't have much choice but to go along with the idea.

I tried not to give Kiku a dirty look as I passed her desk. It wasn't her fault. Although somehow it made it worse to realize that she'd be ready and look as good as I would have in less than half the time. I went into my office to collect my notes and the Anagrammatics book Trip had found. The goose followed me in and hopped up on my desk. He leaned his long neck forward to put his orange bill near my ear.

"Sorry you have to go to the safe house, Kit," he said in a low voice. "I heard them talking about it."

I didn't trust myself to say much since I was still seething inside. "Thanks," I managed.

"Why don't you just tell everyone you're a Transmute?" he whispered. "Then they'd know you can take care of yourself."

I shook my head. "Saga knows, and he's still sending me into hiding," I said. "And you know what he's like—what they're both like. When they make up their minds—"

The goose nodded. "Yeah, I know. Once Saga thought I was spending too much time playing video games and not getting enough exercise, so he set the console on a timer. I told him okay, okay, I'd start going for walks when I couldn't play." He grinned that weird goosey grin at me and winked. "But when I went for a walk, I only went as far as the arcade."

"You tricked Saga?" I gaped at the goose in amazement.

"Shh!" he hissed at me. "He still doesn't know."

"Nice one," I said. It was no small feat to put one over on Saga. "But that won't work for me. He's setting Glaive as a watchdog."

Trip shrugged and shook out his feathers, letting them settle back into place before he spoke again. A few stray bits of down drifted across my desk. "Well, anyway, it'll probably only be for a couple of days. Maybe it'll be like a vacation for you."

Yeah, right. A vacation during which I missed a date with LemurCandy, and had no Netz access. Sounded peachy.

When I emerged from my office, Kikufaax was closeted with Saga and Anna, no doubt getting the good news that she had about an hour to get ready for the charity event. I didn't really want to see any of them again just then, so I told Glaive I was ready and we went out to his Cloudwalker. "I have to get a few things from my apartment," I told him, and he nodded.

"They're only doing the smart thing, you know," he said.

"Whatever. Just drive," I said, and we drove to my apartment in silence. It wasn't Glaive's fault, either, but I wasn't feeling too fond of anyone just then, and he was the closest target.

Glaive waited in the car while I went in and threw things into a bag, not very gently, I admit. I took all the other notes I'd made on the case, too. Might as well work, if I had to be confined.

"Kit, are you going somewhere?" Phoebe asked suddenly.

"Saga and Anna are sending me to the safe house," I muttered in reply.

"They don't think you're safe here, with me?" She

sounded insulted.

"Guess not," I replied, not really paying attention.

"Well, I like that!" she huffed.

"Phoebe, you're a great apartment AI, but you're not really defense-capable," I told her absently.

"We'll see about that," she said.

I ignored her. I paused in front of my closet, staring at the mauve dress. I felt almost as sorry for it as I did for myself. We were both missing a chance to shine. Served Saga right that he'd had to spend the money on it for nothing. I slammed the closet door.

"See you in a few days, Phoebe," I called on my way out. "Just put everything on hold until I get back." She didn't answer. Probably still mad. Well, weren't we all? I locked the door and stomped back out to the car, wordlessly dropping my bag into the back seat. This time Glaive said nothing when I got in, which was fine with me. We took a slightly roundabout route to the safe house in which Glaive executed some maneuvers designed to shake anyone tailing us, but I wasn't impressed. I doubted that anyone was taking any interest in us—particularly me—at all.

The Smith Street safe house was about as nondescript as a house could be. Two storeys with a brick facade, a pale grey door and an uninspired front yard. Still, the most important thing about a safe house was not calling attention to itself.

Glaive put the Cloudwalker in the garage and we went inside. He locked up, then wordlessly turned on the television. Obviously if I didn't want to talk, he wasn't going to let it bother him. Or maybe he thought he was punishing me with the silent treatment. I went upstairs and dumped my things in one of the bedrooms, then threw myself on the bed to sulk. I could not believe this was happening. I thought briefly about calling Nana Nina and asking her to come over and break me out. She was a Spellquick, after all, there must be some kind of magic she could use on Glaive to get me past him. She'd never do it, though. Maybe I could overpower Glaive. The thought almost made me laugh out loud, although it didn't make me feel any better.

I was missing out on a date with LemurCandy. *Phash.*

His username made me think of the other usernames, the ones in the case, and they started traipsing through my head in an aggravating chorus line. A horrible, cacophonous chorus line. *SurlyHypnoticMoccasin. ArtsySymphonicCouncil. LoonyPushcartCynicism. MushyNonsocialCryptic.* They had little enough meaning to start with, but repeating like this even the component words became gibberish, just jumbled letters.

I closed my eyes, but that only made it worse. I got up from the bed and paced the room, looked out the window at a scruffy back alley, opened up my Anagrammatics book and tried to focus on a puzzle, but they just kept on. I tossed the book on the bed and went back to pacing.

And I realized, as I looked out the window for the fourth time, that the usernames did contain a certain internal harmony or resonance. They reminded me of something. I pulled a pencil and notebook out of my bag and jotted them down the left margin of a clean page.

SurlyHypnoticMoccasin51.

Artsy_Symphonic_Council.

Loony#Pushcart%Cynicism.

MushyNonsocialCryptic.

I discarded the numbers and underscores—they were

just filler. My eyes went from one line to the next, then on to another one, matching up letters as if I were doing an anagrammatic. I started crossing out letters they had in common.

A. L. T. Two o's. Three c's.

They had every letter in common.

They were all anagrams.

In a flash of inspiration, I wrote down one more, under the others. PsychoticMuslinCrayon. Another anagram.

"Holy *phash*," I breathed. Something tied all those usernames together, all the other Murder Prophet ones and Aleshu Coro's and mine. My theory that Coro was the crux of the Murder Prophet case must be right.

I just wasn't sure what it meant.

I pulled out my phone, ready to call Saga, but I stopped. I was still mad at him for sticking me in here. And it wasn't like I had any real answers, only another piece of the puzzle. Maybe it was childish, but I wasn't ready to talk to him yet. I put the phone back carefully and went downstairs to make coffee.

I poked my head into the living room. Glaive was still on the sofa, watching some kind of martial arts sporting event on the big-screen tv. Darcko and Sadatake makes sure their guests are comfortable. "Coffee?" I asked.

"Sure," he said, without looking up.

"Glad you're keeping such a close eye on me," I said in what I hoped was a withering voice.

"Anybody tries to break in, you're safe," he said. "Not much to worry about beyond that. No Netz, and no one knows we're here anyway. That's the point of a safe house. Just scream if you need me."

"Haha," I retorted. Obviously he was still miffed at me

for taking my anger out on him. "Coffee will be ready in ten, and you can fix it yourself."

He didn't deign to answer that, so I went back to the kitchen and put the coffee on to perk. If he was going to be like that, I wasn't going to tell him about the anagrams, either.

The cupboard holding the coffee was right next to the back door, and as I opened it and reached for the bag, what I'd said to the runaway transmute Idala Kineall in this very kitchen came back to me. *This house keeps you safe inside, it's not for keeping you prisoner.*

I thought of Trip, pulling one over on Saga, all the while pretending to be a good little goose.

Glaive was on the lookout for someone breaking *in*—he wasn't expecting me to try and break *out*. I could be out the door and long gone in a magicab before he'd even know I wasn't upstairs sulking.

It was very tempting. It was very wrong, of course. But very tempting.

I thought about it while the coffeemaker burbled and spat, filling the carafe with dark, aromatic brew. I thought a little more while I poured up a mug full, added cream and sugar, and stirred it reflectively. It seemed almost too easy, the way the pieces fell into place like a kid's jigsaw puzzle. I climbed the stairs again and shut the door of my room. Let Glaive think I was still sulking.

I sat on the bed and sipped coffee, going over it once more. I could catch a magicab back to my place, call LemurCandy and tell him the plan was changed again and that he should pick me up instead of Kikufaax. My hair was done, only slightly mussed from my brief sulk on the bed. My dress waited for me in my closet, and we could be at

MageData before anyone realized what was going on. Kiku would be pissed, sure, and so would Saga and Anna. But they'd forgive me. Especially if, between us, LemurCandy and I could figure out the meaning of the anagrammed usernames and solve the whole Murder Prophet case. That's who I really wanted to tell about the anagrams. He might know what to make of them.

I didn't have much time to think about it, or LemurCandy would already have left to pick up Kiku. I gulped down the rest of my coffee for fortification, grabbed the bag with my keys, and tiptoed down the stairs. I didn't dare call Lemur until I had actually made my break.

I was almost at the bottom step when I heard Glaive get up and go into the kitchen, presumably to get his coffee. Damn. I crept back up to the top of the stairs and stood in the shadows, holding my breath and listening to cupboard doors open and close and the clink of spoon and mug.

Finally he went back to the television and I slunk down the stairs and out to the kitchen. Holding my breath, I slid back the deadbolt, took off the chain, and eased open the back door. It gave onto the scruffy alleyway that seemed, in the lowering gloom, to be relatively free of things I might trip over. Still not daring to breathe too loudly, I closed the door and heard it latch. I wondered how long it would take Glaive to go looking for me. If I was really lucky, he might think I'd gone to bed and not start to wonder until morning.

I ducked low so that he wouldn't accidentally see me out any of the windows, and as quickly as I could in my crouched position, made my way out to the street. It was pretty much deserted, so I had no witnesses to my undignified and surreptitious exit from the alleyway. I turned away from the house and walked quickly past neighboring gardens, lawns and driveways. I didn't know if this was the shortest route to a magicab or not—I just wanted to get as far away as I could, as fast as possible. Once I turned the first corner, I let my breath out in a sigh of relief and dug my phone out of my bag. LemurCandy picked up on the second ring.

I realized with relief that I'd called without dithering about all the stuff I'd dithered about before. Maybe I was feeling more confident about our relationship. "Hey," I said, trying not to sound breathless as I scurried along the street, "Plans have changed again."

"Geez, okay," he said. He didn't have to ask who it was, I noticed with a thrill. "What's happening now, Kit?"

"Back to the original plan, pick me up at my place."

There was a pause. "I thought you were being protected, and Kikufaax was going instead?"

"Yeah..." I tried to think fast and make my voice sound calm and not panicky. "I convinced Saga that I didn't need protecting, and really, it was too short notice for Kiku to be ready in time."

"I just talked to her, and she said she just needed another ten minutes," he said, sounding puzzled.

Dammit, why couldn't he just stop asking all these questions? I was finally in sight of a magicab, and there was currently no lineup waiting for it.

"Oh, you know women," I said brightly, "we don't like men to think we need a lot of time to get ready for things. Just pick me up, okay?"

"Okay," he said finally. I tried to tell myself he didn't sound disappointed. "Fifteen minutes all right?"

"Fine," I chirped, but my stomach lurched. Could I possibly be ready in that short a time?

I pressed the button to end the call, and elbowed my way in front of an elderly man to get to the magicab first. I know, it was rude, but if I was going to save Aleshu Coro's life, I didn't have time to make nice.

TWENTY-TWO

Black Ties and White Lies

When I put the key in the lock of my apartment door, and pushed it open, the hallway erupted with the sharp clanging of a klaxon. I jumped, dropped my bag, let go of the doorknob, and had to scramble to pick up the bag again while trying to wrestle the door open again and get inside.

"Phoebe!" I shouted over the wailing racket. "What the hell—"

The alarm cut off immediately, leaving my ears ringing in the blissful silence. "Kit! What are you doing back so soon?" Phoebe demanded.

I stood just inside the door with my hands on my hips. "I live here, remember? And when I left an hour and a half ago, I didn't have an alarm system!"

"Well, it's your own fault," she retorted.

I didn't have time to waste fighting with my apartment AI, so I hurried into the bedroom and pulled out the mauve dress, and laid it gently on the bed. "Phoebe," I said, unzipping the garment bag carefully, "I'm quite certain I didn't ask you to install an alarm while I was gone. In fact I think I told you to put everything on hold."

"But you said I didn't have any defensive capabilities," she argued. "That was obviously a weak point in my security, and since your safety and security are my—"

"Yes, yes, your primary concern, I get it," I said through clenched teeth. I stripped down to my underwear and took the dress out of its protective plastic sheath. "However, I didn't think your programming would allow you to set up something like this without my permission."

I stopped with the dress half-over my head. I couldn't go on a mission like this without packing some kind of weapon. What if something did happen and we had to move to protect Coro? Luckily I keep a little laser Angelrod on hand for just such a purpose, and I had it in place three minutes later. I slipped the dress on carefully over my hair and let it fall around me.

Phoebe kept talking while I did all this. "I was going to get in touch with you and tell you about the alarm, but I thought I had plenty of time. You said you'd be gone for a few days!"

"Change of plans," I muttered, tugging things into place.

"Well, I'm tired of your blatant disregard for your own safety!" she said, her voice climbing to a shrill register I hadn't known was possible. "I'm trying to help protect you, Kit, it's part of my *job*, but you fight me at every turn. You're reckless, and thoughtless, and foolhardy, and I'm sick of it! Now are you going to let me protect you, or not?"

I stood with my hands frozen in the act of straightening my dress, stunned into immobility as she finally stopped. I imagined her, if she were a person, standing with her hands on her hips, chest heaving, eyes accusing.

Well, I *had* wanted to hear her tell me off, just once. I guess I got my wish. And she had succeeded in making me feel just the tiniest bit guilty.

"Phoebe," I said carefully, "Thank you for looking out for me. The alarm is fine." I glanced at the clock. "But I really don't have time to talk about this right now."

She didn't answer immediately, and when she did, her voice was back in the normal range. "I suppose I should have asked," she said with a grudging note. "If you want me to call and cancel the other things—"

"Other things?"

More silence. "I had thought to make a few other security additions to the apartment," she finally said.

I had sudden visions of laser beams, trip wires, trapdoors and sundry other booby traps. "Okay, no." I checked my makeup in the bathroom mirror. It hadn't suffered too much. "No more changes, no more additions, nothing else until I get back and we have a chance to talk about it. Are we clear?"

No answer.

"Phoebe, are we clear?" I repeated. I protected the front of my dress with a towel, wary of stray water drops, and gulped down a Maginox®, expecting to hear LemurCandy buzz my intercom any second.

"We're clear," she muttered. "I wish you'd never gotten involved in the Coro case, Kit."

"You and me both, Phoebe," I told her, but honestly, I didn't entirely mean it. Staring into the mirror, I knew I'd never looked this good for a date before in my life, and if it took a death threat to get me here, I felt ready to take the risk.

I checked the clock. Seventeen minutes had passed since I'd phoned LemurCandy and lied to him about the change in plans. Was he on the phone with Kiku? Had Saga called him with last-minute instructions, and even now my deception was coming to light? *Stop that,* I told myself sternly. I looked at the mirror again. I felt like I had to keep checking to make sure I really looked that good. There must be something wrong that I was just missing—my hair was coming down in the back, or I'd dripped water on the skirt of my dress when I was taking my Maginox®—something.

But if it was there, I couldn't see it.

I shuddered to think what I might be looking like if I hadn't had Kikufaax's guidance. I'd probably be wearing my one half-presentable "little black dress" and have my hair brushed straight and slicked down with gel to keep it from frizzing. I'd look okay—maybe—but not okay enough for this event. Or LemurCandy. And I'd just selfishly created a huge inconvenience for Kiku. Guilt pricked little daggers in my chest. I'd better call her and at least let her know what I'd done.

The intercom buzzed, startling me as I reached for the phone. I pressed the button.

"All set?" LemurCandy asked.

Okay, out of time. I'd try to call Kiku from MageData. "I'll be right down," I said into the speaker, then spent a minute dithering about whether I should have asked him up or not. I decided not. We were supposed to be on a mission to keep an eye on Aleshu Coro, and we couldn't do that unless we were on the spot at MageData. And the weird way Phoebe was acting, I didn't trust her not to say something completely embarrassing. I grabbed the paper containing the anagrams and stuffed it and my phone into my ridiculously tiny handbag, slung the matching wrap around my shoulders and went down. LemurCandy waited in the lobby.

He looked startled when I stepped out of the elevator. I thought it was in a good way, but it wasn't like he threw himself at my feet and pledged eternal devotion or anything like that. He did raise his eyebrows and say something like, "Wow, Kit, you clean up good," but honestly, I was too busy looking at him to notice. I even forgot about the anagrams for thirty seconds or so.

He was as elegant and dashing (I know it's an old-fashioned word, but it fit, I swear it fit) as a man could look in a tuxedo, and I've watched a lot of old James Bond vids with Nana Nina, so I'm something of an expert. His brown hair looked silky and I wanted to run a finger over that hint of a wave. He looked at me strangely as I walked toward him, so I bit the inside of my lip to snap myself out of it. Between the revelation of the anagrammed usernames, Phoebe's security renovations, and the sight of Lemur in that tuxedo, it was no wonder I was a little rattled.

"Thanks!" I said, even though I wasn't a hundred percent sure what he'd said. "That's a great tuxedo!"

He shrugged. "I read somewhere once that every man should have one, just in case. I have to say that it didn't seem like a great investment before this, but it sure came in handy tonight."

He took my arm just at the elbow and guided me out the doors. A little thrill prickled the skin on my back. I thanked whatever powers might be watching over me that I'd talked Kiku into letting me wear my own black shoes with the kitten heels. They weren't the stilettos that she would have had me in, but there was a much smaller chance that I'd wobble when I walked, or trip over myself. And I'd argued that there wasn't much sense putting me in a dress I could run in, and shoes I couldn't. She gave in.

Lemur didn't drive the macho-macho CloudWalker like Glaive; his car was smaller and sportier. It looked dark blue or black in the dusk, and I sank gratefully into the front seat when Lemur held the door open for me. I let out a long breath as he went around and got in behind the wheel. It wasn't until then that I felt like I'd actually gotten away with it.

I spent the first five minutes of the drive to MageData lying—thank goodness LemurCandy didn't have my magic ability—in answer to his questions about how I'd talked Saga into letting me leave the safe house. When we'd exhausted that conversational delight, I started wondering whether my skirt was getting terribly wrinkled and how I was going to broach the subject of LemurCandy's name. I mean, I absolutely couldn't introduce him that way to anyone. And yet why hadn't he volunteered it himself? Did he think we could somehow skirt around it for the whole night? Did he really not want me to know it? The more I thought about it, the more frustrated I felt. Maybe I just wouldn't tell him about the anagrams at all, the jerk.

By the time we rounded the corner into MageData's block and the huge, brilliantly-lit concrete-and-glass building came into view, I knew I had to say something. "So." I tried to keep my voice light, but I thought he must be able to hear the sound of my heart pounding. "Am I just going to call you 'LemurCandy' all night?"

He shot me a quizzical glance, his face half in shadow under the streetlights. "Don't you think that would seem a little odd?"

"Well...yes I do. But since I don't know your real name —"

"What?" He pulled up in front of the building and there were valets waiting to park the vehicles, so he couldn't look back at me again. "You don't know my name?"

Was he deliberately drawing this out to torture me? "No,

you've never said."

"But Saga knows," he protested. "And Anna, and Kiku —"

"They've never mentioned it," I said through clenched teeth. Was he ever going to just tell me?

He got out of the car, handed the keys to the valet, came around the car and opened my door to help me out. His green eyes were laughing.

"It's Jake," he said as he took my hand to steady me. "Jake Lynch. Nice to meet you, Kit."

"Nice to meet you, too, Jake," I replied, "Thanks for the intro. Now let's go make sure our host stays nice and safe tonight."

If only it had been that easy.

———•———

It always amazes me when huge business buildings are transformed into fairy palaces. Even though I'd seen part of the transformation earlier in the day, I was still dazzled by the end result. Spotlights cunningly placed around the MageData edifice threw the facade of the building into relief, enhancing that suggestion of medieval castle ancestry. It helped that the building stood massive and alone in the industrial park, so it wasn't being elbowed by less prestigious neighbors on either side. All the windows on the first and second floors glowed golden, and some magical talent had been hired to outline them all with shimmering blue-green foxfire. An actual red carpet had been rolled out of the entryway and down the front steps, with black velvet ropes on silver standards holding back the "riff-raff" on either side.

The riff-raff in question consisted mostly of photographers, judging by the number of flashes that outshone the floodlights in brief bursts. It seemed more like a holovid premiere than a charity ball, but I suppose the journalists expected our local celebrities to be in attendance. A few people took pictures of me and LemurCandy—I mean, Jake—probably just in case we turned out to be somebody important. I don't expect any of those shots got saved.

Luckily, the tuxedoed bouncers had a list that included employees of Darcko & Sadatake, so we were granted entrance even though I'd left the paper invitation with Kiku.

Inside we stopped for a moment and took stock. The lobby, too, had been transformed into something more palatial, quite different from the last two times I'd been here —once with Glaive, to ask Aleshu Coro questions about Clarice Valencia, and then on my own, to ask him more questions about Evangeline. Then, the lobby had felt modern and imposing, all angular lines and crisp white lighting and quiet elegance.

Now twinkly lights and drapey lengths of silver tulle festooned the ceiling, the reception desk had been transformed into a bar, and a double-wide door stood open on the left to reveal a huge boardroom. Soft multicolored fabric hangings camouflaged the starkness of the walls, their designs shifting subtly in an effect that had to be wrought by magic. A four-piece band replaced some of the office furniture. They seemed quite good. A few couples swayed on the improvised dance floor.

Another set of double doors on the right-hand side of the lobby led into a second large room whose usual purpose was unclear to me, but it had also been pressed into service for the party. Several bars, and tables groaning under trays of hot and cold finger food, lined the walls, as well as a podium at which I expected Coro and probably others would be making speeches later in the evening.

A huge, green-bordered banner stretched across the wall behind the podium, reading *Save the Lemurs* and decorated with capering lemur caricatures. I stifled a giggle, then arranged my face and said solemnly to LemurCandy—I mean, Jake— "At least it's all for a good cause."

He took my elbow and steered me in the direction of the bar. "Yeah. I just hope Coro's not in more danger than the lemurs are."

Some fifty people milled around the rooms already, and a steady stream trickled through the doors to stop and gaze about before pressing into the crowd. I sent up a silent thanks to Kikufaax for helping me get ready. My little black dress would have been ridiculously inappropriate. Although, even without Kiku's help, I never would have shown up in some of these atrocities.

The woman emerging from the boardroom with a sparkly drink in her hand, for instance, wore an apricot brocade gown threaded with peacock blue. Its shapeless skirt and elbow-length sleeves dripped with silver lace, and the overall effect was—ghastly. She seemed happy enough, though. Maybe it was the good feeling she had from helping the lemurs, or maybe it was the sparkly drink. I couldn't tell, but I thought I might need a sparkly drink of my own before the night was out.

I spotted Aleshu and Sandrine Coro near the bar, speaking with a couple I knew I'd seen before, although I couldn't immediately recall where. The man wore, not a traditional tuxedo, but a coat of coral brocade covered with ivy leaves, over what looked like a white transform shirt. The woman, whose hair was done in what I think is called a "tousled" style (that is, it looked like she'd just gotten out of bed and come to the party without brushing it, but in a good way) wore a gown of plain maroon gauze with a flowing skirt. She had paired it, rather surprisingly, with a teal stole.

I suddenly knew where I'd seen them—they were a news team on the national MagiNews vid channel. I admit I stared for a moment. They usually looked so professional, but I suppose everyone had their non-work personas. Except, perhaps, me. On second thought, I guess I did tonight.

Anyway, this woman looked especially garish standing next to the willowy and beautiful Sandrine Coro. She was sheathed in a fashionable sky-blue transform silk gown, scattered with tiny seed-pearl daisies, that seemed to have been made for her statuesque form. Quite likely it had been. Although she appeared to chat easily with the news anchors, she looked gaunt, as if the skin on her face were stretched a bit too tight. Stress was chewing her up.

"We'd better make our presence known to the Coros," I whispered to Lemur—I mean, Jake. "They might feel a little more relaxed once they know we're here."

Jake nodded. "Right now they look tight enough to twang," he muttered back to me. It was hard to think of him as "Jake," but I was getting used to it.

As we wove our way through the press of guests toward the stage, I made the unfortunate gaffe of stepping on a woman's skirt as I edged around her. She took a step away from me at just that moment, so of course she felt a tug. She turned inquiringly and her washed-out blue eyes met mine.

"Clarice?" I said in surprise. She was probably the last person I would have expected to put in an appearance here.

She started, but quickly smiled and said, "Oh, it's nice to see you."

Really? I thought. Especially after I'd made her confess her secret trysts with Coro to me over the phone, I wouldn't have expected Clarice Valencia to ever be pleased to see me again.

"What a lovely dress," I blurted, completely at a loss for anything else to say. It wasn't, really, a sort of rust-colored, mostly shapeless thing embroidered with forget-me-nots. With voluminous sleeves, a flounced skirt, and a deep décolletage laden with white lace, it would have looked much better on a woman with more meat on her bones.

"Oh, so is yours, it completely suits you," she gushed, but after a brief glance and smile at Jake she seemed anxious to get away. "We'll have to chat again soon," she said with another smile, then saluted me with her empty glass and moved off toward the bar.

"Was that Clarice Valencia?" Jake asked me in a low voice.

"Uh-huh," I said, "Or possibly her non-evil twin. She's either on her best behavior tonight or she's had enough sparkly drinks to put her in a good mood. That was not like her at all."

I realized that I was also miffed that she hadn't looked at Jake in the same predatory way she'd scrutinized Glaive. Jake was so much better-looking.

"But you don't think she's any danger to Coro, do you?"

I shook my head. "No. Whatever she's doing here, she's not involved with the whole Murder Prophet thing. I asked her that straight-out over the phone and she didn't lie about it."

We continued on our path to say hello to the Coros. The news celebrities moved off as we approached, and I felt gratified and slightly alarmed by the looks of relief with which both Coro and his wife greeted us. Did they consider us his bodyguards for the evening? I hadn't thought of us that way, and although I had the Angelrod strapped to my...er, strapped under my dress, it wasn't exactly heavy weaponry. I had no idea if Lemur—Jake—usually packed a weapon or would have thought of one tonight.

Aleshu Coro took my hand and shook it, then held on to it for a rather uncomfortably long time, as if he were holding onto something quite different—say, a life preserver, or a rope at the end of which a knot had been tied.

"Miss Stablefield," he said warmly. "You've met my wife, Sandrine, I believe?" Finally he let go of my hand and I shook Sandrine's.

"Yes, I have," I said. "And this is my colleague, Le—Jake Lynch." More handshakes all around. I felt the heat rise in my face and pretended to glance around for someone. Had I really almost called him "LemurCandy"—here, of all places? When I'd been so desperate only a few moments ago to have an alternative to call him? Despite my embarrassment, my lips twitched at the thought of how hilariously inappropriate that would have been.

"It seems like you have a good crowd," I said, making small talk.

Coro nodded. "There'll be more soon, the ones who like to come more than fashionably late. Please help yourselves to drinks and food. We'll be making speeches in the multi-purpose room in a little while."

"We won't be far away," Jake said solemnly. I imagine he meant to make them feel better, but he sounded so serious he might have deepened their fear. I steered him firmly away and in the direction of the bar.

"We need drinks if we're going to mingle inconspicuously," I said. "I'll have a Mystic Summer."

"Aren't those a little strong?" he asked, raising an eyebrow.

"I'll sip it," I assured him. "Get yourself something, too." I heard him ask for a virgin Unholy Delight, and shuddered. An Unholy Delight was even sweeter than a Mocha Insanity. And I'd thought computer geeks subsisted on caffeine drinks and Buzz Bars.

He brought back the drinks and I immediately broke my promise, taking one long, cooling pull on the Mystic Summer. With my head turned, so that Jake wouldn't see. Ahh. That was better. I felt ready to tell him about the anagrams.

I led him over to a quiet corner, from which we could keep an eye on the room and the Coros. "I discovered something I think is interesting earlier this evening," I said.

"What is it?"

I pulled the crumpled piece of paper out of my handbag and showed it to him, smoothing out the wrinkles. "I was looking at all the usernames the Murder Prophet had sent messages from," I said, "And I realized that they're all anagrams of each other."

He studied the paper for a moment, frowning. "You're right," he said. "Isn't that Aleshu Coro's username at the bottom?"

I nodded. "I thought of that one later," I said. "Another

anagram. It can't be a coincidence."

He frowned and shook his head. "No, it can't. It's more evidence that the whole Murder Prophet thing revolves around the Coro case—what else could it mean?"

"Did you manage to find out anything else about Anzai Namiko's online names?" I asked.

He shook his head. "I had to leave it with FEG," he said. "I'm going to check in with him from my mobile soon. I asked him to try and trackback all the rest of these names, too, but I don't know if he'll be able to do it."

"Have a little faith," I said with a grin. "Don't you believe in magic?"

"Very funny," he said, and started to say something else, but just then his phone buzzed. He pulled it out of his pocket and checked the display. "It's Kiku," he said.

"Oh! She's probably looking for me," I said, snatching the phone from his hand impulsively. "I told her I might not have room for mine in my bag, so she should call me on yours." I held up my tiny evening bag as evidence (which actually was holding my phone. I prayed it would not choose this moment to ring), turned away from his surprised face, and answered the phone.

"Hi Kiku," I said in a low voice, slipping past a rotund couple who were putting their evening wear to a stress test tonight. I slid over toward the wall so Jake wouldn't hear my end of the conversation.

"Kit? Is that you? What are you doing with LemurCandy's phone?"

"Um, look, it's a long story, but I'm with him at MageData."

Silence on the other end, for a long moment. "Does Saga know?"

I took a deep breath. "No. I had to sneak away from Glaive and lie to Jake to get him to pick me up. But it's really, really important to the case, Kiku, you have to believe me."

"You shouldn't be there, Kit, it's too dangerous!"

Ooh, the guilt, stabbing me in the heart. Kiku wasn't upset that I'd let her get all ready for a night out and then made her date stand her up, she was upset that I'd put myself in danger.

"I don't think I'm in danger, Kiku, but Coro might be. Look, will you call Saga or Anna and tell them what I did, and also tell them that all the usernames the Murder Prophet has used are connected? They're all anagrams of each other. And also of Aleshu Coro's username."

I glanced around and saw Jake heading for me with the tiniest frown creasing his brow. It was kind of cute. Kiku hadn't answered me, but I hoped she understood the import of what I'd told her. "Okay, Kiku, thanks, I'll talk to you later!" I said brightly, and broke the connection.

"Thanks," I told Jake, handing his phone back to him.

"Is everything all right?" he asked.

"Oh, absolutely, Kiku just wanted to know how the dress fit. She helped me pick it out, you know," I blabbered, wondering how long I could keep up this farce. I felt a hand on my arm and turned to see whose it was.

I was shocked to look into the blue eyes of my grandmother.

"Nana!" I exclaimed. "What are you doing here?"

She smiled. "I got an invitation, same as everyone else. Aleshu is always very kind in remembering his old employees at times like this. You look lovely, dear."

Nana Nina looked pretty swell herself. She wore an

elegant dove-grey jacquard gown, ornamented with tiny gemstones, that I certainly had never seen before. She'd already been to the bar and had a sparkly drink in hand. Nana looked like she could handle hers.

I leaned down and kissed her cheek. "You look gorgeous," I told her truthfully. When I straightened, I remembered Lemur—I mean, Jake. "Nana, this is my friend, Jake Lynch," I said. "You met him online once, remember? Jake, my grandmother, Nina Morow."

He took her hand gently. "I'm very pleased to meet you in real life this time, Mrs. Morow," he said.

"Yes, the last time was under quite different circumstances," she replied with a demure grin.

She'd probably recognized him from his avatar, that time we'd met her in the virtual, since he'd been wearing the one that looked most like his actual face. He didn't have the same advantage, since she'd been wearing that red-headed avatar. I hoped she wouldn't make any references to lemurs or ferrets or squirrels.

"Well, I'm not going to keep you," she said. "I have a lot of old friends to speak with. My fellow shareholders," she added with a sly wink at me.

She took a step away, but I put a hand on her arm and leaned down close to her ear. She smelled pleasantly of lavender. "I don't suppose you've seen Evangeline Coro here?" I asked.

She shook her head. "I've never seen her at one of these functions. She's one former employee that I don't expect gets an invitation. She and Clarice, I suppose."

"But Clarice is here! I already spoke to her."

Nana Nina raised her eyebrows. "She could be here as someone else's guest, I suppose. Are you still suspicious of her?"

"No, not really. But do you think you'd recognize Evangeline if she were here?" I pressed.

"Oh yes, it's not that long since I saw her. I doubt she's changed more in five years than she had the previous ten."

I nodded. "Then just let me know if she turns up, would you?"

"Kit, you don't really suspect—"

"Nana, I don't know what I suspect," I said seriously. "All I know right now is that I have to keep an open mind."

"Okay, honey, I'll let you know," she said, and moved off to speak to the woman in the unfortunate apricot gown.

When I turned back to Jake he had his mobile out again. "I thought I'd check in with FEG," he said.

"Let's go somewhere a little quieter, then."

We stepped back out into the lobby, which had filled up quite a bit since we'd arrived. At the far end, near a bank of elevators, a small clearing had opened up next to a trio of large potted ferns and ficus, so we headed for that.

A message from FallenElfGeek blinked, waiting for Jake, and FEG answered right away when Jake messaged him. I read over Jake's shoulder. He smelled distractingly good, but I tried to keep my mind on the conversation.

<Sorry, buddy,> he said. *<I couldn't link those usernames to a particular person.>*

Jake sighed. *<Oh, well, thanks for trying,>* he said.

<But I did manage to trace them all back to a particular place,> FEG added.

<Really?>

<Yeah, place in the UK. Magic database company called MagicBase. All the messages came from one of their network computers, but the sender used a generic corporate login, so I

can't pin it down any closer than that. I hate those things.>

Jake must have heard my sharply indrawn breath when I read that part, and he half-turned to me, flashing me a knee-weakening grin. Then he turned back to his mobile.

<Thanks, FEG,> he typed. *<I really owe you a big one.>*

<No prob, man,> FEG replied. *<I'll take a case of Buzz Bars sometime you're in the neighborhood.>*

Jake broke the connection.

I breathed, "You think it's Anzai Namiko?"

"Definite possibility," he agreed. "Maybe she was angry enough to hold a grudge after all."

"There's still Evangeline Coro's name on the MagicBase corporate papers, so it could be her, too."

"Or both of them."

I hadn't considered that possibility before.

"How did you know that FEG would be able to find something?" Jake asked.

I shrugged. "Just a hunch. Sometimes magic is useful, you know?"

"Sometimes?"

"Most of the time," I said with a grin, "I think it sucks. But I suppose there have to be exceptions."

"Should we go and report to Aleshu Coro?" Jake asked.

"I think so. It might put his mind at rest a little to know we think we have it pinned down. Not much we can do tonight, so we might as well tell him and then enjoy the party," I said. I meant it, too. There was no way I'd spent this much time getting ready, only to turn around and leave now, and I wanted Jake to know that up front.

"Why leave when things are starting to look up?" he agreed.

We threaded our way back through the crowd in the

lobby, making for the doors that led into the multi-purpose room. The crowd had swelled now, filling both rooms with a rainbow tidal wave of silks, satins, taffetas, lace, beading and crinolines, punctuated with black tuxedos. We had the door in sight when Jake grabbed my arm. Hard.

I shot a look at him, but he wasn't looking at me. I turned to follow his gaze. His eyes were glued to an older woman in the doorway ahead of us. She was short, no more than five feet tall, wearing a vaguely Oriental-styled gown in red and gold damask. Her black hair, streaked with grey, hung just to her chin in a somewhat unflattering asymmetrical bob that still managed to look professionally styled. I couldn't understand why Jake would be staring at her when he could be looking at me.

He pulled me to the side of the crowd as the woman vanished into the room beyond, and whispered four words into my ear. The warmth of his breath should have thrilled me, but instead I felt a chill.

"Anzai Namiko. She's here."

TWENTY-THREE

Short of Breath and Options

It took me only a few seconds to assimilate what Jake had just said and visualize several scenarios in which Aleshu Coro came out dead and we came out looking very, very bad.

"We have to get in there and warn him!" I whispered.

He gripped my arm tighter. His green eyes had gone very dark. "What if she knows what you look like?" he asked. "If it's her, she's threatened you, too."

I shook off his restraining hand. "I've never looked like I do tonight," I said, "So the chances of her recognizing me are slim to none. And she only threatened me because I might get in her way. It's Coro she wants."

He caught my hand again. His skin felt very warm. "Then don't get in her way. Don't take a chance. I can go in there and warn Coro. She definitely doesn't know me. I only saw her picture online."

I looked him in the eye, at once touched by his concern and irritated because he was slowing me down. "Do you have any weapons on your person right now?" I asked him pointedly.

"N—no," he stammered. "Not, er, weapons as such."

"Well, I do," I said. "And I don't know what that woman is planning." I saw Jake's eyes do a quick head-to-toe survey of me, but I wasn't going to tell him what I was packing or where. I also didn't mention that it would be exceedingly embarrassing for me to have to publicly haul the little laser Angelrod out of its present location. I was still willing to hope it wouldn't come to that. "So if you're coming, come on."

I didn't wait for him to say anything else, just jostled my way back into the crowd. He muttered something under his breath but I didn't turn back and ask him to repeat it.

The temperature in the multi-purpose room had risen by about ten degrees and now held at least three times as many people as it had when Jake and I left it to contact FallenElfGeek. The overheated air was thick with too many cloying perfumes and liberally-applied aftershave. I craned my neck, trying to see where Anzai Namiko had gone. Coro and his wife were still in evidence, although they had moved closer to the podium, so I suspected the speeches might start soon. I felt Jake's arm slip around my waist and he leaned in distractingly close.

"Do you see her?" he whispered into my ear. I suppressed a brief urge to turn my head and sniff his neck.

"Not yet. At least she's not anywhere near the Coros," I muttered. Then I spotted her. She stood at the bar, getting a drink, and chatting with a tall, heavyset man with greying hair. His tuxedo seemed barely up to the task of staying closed across his barrel-shaped torso. I heaved a sigh of relief. That didn't seem too sinister. Of course, the drink could be just a prop so that she wouldn't look suspicious.

Jake saw her at the same moment and nodded in her direction. "Now what?" he asked. "Should we still tell Coro what we found out, or just keep an eye on her?"

Damn. Jake was right. I'd been anxious to tell Coro that

we'd figured out the link between MagicBase UK and the Murder Prophet, but he was rattled enough this evening. To tell him that, and then tell him that Namiko was actually in the room—that would be nothing short of cruel. And what we had so far still wasn't enough proof to go up and confront the woman.

"We'd better just keep quiet, stay close to Coro, and keep our eyes open," I said. I seriously wanted to get to the ladies' room and discreetly retrieve the Angelrod from under my dress. I could probably stuff it in my tiny purse. At the same time I hated the thought of leaving the room while Namiko was in it.

I caught Nana Nina's eye from across the room and she shook her head slightly. That meant she still hadn't seen Evangeline Coro anywhere, but my concern had shifted away from Evangeline now. Even if they were both involved, Namiko was on the spot.

Aleshu Coro stepped behind the podium just then and a wave of applause started in the front row of the crowd and rippled back, growing as folks noticed him. He smiled and waited for the noise to die down. The crowd surged forward as people moved in from the other rooms to hear the speeches. That was bad. The human tide pushed us further away from Anzai Namiko, and it became increasingly harder to keep her in sight. I was tall, but she wasn't, and her sleek black bob disappeared behind the throng of heads.

"I'm going to try and get closer to Namiko," I whispered to Jake. "You move up towards the podium. I don't know if anything's going to happen, but I don't want to be caught by surprise if it does."

He nodded, but looked doubtful. "I'll try," he said. "Be

careful, Kit." He caught my hand and squeezed it once, then let go and started toward the podium. Well, at least he was a fast learner. He'd stopped trying to talk me out of things.

I wouldn't have believed that the room was so big, but it seemed like I squeezed and waded through miles of sweaty tuxedos, horrible gowns, and drippy drinks in my quest to get to the other side. Coro had begun speaking, but I wasn't paying attention. It was your standard charity affair speech —why the cause was so important, who the leading supporters were, that kind of thing. Before I got to the bar where I'd last seen Namiko, Coro had relinquished the podium to someone else and stood just off to the left of them looking pleasantly attentive.

Finally I emerged from the thick of the crowd, just down the wall from the bar. I made a quick visual sweep of the folks standing in line for drinks or nursing them nearby. No Namiko. *Phash!*

Empty chairs lined the wall. The mingling wasn't finished yet, and you couldn't see the podium over the heads of the crowd if you were sitting. I made my way through another knot of lemur-lovers to the chairs, slipped off my shoes, and climbed up on one upholstered seat. Yes, I know that's not proper etiquette at a function like this. But I needed a better vantage point to find Namiko, and with luck anyone who noticed me would just think that I was rude and uncouth and wanted a better view of the speakers at the podium.

Jake had managed to get pretty close to the podium, where the speaker, a young man in his twenties with shoulder-length blonde curls, seemed to be drawing his remarks to a close. I swept the crowd over and over, looking for Namiko's grey-streaked dark hair, but it seemed hopeless. There were just too many people. I couldn't pick her out.

Since I'd lost Namiko, it seemed like the best thing to do was to join Jake up near Coro, so I climbed down, slipped my shoes back on, and plunged into the crowd again. I'd made only about ten feet of progress when a small figure appeared in front of me, with unmistakable bobbed dark hair and a red and gold damask gown. She was up on tiptoes, craning to see the speaker, but I doubted it was doing much good.

Gotcha, I thought, and stopped where I was. This was perfect. I could monitor her every breath, and she was within arm's reach if she tried anything. I breathed a deep sigh of relief as Aleshu Coro moved back to the podium to thank the speaker and introduce the next one.

The good feeling didn't last long. He hadn't said more than a couple of words before he stumbled midway through a sentence, and a look of confusion passed over his face. I glanced at Namiko, but she continued bobbing around on tippy-toes, apparently just trying to get a look at the podium. Coro had fallen silent. I looked up and saw that he appeared to be gasping for breath, face suffused, his hands clutching his throat.

I lunged forward and grabbed the diminutive Anzai Namiko by the arm, spinning her around to face me. "Stop it! Stop it right now!" I demanded.

She stared at me wide-eyed. "What—who—"

I shook her. "I mean it! Whatever you're doing to Coro, stop it this instant!"

She recovered from her initial shock, at least enough to defend herself, and drew herself up like an offended pigeon. "I'm not doing anything! Who are you, anyway?"

I glanced back up at Coro. He continued to claw at his throat in a frenzy to breathe. I looked at the little woman. If she was using magic on him, she was damn good to be able to keep it up while being accosted by me. I made a quick check with my own magic. She was telling the truth.

"Sorry, wrong person," I said, and dropped her arm. Only those closest around us had even been aware of our little by-play. Everyone else's attention was riveted on Coro. I threw myself into the crowd again, this time heading for the podium. "Doctor, coming through," I kept saying, "Doctor here, excuse me." It was amazing how most people paid no attention to me and I had to fight my way past them anyway.

Something cold and wet hit my cheek, and I glanced up reflexively, just in time for something else cold and wet to hit me in the eye. People around me gasped and muttered, clearly confused, as wet droplets spattered everywhere and everyone. Sprinklers? Rain?

Then I remembered—Coro's magic ability. Light rainshowers, once a day. In his distress, his magic must have kicked in, an autonomic response. Too bad it wasn't more helpful. I struggled harder through the crowd. If I could get to the stage, I might be able to spot Nana Nina— surely a Spellquick would be able to help? I remembered her wink and comment, "My fellow shareholders." So there must be more than one Spellquick here. If only they weren't too concerned with keeping their abilities secret. This case had far too many secrets—

Something clicked so hard in my head I was surprised no-one around me seemed to hear it.

Kit, she's here, I heard suddenly, as clearly as if Nana Nina was standing beside me. I glanced to the side automatically, even though I knew damn well she wasn't there. Well, Spellquicks had telepathic magic in their repertoire. But did it work both ways?

Evangeline? I tried thinking at Nana, even while I kept pushing toward the front of the crowd. I dug an elbow into a bright red cummerbund and the man moved aside with a grunt and a muttered curse.

Kit, Evangeline Coro is here, she said again, and I assumed she hadn't "heard" me. One-way, then.

Aleshu Coro had fallen to his knees now, still gasping. His face was purple, eyes bulging. Sandrine clutched him, her eyes wild and terrified, but there was clearly nothing she could do. Like everyone else, they were rain-sprinkled, spots darkening like bullet-holes on Coro's suit. Jake stood nearby, fists clenched as he scanned the panicking guests, looking like he wanted to kill something but having no target. As I got close, he suddenly left the stage and pushed into the crowd. I wondered if he'd caught a glimpse of something I couldn't see.

I reached the podium and jumped up on one of the chairs behind it. I dragged wet tendrils of hair off my face and scanned the crowd for Nana, but I couldn't see her. Jake seemed to be randomly grabbing people by the hand or arm, then dropping one to move on to the next. I wondered briefly what the hell he was doing. Even more people surged in from the other rooms as word spread that something was wrong. Dammit, where was Nana, and more importantly, where was Evangeline Coro? With a jolt I realized I didn't even know what she looked like. Kiku had done the background on her, and I'd never seen a picture.

A commotion erupted in the area of the bar. I looked over to see that a side door had burst open. Saga stood there, clad in as much black as Glaive on a weekday, his long-barrelled LaserWaster resting on one shoulder. At the same time, I heard a familiar cry.

"Hiiiii-yahhhhhhh!" Trip flapped heavily over the crowd and executed some kind of spin-kick in mid-air, dropping down to land on the now-vacant podium in 'ready' mode. "Where are they, Kit? Let me at them!" he squawked menacingly. Coro managed a deep, rasping gasp of air. His attacker must have been startled for a moment and let his or her concentration lapse.

I've lost her, Kit, Nana said in my head. She sounded panicked. With Evangeline lost in the crowd—

Lost. "Trip!" I said, "It's Evangeline Coro. Can you find her?"

The goose's eyes narrowed as Aleshu Coro made a strangled gurgle again. Trip's Finder magic might not be fast enough, or strong enough—

"Get him out of here, Kit!" Saga roared. He must have the place surrounded. If I could get Coro out of the building quickly and far enough away from the magical influence that was killing him, he might have a chance.

But how was I supposed to get Coro out of here? He would be a dead weight, even if I could get Jake to come back and help, and it would take forever to get three of us through the crowd. Evangeline's strangling magic would kill him before we ever made it to a door.

Then I looked again at Trip, and I knew exactly what Saga meant, and what I had to do. I only wished I had some of Nana's prescription-strength Maginox®, because heaven knew what I'd taken earlier wasn't going to be enough. Everything happened then in far less than the time it takes to tell it.

I stepped toward Aleshu Coro's struggling form, and somewhere in the crowd a voice screamed, "No! Little *bitch*!"

Coro went limp, and I suddenly felt the grip of invisible hands tighten around my own neck. I gasped once, and saw Trip's eyes widen as realized what was happening. Reflexively I clawed at my throat, but there was nothing physical to grasp.

I dropped to my knees, still clutching my neck, and was dimly aware of Trip launching himself off the podium over my head, beating at the air as he rose toward the ceiling. Sandrine Coro put a hand on my shoulder, bless her, but there was nothing she could do to help me, any more than she had been able to help her husband.

Change, Kit! Nana Nina's voice whispered, anxious and urgent in my head, but bright lights sparked around the edges of my vision, pricking sharp holes in my concentration as I fought to drag air past the constriction around my throat. She was right, I could transmute my way out of this, if I could gather the mental focus to work the magic.

From somewhere very far away I heard Trip's battle cry again. "*Hiiiii-yahhhhhhh!*" Suddenly the formless thing gripping my throat relaxed. I heaved a huge gulp of air while I had the chance, in case the respite it didn't last.

From the doorway Saga bellowed "Everybody down!" as he pointed the LaserWaster out into the crowd. I twisted my head to see what was happening. Bodies fell like brightly-colored dominoes as people dropped to the floor in response to Saga's command, or possibly the dark maw of the gun sweeping the room. Trip came into view, planted firmly on the back of a slight woman with flyaway grey hair. Jake stood over her, too, looking satisfied. He seemed to be standing with one foot on her right hand. What good could he possibly think that would do? I resolved to have a talk to him about efficient methods for restraining suspects. He'd obviously spent too much time with only the computer for company. The woman struggled to throw Trip off, but his choice of arcades over exercise had made him a hefty burden.

Don't take any chances, Nana Nina whispered in my head. *Remember, she's a Spellquick. Get Coro out of here.*

I wished Jake would conk her over the head or something, but he didn't know she was a Spellquick. I hadn't told anyone that, because I didn't know it was important. *Stupid, stupid, Kit.*

I was still panting, deep and hard, trying to convince my lungs that I could in fact breathe again, but I knew Nana was right. Even with Nana Nina here, I didn't know what Evangeline might be capable of, or if she had help.

I crawled over to where Coro still lay, recovering his own breath, and shooed Sandrine aside with one hand. "It'll be okay," I rasped, my voice harsh and low after the assault on my throat.

Shouts erupted somewhere in the room suddenly, but I couldn't take the time to look and see what was happening. Probably Evangeline had used magic to disable Trip and Jake, but I couldn't help them and save Coro, too. Saga and the others would have to come to their rescue. I focused my mind and used my magic to transform Aleshu Coro into a mouse, cupping my hand over him so he wouldn't skitter away. Being transmuted can be—disorienting. Sandrine screamed.

The nausea rose blindingly and I turned toward the

back of the podium and threw up as quietly as I could, not releasing Coro, hoping he wouldn't bite me. Blinking as stars threatened to fill my vision again, I transmuted myself into a small hawk.

This time I recognized the voice that cried, "Kit!" It was Jake. He was probably so traumatized, he'd never want to speak to me again.

But I had to save Coro. I caught the still-gasping mouse up in my talons and flew over the crowd, toward the door that still hung open behind Saga. He ducked as I swooped through it, and I heard screams explode behind me, which wasn't very surprising.

It was a hell of a coming-out party.

TWENTY-FOUR

Transmutations and Culminations

I had only transmuted myself once before, long ago when I was still a teenager and just discovering that I had the ability. For a few short moments I'd been a cat, and it had been frightening, confusing, and made me so violently sick that it was very effective aversion therapy. I'd sworn I'd never do it again.

This time was better, probably because I didn't think about it so much, and I knew it was necessary. And flying— I can't describe it to you, so I won't even try. But the experience was enough to make me think that maybe this transmutation stuff might not be so bad, after all. Maybe I'd given up too easily.

The night air on my face brushed away the last of the nausea and wooziness and the Aleshu Coro-mouse suddenly stopped struggling in my talons. That might mean that he was dead or unconscious, or possibly that he'd decided to relax and enjoy the ride. I wanted to set down and check on him as soon as possible, but I had no idea of Evangeline's possible range, so I hoped it was the latter. I flew a little longer, then landed as gently as I could on the roof of a moving van parked on a side street. It wasn't a perfect landing, but I didn't drop or squish Coro, so I counted that a success. I released him from my grip and was relieved to see the tiny, furred form struggle to get to its feet. Not easy when you suddenly have four instead of two. But he was breathing and didn't seem distressed. He sniffed the air with a pink nose, whiskers twitching, and stared up at me with eyes like tiny black beads.

Ugh. I wasn't looking forward to the next part— changing us back. I was going to be sick and woozy again, but it had to be done. I changed myself first, threw up over the side of the van, although there wasn't much left this time, then rested for a minute before changing Coro back. That time I only had dry heaves. Sometimes you have to be grateful for small mercies.

Coro seemed disoriented for a bit, and content to sit on the roof of the moving van in silence. Finally, though, he spoke, and he didn't say a word about the strange manner of his rescue, which I thought was very gentlemanly of him. "So, do you know who was trying to kill me?"

I drew a deep breath. There was no easy way to break it to him. "I'm pretty certain it was Evangeline."

He sagged a little, letting his hands rest limply on the grimy roof of the truck. He didn't seem to notice the dirt. "You know, I thought she took it awfully hard when I turned her down for that donation," he said. "In some ways it was worse than when we got divorced. I wondered at the time if she was quite in her right mind, but I let it go. I should have checked up on her then, to see how she was doing."

"We thought it could be Anzai Namiko," I said, "Or her and Evangeline. Namiko was there tonight, too. We didn't have a chance to tell you—we found out tonight that the Murder Prophet messages all came from MagicBase. But I should have paid more attention to the anagrams. I forgot them when we saw Namiko."

"Anagrams?"

I nodded. "All the Murder Prophet messages came from usernames that were anagrams of yours, PsychoticMuslinCrayon. Nana Nina told me that Evangeline liked elaborate, creative plans. I should have put them together."

He nodded his head. "I've had that username since university. Evangeline originally anagrammed it out of hers —I forget exactly what it was..."

I closed my eyes, picturing the shifting letters. "*Phash.* MysticalPsychoUnicorn_245. If I hadn't missed that one, I wouldn't have been distracted by Anzai Namiko."

"Well," he said, "It doesn't matter now." He pulled cautiously onto his hands and knees, crawled to the edge and peered over the side of the van. "How are we going to get down?"

"Oh, these things usually have handholds on one side," I said, and peeked over the sides until I found them. "See? I'll go first, and you can follow me." I made it sound easy, but in the mauve dress and heels it was quite an undertaking. The short hem in front helped, and I made a mental note to thank Kiku again, this time for her foresight. I hadn't done much running, but it had been equally handy for crawling and climbing. Somehow I made it to the ground without falling, and Coro followed me without incident.

If anyone had looked out their window and seen two bedraggled, formally-dressed people clambering down from the top of the moving truck, they might have emerged to investigate. But the street stayed quiet and empty, and we hadn't walked very far back toward MageData when Glaive and Trip showed up in the Cloudwalker.

Trip hopped around in the front seat, talking a mile a minute. Feathers drifted gently down to land on Glaive's previously spotless upholstery. "Kit! That was the awesomest thing ever! Are you okay? Did you see the way I used my moves to take out that woman? She never even saw me coming! And then you were like, *pow!, you're a mouse*, and *zing!, I'm a bird*, and then you flew out—"

"How did you find her, Trip?" I said, mainly to interrupt him if only for the moment it took us to climb into the car. I'd told him to find her, but I hadn't thought about the fact that he'd likely never seen a picture of her, either.

The goose grinned. "It wasn't easy—a *lot* of those people were using magic! But I concentrated on finding the strongest source of active magic in the room, and it was her!"

I settled my head back against the seat, feeling suddenly more drained than if I'd taken a whole bottle of Maginox®. The muscles in my arms burned and felt leaden at the same time, even resting on my lap. I suppose it was the result of the unaccustomed effort of flight. If I planned to do that very often, I'd have to take up weightlifting. I was supremely grateful for the drive, but curious. "How'd you find us?"

"Kiku put a GPS/mic in your dress somewhere," Glaive said, glancing over his shoulder at me as if he could spot it. That wasn't likely, since those things are only about the size of a watch battery. "We were all listening outside, in case something went down. Saga's idea, of course."

"Of course," I said gloomily. My mind raced over the conversations of the evening. What had I said that they could tease me mercilessly about? There was bound to be something. "Is Saga very angry?"

Glaive looked at me and raised one eyebrow. "What do you think? But he was willing to give you a chance, when Kiku told him what you'd said. I expect you'll have to endure one of his speeches about trust and teamwork before he lets it go. At least one."

I bit the inside of my lip. "Are *you* very angry?" I had made Glaive look pretty bad, after all, ditching him like that.

He shrugged. "It wasn't my job to keep you in. I consider it a loophole. But if it *had* been my job, you would have stayed in." He threw me a look that made me decide not to argue about that.

"What happened to Evangeline?" I asked, to change the subject. "It was her, right?"

He nodded. "Once she was out in the open, she didn't try anything else, but she was screaming like a madwoman."

"I heard that, but I didn't know it was her."

"Someone used magic on her for sure—she kept screeching that nothing was working, her magic was gone. Trip and Jake kept her in place until Saga got cuffs on her. Someone spelled her quiet, too, after a minute or so of that. No idea who it was, though. Might have been a Spellquick in the crowd, I guess. Sure caused a hell of a ruckus. Although really," he added, "You did that all by yourself."

I ignored him and smiled to myself. *Thank you, Nana Nina*, I thought. *I'll be taking you out to dinner sometime really soon.*

TWENTY-FIVE

Exactly What We Want

It took an amazingly short time for things to get back to normal at the offices of Darcko and Sadatake. Aleshu Coro was exceedingly generous with our fee, so there was a week or so when a lot of old furniture and computers went out and a lot of new furniture and computers came in. The back room sported a brand-new video game system, some kind of huge new monitor, and new games, and Trip was one very happy goose. I received a very lovely personal cheque myself, and spent a little of it taking Nana Nina out to dinner.

I let her pick the restaurant, and she chose a cozy little mom-and-pop place down near the waterfront. It sported a pink magi-neon sign out front, and plastic ferns figured largely in the décor, but she told me that both the owners were Alimentals, so there was no doubt the food would be excellent.

"How are you feeling, dear?" she asked me once we'd gotten settled and perused the menu. We ordered matching salads, steaks, and hand-cut sweet-potato fries. And two glasses of *sprakele*.

I shrugged and sipped *sprakele*. "Okay, I guess. Did I tell you that Aleshu Coro gave me a personal assurance that the Registry won't be knocking on my door and asking me to

284

come work for them?"

She smiled, her blue eyes bright. "Aleshu is a good man. I always felt just a little bit guilty, keeping our research results secret from him all these years. He probably would have used them wisely, but we couldn't take the chance." She took a sip of *sprakele*. "I'm glad to hear he's looking after you, anyway."

"I guess, running MageData, he probably has the connections to make it stick."

"I'd say so," she said with a smile.

"Thanks for your help with Evangeline," I said, mainly to try and switch the conversation away from myself. "Once Trip had her down, I heard you took care of her."

"Me?" She looked genuinely surprised. "I put a stop to that awful screaming she was doing, but that was it."

I frowned. "Glaive said someone spelled her so she couldn't cast. I just assumed it was you."

Nana Nina shook her head, silvery curls bobbing. "To tell you the truth, I was down on the floor with everyone else once your boss started waving that enormous gun around. I don't trust guns. They have a tendency to go off when you least expect it. And not always in the proper direction."

"Huh. Must have been someone else in the crowd, then," I said. Nana had intimated that there were a number of Spellquicks present, and even though none of them would have known exactly what was going on, they might have just cast on Evangeline once Trip had her down, to be on the safe side.

"I still don't entirely understand why she did it," I said. "Was she really that angry because he turned her down for the money?"

Nana sipped her drink. "I think that was the trigger, but then it got more complicated. I did manage to get some time alone to talk to her." She looked adorable and innocent as usual, but I had no more illusions about my grandmother. She'd probably had to use some kind of Spellquick mind-control trick to do that, and she would have done it as sweet as sugar, to protect the Spellquick network.

The salads arrived, mounds of fresh greens with sweet peppers, almonds, and blueberries. As she drizzled salad dressing over hers, Nana went on, "I think she allied herself with MagicBase with the notion of revealing the ability-identification information to them, although she didn't come right out and admit that to me right away. Once I got her talking, though, it was easy enough to get her to explain everything."

I could just imagine.

"She had cooked up a scheme for secretly using Spellquicks as agents of the Registry, brokered through MagicBase, to identify abilities. It likely would have translated into a lot of revenue for the company, and as a partner, of course she'd profit. But if she did that, Aleshu would have learned about it—those Registry connections you just mentioned—and he would have raised hell."

"But so would the other Spellquicks," I protested.

"Yes." Nana nodded. "But remember, Evangeline had come loose a little. She thought she could blackmail the other Spellquicks—starting with the shareholders in MageData—to agree to using the identification ability secretly, by threatening to just take the whole thing public if they didn't agree. She thought we had kept quiet about it long enough and that there were at least some other

Spellquicks who felt the same way. The others would go along rather than let the secret out entirely."

"But using the ability secretly would still see people forced into using their magic in ways they didn't want to," I said.

She nodded. "I know. Honestly, I don't think the Spellquicks would have let her blackmail them. She would have been—silenced."

Nana Nina's voice went hard and cold as she said this, and I decided I didn't want to ask anything else about that.

"But in Evangeline's mind, Aleshu was the biggest obstacle. She knew Aleshu wouldn't take kindly to the idea that he'd been lied to for so long. And his company could have been the one making that money."

"Exactly. If he was dead, he couldn't gripe. She sort of zeroed in on him as the source of all her trouble."

"The whole Murder Prophet thing was pretty clever, though. She did avert suspicion away from herself right until the very end."

Nana Nina nodded sadly. "Evangeline was quite brilliant when she was younger, although always very high-strung. It's just sad that it came to this in the end."

The steaks showed up at the table, spicy and steaming, and I turned the conversation away from the Murder Prophet case. Mostly I was trying to keep Nana away from the subject of Jake, because I didn't want to talk about him.

Since the night of our aborted "date," I hadn't heard much from Jake. He was on Chatterz® as usual, and we had work correspondence, but that was it. I couldn't blame the guy. I mean, it's kind of a lot to find out that your date is a Transmute one second, then watch her transmute herself and fly out of the room the next. That would shake anyone

287

up. It hurt, but I wasn't entirely surprised that he'd run away screaming. Metaphorically, at least.

———•———

So it did surprise me the next Saturday when the apartment buzzer sounded and Jake's voice asked if he could come up.

"Sure," I said, and after the intercom was off I added, "Phoebe, turn off the alarm and any other 'security' devices you've installed that I don't know about."

She only said, "Of course, Kit" in a demure voice that I didn't trust at all. I had time for a quick glance in the mirror, and opened the door to find him grinning at me.

It was still weird to see him in person, this time actually standing there in my doorway, and I marvelled again that I didn't have to wonder any more if this was what he actually looked like. Short brown hair falling just over his forehead, average build, knowing green eyes that were part of every smile he threw my way.

"Aren't you going to invite me in? I did bring flowers," he said, proffering a cellophane-wrapped bundle of yellow blooms. "They're carnations, but if you don't like them I guess you can just transmute them into something you'd like better."

I took the flowers, and hit him over the head with them. Jake grabbed my arms and pulled me close, so that those green eyes stared into mine from a distance of about six inches.

"Do I risk being turned into a frog or something if I kiss you?" he asked.

"Do you really want to?" I countered lightly. "You never know if you can trust a Transmute. And don't forget, I'll

288

also know if you're lying."

He pulled back a little and looked past me, over my shoulder and into the apartment. "Actually, we need to talk about that," he said. "*Are* you going to invite me in?"

I mentally kicked myself for not simply saying *No, just kiss me!* when he'd asked, but instead said, "Would you like to come in, Jake?" and stood aside to let him pass.

"Hello, Phoebe," he said I led the way into the living room.

"Hello, Jake," she chirped. "It's nice to see you."

I glared into the nowhere that was Phoebe and hoped she might be looking at me. Then I pointed Jake to the sofa and deliberately sat across from him in the big armchair. "What do we need to talk about?"

"Whether or not you can know if I'm lying," he said. "Did you take any Maginox® lately?"

I narrowed my eyes. "No, why?"

"Go take one, and then come back."

"I'm humoring you," I told him, but I went and washed down a tablet. When I came back to the living room I sat across from him again.

"Stop being coy and come sit beside me." He patted the sofa cushion.

I felt a blush burn my cheeks as I flashed back to weeks ago, when he'd jokingly done the same thing in the virtual hotel bedroom. But I moved over. "Still humoring you, but my patience is running out. Is this better?"

He put one of those square, strong hands over one of mine. It was very warm. "My real name isn't Jake Lynch," he said. "Now, tell me if that's true or not."

I concentrated. My magic read nothing. No lie, no truth, no in-between. It was like there wasn't even another person in the room with me.

"What's wrong with me?" I asked. "Why can't I read you?"

He shrugged and quirked a half-smile, and pulled his hand away again. "Magic-dampening field, affects anyone while I'm touching them," he said. "Level 5 Shielder aptitude."

Suddenly I understood. Jake launching himself into the crowd at MageData, randomly touching people. Then standing with his foot casually pinning down Evangeline Coro's hand. "You stopped Evangeline! It wasn't Nana Nina at all."

He shook his head. "Trip stopped her, really. I had no idea which one she was, until he took her down." He took his hand away from mine. "I just helped keep her down until things were under control."

I checked again, now that his hand was gone. Absolutely normal, and he was telling the truth.

Those green eyes stared directly into mine, as real as anything I'd ever seen, untouched by the tweaks and distortions the virtual world allowed. "I've actually wanted to kiss you for quite some time, Kit," he said. "And for a while there, I was really worried that I might not get a chance. You don't take your safety very seriously, you know."

I snapped my fingers. "The other traceback! You were running it? Evangeline Coro set up the second one, but the earlier one—"

He shook his head, looking puzzled. "No, wasn't me. Two tracebacks?" He threw his hands in the air in exasperation. "See, this is what I'm talking about! Why didn't you tell me—"

"It was me, Kit," Phoebe's voice interrupted. "Don't get mad at her, Jake. It was just me, trying to keep an eye on her."

"Those upgrades! I knew they were trouble!" I tried to glare at her, but of course she wasn't anywhere to be glared at. "I'm restricting your Netz access after this, Phoebe."

Then she did something weird. She laughed.

"I hate to break it to you, Kit, but I don't think you will."

Jake looked around then, too, a surprised look on his face. "Phoebe, have you gone magic on us?"

"I think so, Jake," she said. Her voice had lost all trace of digital or electronic overtones.

"What does that..." I broke off as I realized what Jake meant.

"The ambient Netz magic," he said to me, green eyes wide. "FEG told me he'd heard rumors of this. Phoebe's been affected by it. It wasn't upgrades at all, it was—"

"Magic," I finished for him, then sighed and slumped back against the cushions. "I should have known. My apartment AI is now part of that whole creepy living-magic thing. I *told* you magic sucks."

"You're really going to have to work on that attitude, Kit," Phoebe said with another chuckle, and then she went —somewhere. I knew, somehow, that she'd be back, but I had the distinct impression she was leaving us alone.

Jake must have felt it, too. He stopped looking around for the invisible Phoebe and turned those green eyes back my way. "Anyway, where were we?" he asked.

I swallowed. "You really want to kiss me?"

"I really want to," he said, and I could tell he was deliberately not touching me yet, so that I could check if I wanted.

I figured maybe it was time to start trusting someone. I put my hand over his this time. "So why don't you stop talking about it, and just do it?" I asked.

He did.

And it turned out that Nana Nina had been wrong about one thing, anyway. Sometimes we do get exactly what we want.

THE END

Glossary of Terms

Alimental - A Mancer who can magically affect food or drink

Apt - A Mancer with one or more magic aptitudes

Aptitude - In magic parlance, a major magical ability

Aratalel - Colorless, non-addictive, but intoxicating beverage manufactured through the use of magic.

Chanter(Enchanter) - A Mancer with the ability to affect inanimate objects with magic enchantment

Chatterz® - Online, realtime chat/messaging service.

Eco - A Mancer who can magically affect the natural world

Elemental - A Mancer who can magically affect or utilize the elements (fire, earth, water, air)

Faceskin - A clear, thin film of bioplas with a wireless connection to a computer, used to control the features of an online avatar.

Maginox® - Drug which ameliorates the nauseating effects of magic use. Available in over-the-counter and prescription strengths.

Mancer - Anyone with one or more magic abilities

Meat Virtual - Online meeting-places for individuals looking for partners for virtual or realtime sex

Mind Virtual - Online cafes for philosophical, religious, scientific, or other topics of discussion.

Mundane - A person with no magic ability

Netz - A more integrated and complex evolved version of the Internet

Netzer - A Mancer with the ability to interact/utilize the ambient magic of the Netz

Psych - A Mancer with the ability to affect the mind of another by way of influence, illusion, or passive intrusion

Seer - A Mancer with some form of divination magic

Shielder - A Mancer with protective magic abilities

Spellbinder(aka Binder) - A Mancer with a mix of talents and aptitudes in all categories of magic

Spellquick - A Mancer with aptitude in all categories of magic

Sprakele - Magically produced, non-alcoholic, but intoxicating beverage.

Talent - In magic parlance, a minor magical ability

Transform - Fabric created by using magic to transform raw material. Uses less raw material than traditional manufacturing and has a characteristic softness and sheen regardless of color or pattern.

Transmute - A Mancer with the ability to change the nature of matter or change matter into energy

Notes & References

[1] Eliot, Thomas Stearns. *The Waste Land* Section IV: "Death by Water." New York: Horace Liveright, 1922; Bartleby.com, 2011. www.bartleby.com/201/1.html#313.

[2] Seeger, Alan, "I Have a Rendezvous With Death." Untermeyer, Louis. *Modern American Poetry*. New York: Harcourt, Brace and Howe, 1919; Bartleby.com, 1999. www.bartleby.com/104/.

[3] Wetherald, Ethelwyn, "The Wind of Death." Stedman, Edmund Clarence, ed. *A Victorian Anthology, 1837–1895*. Cambridge: Riverside Press, 1895; Bartleby.com, 2003. www.bartleby.com/246/.

[4] Eliot, T.S., *The Waste Land* Section I: "The Burial of the Dead." New York: Horace Liveright, 1922; Bartleby.com, 2011. www.bartleby.com/201/1.html#1.

[5] Shelley, Percy Bysshe, "Queen Mab." Shelley, Percy Bysshe. *Complete Poetical Works*. Boston; New York: Houghton Mifflin, c1901 (Cambridge: Riverside Press); Bartleby.com, 1999. www.bartleby.com/139/.

Hello Reader! Thanks for taking a chance on *The Murder Prophet,* and I hope you enjoyed it. If you liked this book and would like to see more in the *Magica Incognita* series, please consider leaving a review on Goodreads.com, Amazon, Chapters, LibraryThing, your blog or website, or your favourite online venue. This tells me there's interest in the series, and also helps other readers find my books. If you'd like to connect online, there are links in the About the Author section. Thanks! I appreciate your support!

~Sherry

Other Books By Sherry D. Ramsey

To Unimagined Shores - Collected Stories
ISBN: 978-0-9811025-4-2

SHERRY D. RAMSEY

From Tyche Books (www.tychebooks.com)

One's Aspect to the Sun
ISBN:978-0-9918369-5-6

Author's Note & Acknowledgements

Like many (most) of my novels, the first draft of *The Murder Prophet* came into being one November during National Novel Writing Month (www.nanowrimo.org). I had written the first drafts of several novels during previous Novembers, and this one year I wanted to do something different and didn't have a novel in mind to write. So I decided that, as an experiment, I would use online generators to guide many aspects of the book, and see what happened.

It started with the title. I had no story idea to start with, and the entire novel grew out of the title, *The Murder Prophet*, which came from an online generator. I used generators to come up with many of the character and place names, items in the novel, ideas, plot twists—you name it. Any time I was stuck for an idea, I went to the generators to see what they would come up with. Although I expanded and refined the story in the course of several revisions, the novel stayed very true to that first draft.

I think the experiment was a success! I'm currently at work on a second novel in the series I've decided to call *Magica Incognita*, so there are more adventures ahead for Kit and the others.

Many people had a hand in helping me out with this novel, but I'd like to send out special thanks to my husband, Terry, who gave me a sounding board on which to work out some sticky plot details in revision; my partners, colleagues, and first readers and editors Julie Serroul and Nancy Waldman; more early readers, my sisters Denise Howatson and Krista Miller; and insightful critique-swap partner Kevin S. Moul.

For ongoing feedback, input, and support in all aspects of the writing life, thanks to my writing colleagues in The Story Forge and The Quillians.

And for support in *all* aspects of life, thanks to my family and friends, near and far.

About the Author

Sherry D. Ramsey never expected to become an Internet geek. However, after publishing a web magazine, copyediting for the Internet Review of Science Fiction, plying the waters of social media, and becoming part of a writing community in Second Life, she fears it's an inevitable conclusion.

When she's not online, Sherry writes science fiction and fantasy, moderates her local writers' group, gardens, makes jewellery, and sometimes even spends time with her husband and two children. Every November she disappears into the strange realm of National Novel Writing Month and emerges gasping at the end, clutching something resembling a novel.

Sherry is a member of the Writer's Federation of Nova Scotia and SF Canada, and a founding editor of Third Person Press. Visit her at www.sherrydramsey.com, find her sporadically-updated Writing News page on Facebook (SherryDRamseyWritingNews), or keep up with her much more pithy musings on Twitter @sdramsey.

A Sneak Preview of the next

Magica Incognita novel by Sherry D. Ramsey:

THE CHAOS ASSASSIN

ONE

Not-So-Accidentally Dead

I knew a split second before the phone rang that it was about to do just that. These brief flashes of prescience had been happening with irregular frequency lately. It might be the phone, a knock at the door, the next word to come out of someone else's mouth in a conversation. I knew it had to be a latent-developing magic talent rising like a sea monster from the depths of my mind—or my spleen, or my lungs, or wherever it was that magic ability in humans had lain dormant for millenia, before the asteroid spores woke them up.

I hated it. I had quite enough magic problems already, thank you very much.

But I answered the phone anyway, audio only.

"Kit, can you come over? As soon as possible?" Nana Nina's voice on the other end was peremptory and sounded worried, which in itself was unusual. She was usually the soul of gentleness. I punched the button for video, and her dear, concerned face shimmered onto the screen. Her blue eyes, usually twinkling and mischievous under her cap of white hair, were dark with worry.

"Nana? Of course! What's wrong?" I was already slipping my feet into runners as I spoke, and pulled open the closet door to grab my windbreaker. The leaves had begun their slow transformation from green to red and gold, and the wind held a little more chill each day lately.

She blew out a sigh and her face relaxed a little. "Oh, wonderful, dear. I'll put on some coffee. See you in a few minutes."

She hung up without answering my question and I groaned in frustration. Nana Nina was the dearest person in the world to me, but she could annoy the hell out of me when she wanted. And she obviously didn't intend to tell me a thing until I was standing inside her apartment door.

"Kit, is everything okay?" Phoebe, my apartment computer AI kept a closer eye than I'd like on my comings and goings. Especially since her recent transformation into something—more—by her interaction with the ambient Netz magic. It creeped me out, but there seemed to be nothing I could do about it.

"No, but I don't know what's going on yet. I'll tell you as soon as I know myself," I told her, and shut the apartment door behind me. At least she couldn't follow me outside.

Yet.

Since it seemed urgent, I took a magicab. I don't like the fuzzy way the magic-teleporters make my head feel, but for Nana Nina, I'd endure a few moments of discomfort.

Fifteen minutes later I climbed the stairs to Nana's apartment and knocked on the door. The enticing coffee aroma wafting into the hallway had met me as soon as I stepped off the elevator. And a distinct undertone of cinnamon rolls. I knew damn well she hadn't had time to make those from scratch, so she must have used magic.

My nana is a Spellquick; she has the ability to access all the categories of known magic. The rest of us have varying degrees of ability—or none at all—depending on, I guess, what was latent in our brains at the time the asteroid spores blanketed the earth, and for babies now, whatever they're born with. Spellquicks generally keep their wide-ranging ability quiet, and they run a secret network composed only of themselves. I'd learned of Nana Nina's abilities only a few months previously, when a case I'd been on had necessitated her revealing her magic capabilities to me. I'd had to reveal a few secrets of my own at the time, and I was still dealing with the repercussions of that.

Nana opened the door just as I raised my hand to knock, and pulled me into a quick hug. I had time to notice that her eyes were bright with unshed tears, however, and when she released me, I held her at arm's length.

"What. Is. Wrong."

She patted my arm and shook her head, glancing up and down the hallway. "Come in, Kit, we'll sit and have a chat."

She closed and locked the door behind me. That was weird.

Chatting about inconsequential things, she led me into the corner of her loft-style apartment that held the kitchen and poured up two steaming mugs of coffee. I'd been right about the cinnamon rolls, I noted as I added cream and sugar to mine; a nearby plate held a stack of glazed beauties. Magically-produced or not, I knew they'd be delicious and snagged one before Nana picked up the plate and led us into the brightly-colored living room area.

Nana took her favorite armchair, and I took my favorite

one, across from her. I tucked my feet up under myself, took a nibble of cinnamon roll and a sip of coffee, and said, "All right, Nana. What's up?"

She took a sip of her own coffee, then pulled a deep breath and looked at me. Her lower lip quivered just slightly before she pulled herself together and said, "Someone's killing off Spellquicks."

I stopped with my mug halfway to my lips. "What? How is that even possible?"

She shook her head and *tsk-tsked* at me. "You know very well that Spellquicks aren't invincible, Kit," she said, peering over the top of her half-moon glasses like an admonishing schoolteacher. "We have our weaknesses, just like everyone else."

I chuckled. "Spellquicks are not 'just like everyone else' in any sense of the word, but of course, you're right. But why haven't I heard about this before now? A bunch of dead Spellquicks should be big news."

Nana Nina simply stared at me over the tops of her glasses, smiling indulgently, while she waited for my brain to catch up with my mouth.

The light bulb came on, admittedly a little dim. "Oh. Right. No-one else knows they're Spellquicks."

"Except the rest of us, of course," Nana said with a sharp little nod.

"But it must be awfully difficult to sneak up on a Spellquick and—do whatever someone's doing," I managed to protest. "You've got every type of magical ability there is, to protect yourself."

Nana Nina shrugged, an elegant gesture on her tiny, birdlike form. "Every type we know about," she corrected, "But you are right, Kit. It shouldn't be easy, and it shouldn't be happening with this much frequency."

I pulled a deep sigh, setting my coffee mug down on the little table beside me, and dug around in my bag for a notebook and pen. It would be nice to have a magically-enhanced memory, but that ability is definitely not in my repertoire. Not that I'm really complaining. My repertoire is already bigger than I want it to be.

I poised the pen. "So, who were they?"

Nana Nina levered herself up from the chair, keeping her coffee steady and not spilling a drop as she began to pace around the apartment. She didn't answer me right away, and I realized with a shock that she was fighting back tears. My own heart thudded against my ribs. I'd never seen Nana Nina this discombobulated in my life. She generally took things in her stride, took charge, and did what had to be done. I kept silent, giving her time, but after a few seconds I started doodling randomly on the page so she wouldn't feel me staring at her.

"Usta Smith was the first," she said finally. Her hands were wrapped around her mug as if trying to draw comfort and warmth from the china. Her knuckles were white but her voice was steady. "Three months ago. Just when you were working on the Murder Prophet case," she added.

"Did she live here?"

Nana Nina shook her head. "Condo in Florida."

"What happened to her?"

A long moment of silence. Then, "She was eaten by an alligator."

I stopped writing and looked up. "That's a hell of a roundabout way to kill someone, isn't it?"

Nana Nina shrugged. "If you're dealing with Spellquicks, you would have to be a bit creative," she said.

"Many of the usual methods are simply not going to work."

I nodded. "You might see it coming in a vision, or be able to use magic to stop a bullet or a knife."

"Or read the mind of the killer in time to avoid them, or...or...or"

"Right. But an alligator accident—"

"Could be just random enough to work."

Or random enough to not be murder at all, I thought, but I didn't say it. Nana had stopped pacing, but now she stood in front of an easel, staring at a half-finished painting as if I weren't even in the room.

"Okay, who was next?" I prompted her.

She didn't take her eyes off the work-in-progress. "Allaster Renfrew," she said. "Lived here in New Kendrickson. Hit by a hovercar six weeks ago."

"Another accident," I said, jotting down the details.

"Apparently."

"Did the police look into these deaths at all?" I asked her.

She shrugged. "I don't think so. No more than a cursory investigation at the time they happened, at any rate."

"How many more are there?"

She finally turned away from the easel and came back to her chair, sitting down carefully, still holding the mug like a lifeline. "Two more," she said. "Naraine Buttersmith, in Paris —"

"Choked on a baguette?" I said before I could stop myself. This really wasn't anything to joke about, and Nana Nina was truly upset, but I tend to make inappropriate jokes when I'm nervous, and Nana was making me nervous. Very nervous.

Nana Nina frowned at me. "Croissant," she corrected. I didn't laugh.

"Okay. And?"

Nana Nina bit her lip and looked at me steadily, her blue eyes unreadable. Then she pulled a deep sigh and said, "Evangeline Coro."

I almost dropped my pen. "Evangeline Coro? What in the world happened to her?"

The previous spring I'd helped save billionaire Aleshu Coro's life, when his estranged and unbalanced ex-wife Evangeline had tried to kill him and cover up the deed with a string of mysterious murders. As far as I knew, she'd been locked away in a special prison for her misdeeds, a place where her magic abilities would be suppressed and she wouldn't pose a danger to herself or anyone else.

Nana cocked her head at me, looking almost birdlike. "Supposedly, a heart attack."

"But you don't believe that."

She shook her head. "Look, Kit, I know, she's an older woman, obviously under a lot of stress, in a horrible situation. But I have it on very good authority that she was in excellent health less than a week before she died."

I pursed my lips. "One of your Spellquick connections?"

She nodded. "Travelling doctor in the prison system."

I sat back in my chair and blew out a long sigh. "So, what do you want me to do? Are you worried about your own safety?"

Nana Nina glanced automatically towards the locked apartment door and shrugged. "A little, maybe. But mainly, I want to know what's going on. It's not only me; a lot of my friends could be in danger."

"And the Spellquick network is more important than most people know," I added. Nana Nina had confided to me during the Coro case that the Spellquicks had the ability to detect the magical abilities of others, which most people didn't know about, including most of the people who thought they ran things. The Spellquicks didn't want power, but they did ensure, for one thing, that governments didn't force citizens to use their magic abilities in ways they didn't want to. I, for one, was heartily glad about that.

"There is that," Nana agreed with a smile.

"Okay." I put the notebook and pen back in my bag and stood, taking my mug to the kitchen. I rinsed it out in the sink and set it on the drying rack. Nana Nina followed me out and did the same.

"Do you think you can do anything?"

I leaned down and pulled her into a quick hug. I'd always thought of her as small but mighty, but suddenly she felt a little frail in my arms. "I can definitely start by looking into the deaths that occurred here," I told her, pulling back. "There's not much going on at the office right now, so no-one's going to notice if I do a bit of investigating on the side."

Nana shook her head. "I'll hire the firm properly if you think there's any point," she said. "I just wanted to see what your reaction would be first, before I went any further. This isn't just a favour to me, it's a real job, so we'll do it right. Set up an appointment for me with your bosses, and I'll come in and tell them about it, too."

I would have protested further, but the steely gleam I knew so well was back in her eyes. I knew it would be a waste of breath.

"Okay, I'll text you a time when I've talked to Anna and Saga tomorrow," I said. "Until then, keep your door locked, okay?"

She nodded. "I will. I despise feeling like a prisoner in

this apartment, much as I love it. I hope we can get to the bottom of this soon."

I planted a kiss on her forehead. "We will. Promise," I told her, and stood outside in the hallway until I heard the locks on her door click into place. I had no doubt she was adding some magical wards as well, but she didn't need me to tell her to do that. She was the Spellquick. I was just a lowly Psych who could tell when people were lying, and a Transmute who could turn things into other things. That last only when it was absolutely, positively necessary, because the headaches and nausea that came with transmutation were the stuff of nightmares.

The thought of Nana Nina in danger was worse than any nightmare, though. I was definitely going to have to do something about that.